DABNEY'S REEF

Robert Standish

PETER DAVIES : LONDON

Peter Davies Limited
15 Queen Street, Mayfair, London W1X 8BE
LONDON MELBOURNE TORONTO
JOHANNESBURG AUCKLAND

Printed in Great Britain by
Northumberland Press Limited
Gateshead

DABNEY'S REEF

PROLOGUE

During the interminable seconds between being catapulted out of the burning 'plane and the opening of his parachute, he found time to wonder at his own remarkable lack of fear. By nature, as he would have been the first to admit, he was a fearful man, but the paradox of having conquered his fears made him by normal standards a brave man. This last, however, did not occur to him. Surveying the heavily wooded country below, he calculated his chances of survival grimly. But even when in imagination he conjured up the vision of a tombstone on which was engraved

JONATHAN DABNEY

1922-1941

he was still strangely unafraid.

In wide pendulum swings he floated earthwards into the upper branches of a fine beech, where he remained hanging by the cords of his parachute. At this stage, apart from a few bruises and scratches, he was more or less unhurt. It was the last thirty of his twelve thousand feet fall which were to be his undoing. Two stretcher bearers who arrived on the scene so quickly that it seemed they were waiting for him, lifted him into an ambulance which bumped across the greensward towards a huge turreted country house. Five minutes later he began to feel the pain from a compound fracture of the left leg. He must have swooned because the next thing he remembered was the prick of a hypodermic needle and a fruity baritone voice saying: 'Have a good sleep now. In a few weeks we'll have you good as new.'

When he came out of his drugged sleep some hours later,

it was to see bending over him a young woman clad in nurse's uniform. She was so breathtakingly lovely that for a moment he imagined it was a dream. Her cornflower-blue eyes brimming with compassion, she asked: 'How do you feel now?'

'Like hell!' he replied as pain took over.

An older nurse appeared on the scene, brisk, starched and competent, who said to the younger one, her voice edged with impatience: 'On your way! There's work to be done and there's no room for you here.'

The vision of loveliness faded, leaving Pilot-Officer Jonathan Dabney to wonder how anyone could treat a goddess so brusquely.

'Where am I?' he asked.

'This is Ashpole Manor Hospital ... in Buckinghamshire....'

'I remember the Buckinghamshire part from the map....'

'You dropped right at our back door, so to speak ... now go to sleep.'

On his next awakening, two orderlies lifted him gently on to a stretcher and a middle-aged woman he took to be the matron, or someone in authority, said: 'We're not properly equipped here, so you are being sent to a hospital where they have everything. This is really a convalescent home....'

'Will I be allowed to convalesce here?'

'No harm in asking.'

1

History was repeating itself. Ashpole Manor had been turned into a hospital-cum-convalescent home during the 1914-18 war. When in 1919 it had been returned to the possession of its owners, the place had been in such a state of dilapidation that they had not thought it worth while to repair and restore the old house. Accepting the sum paid by way of compensation, they had vanished from local ken. Ashpole Manor remained semi-derelict for several years.

One of the boundaries of Ashpole Manor ran with Crompton Farm, owned by a disgruntled and unsuccessful man named Jabez Fook who, having given up the struggle of arable farming on the poor land some years previously, had turned the place over to the breeding of Aylesbury ducks, which flourished on the ponds and waterways of the farm.

With the end of the war opportunity was about to knock at the door of Crompton Farm, but Jabez Fook did not live to hear it. His son James, who had been demobilized just in time to bury his father, had had his wits sharpened by war which had seen him rise from private soldier to quartermaster sergeant and finally to commissioned rank. In this latter capacity any fine distinction between *meum* and *tuum* had become somewhat blunted. Just how it was all managed can be left to imagination, but on his return to civilian life the loot of the war years was dispersed in five bank accounts.

Crompton Farm, from which Jabez Fook had been able to scratch only a bare living, was a potential goldmine, a fact which was soon apparent to the acquisitive James who, working with former colleagues at the immense dump of military transport vehicles at Slough, was soon the possessor of a fine fleet of army lorries bought at auction for the proverbial song. In the knowledge that essential parts of the vehicles were missing and irreplaceable, there was little competitive bidding. James Fook, secure in the knowledge that the missing parts were in the barn at Crompton Farm, bought with confidence, becoming the possessor of a big fleet.

In 1919 and for some years afterwards there was a building boom in Britain. Crompton Farm being overlaid with fine gravel and sand to a depth of some 16 feet, James Fook was in a position to supply the enormous demand which had been created. With the added advantage of being able to deliver the gravel wherever required, he was 'sitting pretty'.

In 1921 James Fook was passing rich. In that year he married Doris Lockett, the junoesque barmaid at the Ashpole Arms, of which since his return from the war he had been one of the principal props. In 1922 and 1923, respectively, Doris produced two daughters, the older named Jean and the younger Gloria, the latter name discovered in a novelette.

By this time James Fook, having sold more than 700,000 tons of gravel, was filthy rich. Learning that Ashpole Manor was on the market, Doris gave him no peace until he had bought it. Doris had social ambitions. Whatever social inclinations James had had found fulfilment in the saloon bar of the Ashpole Arms where, being the star customer, he enjoyed privileged status.

Doris in the meantime, learning that Fook, Fulk, Fewkes, Fuke, Foulkes and ffoulkes were merely variations of the same name, arising probably out of illiteracy, decided that she liked the last. It was an improvement on Fook, which she regarded as rather common. Privately, she thought the ff 'a bit daft'. There began a campaign to persuade James to agree to the change of name. James, who had learned by experience that when Doris was on the warpath there was no peace until she had what she wanted, gave way. Although the change from Fook to ffoulkes was made by deed poll, he continued to call himself Fook and to insist upon being so addressed outside the home. Neither the relative magnificence of Ashpole Manor nor the change of name improved his earthy speech nor primitive table manners.

Crompton Farm, the source of the new-found wealth (if one

forgets the earlier larceny which made it all possible), was the real love of his life, and when Doris suggested that he move back to the old farmhouse without her and the girls, he agreed with alacrity. Apart from the thieving propensities acquired or developed as a quartermaster, James was a man of parts. There was even about him something which approached greatness. When the gravel had been stripped from the farm, leaving a series of huge pits linked by connecting waterways, a lesser man would have sat back to enjoy his wealth and called it a day. There was, as he expressed it, still some juice left in the old farm and he set about squeezing the last drop from it. Almost overnight it seemed he blossomed into a watercress king, and when he deemed that the market would not absorb any more, he stocked the gravel pits with trout, which were soon finding their way in thousands to London's better hotels and restaurants. His final venture was nothing less than a stroke of genius, the Crompton Angling Club. Every weekend scores, sometimes even hundreds, of ardent anglers at two guineas the rod, came to flog the waters for trout which cost them a great deal more than they would have cost retail. The bonanza came to an end when the trout were stricken with a disease which killed them in thousands. Then it seemed that both Crompton Farm and James Fook had fulfilled their destinies.

On the way back from the Ashpole Arms one evening, staggering under an impressive load of whisky, James tripped and fell into one of his trout ponds, where he drowned. The estate which he passed on to Doris and their two daughters was not far short of seven figures, which in the 1920s was solid wealth.

If James were not greatly mourned at Ashpole Manor, he was at the Ashpole Arms where, as a mark of respect, his usual stool at the saloon bar was draped in black crêpe on the evening after the funeral. Everything that can be said about him having been said, he now passes out of the story. Ashpole Manor, which barely noticed his presence, was seldom reminded of his absence. Doris, whose standards of gentility had been acquired behind the saloon bar, filled the old house with noisy riffraff amongst whom shrillness took

5

the place of wit. As soon as the girls were old enough, she packed them off to boarding school, where they acquired a certain elegance of deportment which they could not have acquired at home.

When the minimum permissible interval had elapsed, Doris achieved her life's ambition by marrying a shop-soiled baronet, Sir Eustace MacNiven, becoming in the process Lady MacNiven.

Sir Eustace proved an expensive luxury, for soon after the wedding a procession of process servers arrived at Ashpole Manor and it was only by paying off sundry creditors and redeeming bad cheques that criminal charges were averted. It cost her some £25,000, but as she saw things it was worth it.

Nevertheless, the quality of the guests who accepted Lady MacNiven's invitations was not conspicuously better than when she was plain Mrs ffoulkes or, for that matter, Mrs Fook.

Lady MacNiven was finding Ashpole Manor far too big for her needs. She, her daughters and the occasional house guests rattled around in it and it was only by employing more servants than were called for that its seemingly endless corridors came to life. When war broke out in 1939, Doris saw in it a heaven sent opportunity to unload this costly white elephant on to the shoulders of the taxpayer. Keeping a fine suite of rooms for herself in the west wing, she 'lent' Ashpole Manor to the government for use as a convalescent home for officers. It was a master stroke, which earned for her at no cost the reputation of being a patriotic benefactress, with always the possibility that among the convalescents there might be some well-born, eligible bachelors. In 1940 and 1941, when gallant young men were being shot out of the skies in hundreds during and after the Battle of Britain, the convalescents began to arrive. Jean, the older daughter, was then nineteen. Gloria was one year her junior. They were both ravishingly beautiful, charming and a credit to the excellent schools they had attended. They were fair-haired and had the same dazzling cornflower-blue eyes.

The more disagreeable tasks necessitated in ministering to

the needs of the convalescents, many of whom were barely mobile, devolved upon the nursing staff. Lady MacNiven and her daughters confined themselves to social duties. As it would not look well to be seen draped about the place in fashionable clothes, a West End couturier designed for the three of them a nursing 'uniform' which looked remarkably like the real thing only better. It was a great success ... with everyone but the nursing staff, where resentment ran high and contempt was barely concealed. Doris, never over-sensitive, had found it expedient during her years behind the bar of the Ashpole Arms to stifle what little sensitivity she possessed.

If Doris is being portrayed unsympathetically, she has no-body to blame but herself. She had her qualities, but they were not of the kind suited to the needs of an aspiring lady of the manor. If only James Fook had left her where she was behind the bar, she would have continued to be an ornament to her occupation.

*　　*　　*

By dint of much persistence and a little luck, Pilot-Officer Jonathan Dabney managed to get himself sent back to Ashpole Manor for convalescence and he was in a very low state when for the second time an ambulance brought him to its door. The compound fracture of his left leg had proved more than ordinarily troublesome, added to which he had suffered from delayed shock. He would always walk with a limp, the doctors had told him, but on the credit side was the near certainty that he would be grounded for the duration of the war.

Jonathan, one of a score of convalescents reclining in long chairs under the vast dome of the conservatory, saw the well-remembered vision of loveliness as soon as she came into view. She paused from time to time as she made the round, now to touch her cool, well-manicured hand to a possibly fevered brow, and then to study her wrist-watch intently as she felt a pulse, wondering as she did so how many heart-beats there should be to the minute and registering a mental note to ask someone. Jonathan looked up eagerly as she came abreast of him, shivering with delight in expectation of finding himself once more in the gaze of those lovely, sympathetic cornflower-blue eyes. But to his chagrined amazement and horror, she passed on without a sign of recognition.

'Isn't she a smasher?' he asked of his neighbour. 'Who is she?'

'Jean ffoulkes,' was the reply.

'So does her sister, or so I'm told,' said another voice.

Jonathan squirmed as he heard the chuckle that went the rounds. If there had been a white charger available, he would have done his best to mount it and slay the coarse-minded brutes who could not recognize loveliness and sweet innocence when they met it.

It was a full week before the lovely Jean ffoulkes noticed Jonathan's existence and even then, of course, they met as strangers. Their first encounter had been forgotten, all in the line of 'duty'. To Jean the love-light which shone from Jonathan's eyes was no novelty. She had come to regard it as an occupational hazard and after a time it became boring. There was no future in forming attachments to pleasant, sometimes delightful young men who were liable to be moved out of her orbit in a matter of days or weeks, probably never to be seen again. Her mother did not make things easier. Having landed a titled husband for herself, she was hopeful that her daughters would make 'good' marriages. Sentimentalizing over doubtless brave young men with broken limbs and no prospects was not going to help. In this attitude Doris regarded herself as being practical, but not hard; a fine distinction not always apparent.

A fact which has not been mentioned is that Jonathan Dabney was a good-looking young man, easy mannered and with an air of distinction probably inherited from an eighteenth-century French ancestor, together with the parrot-beak style of nose so greatly prized in France. While Jean ffoulkes was not as infatuated with Jonathan as he was with her, there was a mutual attraction. She was spending at least a half-hour daily with him and only mother's watching eye

8

prevented her from spending more. Then, just as things were falling nicely into place, the doctors pronounced Jonathan fit for ground duty and he was posted to an airfield in Scotland, where he was given a desk job in the operations room.

It seemed unlikely that they would ever meet again.

Nineteen forty-one merged into 1942. Jonathan was posted to another ground job, this time in North Africa. In a dive-bombing attack on a munitions dump he was wounded by shell or bomb splinters. None of the wounds was serious, but in the aggregate they were bad enough to keep him in hospital for several months, during which sundry pieces of metal were removed from him. At the end of 1944, after a spell of convalescence in Durban, he reached England in a poor state, physically and morally.

All this time his devotion to Jean ffoulkes had not diminished. He wrote to her constantly and received several letters in return, some of which he found rather bewildering because of a certain confusion existing in her mind between him and a young Canadian, also named Jonathan, who wanted her to return with him to Pincher Creek, Alberta, when the war was over. In one of her letters to Jonathan, i.e. Jonathan Dabney, she said:

> However hard you try to make Pincher Creek sound attractive, it sounds perfectly grim to me. Just fancy receiving letters addressed to Pincher Creek. No thanks!!

Even when he received this, the scales did not drop from our Jonathan's eyes. So sweetly was she enshrined in his heart, he could not believe that Jean was playing fast and loose with his affections.

Doris steamed open and read all letters addressed to her daughters. It was, she insisted, her bounden 'duty'. Far from discouraging this supposedly clandestine correspondence, she was delighted. At one time Jean had eleven suitors on a string in every theatre of war, and when mortality reduced their number to five she remarked sardonically that her daughter seemed to have the kiss of death. There was, as the saying went, safety in numbers until someone 'suitable' came along.

Jonathan's greatest worry for some while had been something too indelicate to put in a letter and most certainly not calculated to enhance his desirability in the eyes of any nubile young woman, still less one of Jean's lusty habit. One of the splinters from the bombing of the munitions dump had struck Jonathan in what a jovial surgeon described as 'the family jewels'. 'You may have pride of ancestry, my boy, but like the mule, your hopes of posterity rest upon a very flimsy foundation. Let's hope for the best.'

On arrival in England Jonathan went directly to a convalescent hospital not far from Guildford in Surrey. It was another huge private house – Pilgrims – 'lent' for the duration of the war. Here, driving a smart van wangled by Lady MacNiven for the transportation of 'hospital supplies', Jean ffoulkes came to visit him.

On this occasion, greatly to his joy, Jean greeted Jonathan effusively. The old offhandedness, to which he had grown inured, was put aside and for the first time he did not have to indulge in too much self-deception to believe that his love was reciprocated.

On Jean's third visit to Pilgrims, Jonathan tremblingly produced an extremely modest engagement ring, bought the day before in Guildford. 'It isn't much in itself,' he said, 'but it's what it stands for that counts.'

When he was allowed to slip it on the correct finger, Jonathan admitted to being the happiest man in the world.

2

A film casting director needing someone to play the part of a languid French aristocrat taking his last ride in a tumbril to the guillotine, would have seized on Mr Edouard St Laurent Dabney with avidity. The services of a make-up man would not have been needed, except perhaps to adapt skin colouring to the lights. His luxurious sideburns and drooping walrus moustache were almost too good to be true.

As he paced the long gallery in the dying rays of the westering sun, the sadness of his bearing seemed to speak aloud. La Bastide, the big ugly stone plantation house, which had been in the possession of the family since 1781 when Newcastle Island, as it was now called, had been known as Châteauneuf, was likely to pass into other hands unless some unlikely financial miracle were to bring respite. In the old ballroom rum casks, most alas! empty, were stored. In sixteen of the eighteen bedrooms rats were nesting in the mattresses. His own bedroom still retained some of its shabby magnificence and that of Jonathan Dabney, away at the wars, was kept ready for his immediate occupation when and if he should return.

La Bastide had been built on the highest point of the island, commanding on three sides a sweep of sugar cane down to the palm-fringed beaches beyond which the incredibly blue blueness of the Caribbean stretched away to the horizon, like some vastly exaggerated picture postcard brought to life. Five generations of his forebears had looked down on this scene, secure in the knowledge that with the exception of the relatively small holdings of land on the north side, it was all theirs. But for reasons which even he did not fully understand, during his father's and his own generation it had almost all passed from Dabney hands. The explanation was simple enough. The momentum possessed by the family in the late eighteenth century had not been great enough to survive into the twentieth and, in modern terms, it had just run out of steam.

Dabney turned sadly from the gallery into the house and, seated at a Louis XV escritoire which collectors would have fought to possess, he began to write what was in effect the epitaph of the Dabneys. It was the first of a series of articles he had undertaken to write for the *Novocastrian*, the island's weekly and only newspaper, and since out of a total population of something over 70,000 approximately eighty-nine per cent was illiterate, it could not afford to pay its rare contributors. For Dabney it was a labour of love.

HISTORICAL NOTES

Since the fateful day in 1781 when, as the representative of King Louis XVI of France, Comte Armand Saint-Aubin d'Aubigny first set foot on these shores, the story of his descendants and that of the island itself have been inextricably mingled. Twice during the eight years which elapsed between his arrival and the French Revolution, the French flag was lowered and replaced by that of England, only to have the process reversed until in 1802 the French flag was lowered for the last time. But although England was the dominant power, the heart and soul of Châteauneuf, anglicized to Newcastle, remained French. The language of the people remained French for two whole generations. Despite other influences at work upon their Faith, their religion continued to be Roman Catholicism.

Under who can guess what pressure d'Aubigny dropped his title of nobility. His grandson under like pressure dropped even the name, becoming plain Mr Daubeney, which in turn gave way to the even simpler form of Dabney....

He might have added that by a brilliant feat of gymnastics and balancing, the family succeeded in walking the tightrope between French sympathies and British loyalties, but preferred for his own good reasons to slur over it and the further remarkable fact that by these means they managed to survive the storms with their lands intact.

The truth of the matter was that this eminently practical family, once satisfied that Anglo-Saxondom was firmly in the saddle, quickly came to terms with the new régime, which was not at all difficult as the British were only too glad to have the most influential French family on the island ranged on their side.

Summoning an aged coloured retainer and instructing him to harness the pony to the rickety dogcart, Dabney donned his best black-alpaca suit, used only on important occasions, and drove into the squalid little town of Port Lewis, formerly Port Louis. Arrived outside the two-storey structure which housed the *Novocastrian*, he hitched the pony to a rail and climbed the sagging wooden staircase, pausing at the wooden door marked 'Editor'. When his knocking produced no result, Dabney opened the door to see Robbie McAlister – owner, editor, business manager, typesetter and proof-reader – snoring in a long cane chair beside the open french window.

From below came the rhythmic thudding of an ancient flat-bed printing press. It was Thursday evening: the *Novocastrian* had gone to press. As Dabney should have known, without troubling to pay the call, Robbie was drunk.

Disinclined to leave the first instalment of the 'Historical Notes' on the desk at the mercy of the rising trade wind, Dabney put it in his pocket, picked his way downstairs with care, unhitched the pony and resumed his seat in the trap, where he sat for a few minutes in a mood of indecision. To go or not to go to the Tucker House, the town's only bar and eating place worthy of the name: that was the question. There was plenty of rum at La Bastide, plenty that is to say for non-commercial purposes, and of infinitely superior quality to anything obtainable in the town. But he was in one of his rare gregarious moods and, tired of his own company amid the faded grandeur of his home, passionately desired the bonhomie of the bar to help lift the cloud of sad nostalgia which had settled on him since writing the article.

Dabney had no money. He would have none until the end of the month, when certain small sums were due to him. But in the interim the big question in his mind was whether his credit would be good at the Tucker House, or not? To be refused credit by a coarse, ill-bred man like Tucker was unthinkable, the ultimate humiliation. Sadly, he turned the pony's head in the direction of home.

On arrival, hand trembling with eagerness, he lit a candle with whose aid he fumbled his way across the littered ball-room where, from the last but one cask of old rum, he filled a splendid cut-glass decanter. The smooth golden spirit restored to the drab realities of the present some glitter of years which were gone forever. The decanter empty and the beloved trade wind cooling his fevered brow, Dabney fell into a dreamless sleep, unbroken until the sun rose to begin the climb to its brazen zenith. The problems of yesterday, being insoluble, remained to be faced all over again.

Over his early morning coffee and fruit, Dabney came near to deciding to accept the post of librarian which, together with the pittance it carried had been offered to him some days previously. Since it meant being the custodian of such of the archives as had not been destroyed by damp, white ants, rats and clumsy hands, he hoped the stuffy little bureaucrats would accede to his request and call him archivist, which sounded so much better than librarian.

The morning began well with a letter from his son Jonathan, who announced his forthcoming marriage to Jean ffoulkes, the 'sweetest and loveliest girl I have ever met'. Knowing his son's romantic nature, this left him unimpressed. But what did impress him came later in the letter:

... Jean's mother, Lady MacNiven, seems to be a very wealthy woman. She evidently approves of me as a son-in-law because she holds out the prospect of a job in a company in which she owns a controlling interest. Just exactly what the job is she does not say, but quoting her it is 'to keep an eye on my interests'. These must be important because the salary mentioned, £2,000 per annum, seems a lot for someone as inexperienced as I am. We plan to be married as soon as I am out of the hands of the doctors....

Undaunted by the fear that credit would be refused, Dabney joined a few of his cronies at Tucker's bar just before noon. 'Gentlemen,' he announced in a firm and confident voice, 'I ask you to join me in a toast. My son Jonathan writes to say that he is recovering from his wounds and will shortly be married. Jean, the bride-to-be, is a considerable heiress, daughter of Lady MacNiven ... *the* Lady MacNiven.'

Credit re-established, Dabney was still propping up the bar when the shadows lengthened and the curtain of tropical night enfolded the squalid little town, and it was left to his friends to drive him up the hill to La Bastide.

There were those who regarded Dabney *père* as a drunk and in a sense he was that, but he was the kind who drank less for the drink itself than for the way it softened the harsh outlines of life. Under its influence he had never been known to behave badly. His tongue might slur over certain words, his feet might have to be lifted somewhat high to enable him to cope with the big fluffy balls of cotton which unaccountably attached themselves to his soles. Always somewhat formal in his manner, he became more so. His vocabulary, always impeccably clean, tended to become archaic, while his manners would not have disgraced the ancestor who, as he strolled through the *Salle des glaces* at Versailles, was in the habit of surveying the details of his attire before being ushered into the royal presence. The story may well not have been true, but the manners were indisputably so. When invited to Government House, his courtesy towards Their Excellencies was indistinguishable from that he accorded to the great-granddaughters of former d'Aubigny slaves encountered in the streets of the town. For these and many other endearing qualities, Edouard St Laurent Dabney was a well-loved man. People were inclined to laugh at him, but if they pitied him they did not show it.

3

Ashpole Manor had served its purpose and when Lady MacNiven drove out of the gates for the last time, she had no regrets. It was April 1945. When the last of the convalescents had departed, and she had regained possession of the house, she intended to accept the offer of an insurance company whose intention was to transform it into an office and storage place for files. What now pleased her most was that she would no longer be haunted by the spectre of the Ashpole Arms and the degrading years which necessity had caused her to spend behind the bar, years which Ashpole neighbours could not be expected to forget. All that, she hoped and believed, belonged to a past now finally buried. It served only to show how true nobility could survive the most demeaning circumstances.

In the twelve-room flat in Park Lane, whose lease she had just purchased, unhampered by the petty considerations of what she regarded as near-suburbia, her daughters would be launched into the social whirl to which their beauty and their mother's wealth and position entitled them.

Jean, the naughty girl, had been doing some shooting before the Twelfth, as the saying was, but with Jonathan Dabney out of hospital and their imminent marriage, that worry was off her mind. Nevertheless it was going to be a near thing, mused Lady MacNiven. Seven months could be explained away. Six caused raised eyebrows. But five, no, and that she greatly feared was Jean's coming problem.

But what puzzled Lady MacNiven was the question of how and when it had happened. Certainly not on drives in a two-seater car, swathed in bandages and with a hip set in plaster. An equally improbable theatre was a single bed in a dormitory shared with a dozen other men. Then how and when? She would have to think up some delicately phrased formula for asking Jean herself. The answer could be extremely interesting and informative. The things these modern young people got up to! Small wonder that in the days of iron-bound stays and crinolines girls were so inhibited. Not that such considerations had weighed in her family. She herself had been conceived under a hedge on a hop-picking fortnight near Paddock Wood and, so she had learned many years later, her mother had married the wrong man.

In the beginning of their association Doris had had some doubts as to the suitability of young Dabney as a husband for Jean. But in the light of the first instalments of the 'Historical Notes' which Jonathan had just received from his father, the doubts had been dispelled. What could be more distinguished than an ancient family of French aristocrats compelled by the brutal English to relinquish their title, former owners of eight hundred slaves and countless acres of sugar land?

If d'Aubigny had been vulgarized to Dabney, what was to prevent the process being reversed? The Comtesse d'Aubigny would rank above even Lady MacNiven. It would be a triumphant outcome to what might have been a sorry *mésalliance*. There was a song in her heart on the drive back to London.

There was more good news when she arrived in Park Lane. Sir Eustace MacNiven, who for two years had been battling pink elephants and other zoological manifestations, had suddenly taken it into his head that he was a pigeon and had flown out of a fourth floor window in Aberdeenshire.

All was merry as a marriage bell: but was it?

Jonathan announced himself from the lobby of the Park Lane flats. Would it, he asked his mother-in-law-to-be, be convenient for her to receive him privately?

'I suppose you mean without Jean hearing. Is that it?'

Yes, that was it.

'Well, come up and get it off your chest, whatever it is,' she said heartily. Young men had always shown a tendency to confide in Doris, dating back to before the saloon bar days. They always talked bloody nonsense and it always added up to nothing. Here was just one more.

'I intended to say what I have to say to Jean,' Jonathan began uncomfortably, plumping into his half of a Darby and Joan chair, facing the window overlooking Hyde Park.

'Well, why didn't you?'

'It wasn't the kind of thing I could discuss with an innocent girl. . . .'

It was only iron self-control which prevented Doris from a loud guffaw.

'You see,' he continued, 'when I was wounded in North Africa, a shell splinter hit me in . . . well, a rather awkward spot, and the surgeon who removed it warned me that I might never be . . . a father.'

'D'you mean you're impotent? This is the hell of a time to announce that. . . .'

'I don't think so . . . that is if impotent means what I think it does. . . .'

'You don't think so!' roared Doris in high indignation. 'Don't you think it's about time you found out and set your doubts at rest? God Almighty! boy, you're going to be married in a couple of weeks. D'you realize what that means?'

'Yes, that's why I'm here now . . . I'm trying to do the – er – decent thing. I've come to you for advice. What shall I do?'

'What shall you do? God strike me pink! What a question! Find out for sure whether you are or not, then let's take it from there. . . .'

'But how?'

'How?' she echoed with unnecessary loudness. 'Well, for crying out loud there *is* only one way . . . the old-fashioned way . . . give the dog a swim!'

Jonathan winced. He had never heard the expression before, but its meaning was painfully clear and it occurred to him for the first time that the veneer of gentility she wore was very thin.

'You're surely not telling me to be . . . unfaithful to Jean?' he asked in shocked amazement. But he was far less shocked than Doris was when the full implications of the situation became apparent to her. Jean, as her mother was only too well aware, was as she put it, a member of the 'pudden club' in good standing and had been for at least three months, possibly more. This did not in itself faze Lady MacNiven, for Jean had been born a bare three months after Doris's own wedding ceremony. But the pill she was finding difficulty in swallowing was that if this embarrassed young man were speaking the truth, and she believed he was, he could not be responsible for Jean's condition, as she had all along assumed to be the case. Jonathan, as she well knew, was green as grass, but Doris was too worldly-wise to confuse inexperience with stupidity. He was far from stupid. His kind was somewhat beyond her ken and although she did not know what made him tick, she recognized him as an idealist. She had heard about such people, knew they existed, and had the wit to understand that when their illusions were shattered they themselves were shattered too.

Doris had a very kind streak in her. She liked Jonathan and did not want to see him hurt. But how to avoid it? Her eminently practical mind wanted to tell him to have a romp between the sheets with Jean, which would clarify everything. If Jonathan turned out to be incapable of rising to the occasion, the engagement would have to be broken. If, on the other hand, his pessimism about himself proved to be without foundation, he would be so proud and delighted to be a prospective father that little inconsistencies of the calendar would escape his notice. Jean would be able to explain all that away. Trust Jean.

It seemed to Doris that whatever she might do at this juncture was sure to be wrong, which was a very wise summation of the matter. There was no way in which she could advise Jonathan. Advice, if she had any to give, must be reserved for Jean. What Jean did, or did not do, must decide everything.

Telling Jonathan untruthfully that she had an important engagement, Doris looked anxiously at her watch, disappeared into another room to change for the street, and left him to wait for Jean, who was supposed to be with her hairdresser.

Five minutes after Doris had closed the door of the flat behind her, Jonathan, still sitting glumly by the window in the mood of indecision, heard the handle of a door turn behind him. Turning to look, he could hardly believe his eyes.

Gloria, Jean's younger sister, her back towards him, was preening herself in front of a mirror, clad in pink silk panties of a kind soon to be called bikinis and more or less nothing else.

Jonathan being Jonathan coughed gently and resumed his study of the double-decker buses on Park Lane.

Gloria shrieked in mock terror and fled. The encounter, she was sure, would have a greater impact on Jonathan if he believed it to be accidental.

Now Jean and Gloria resembled each other very closely. In fact, during his first convalescence at Ashpole Manor, seeing them apart, he had more than once mistaken one for the other. They were both exceptionally beautiful girls, but latterly it had been easy to tell them apart.

It had always seemed to Jonathan that Gloria disliked him. Where possible she had avoided him. Being so infatuated with Jean, the other's disdain had not troubled him. But the truth had been quite otherwise and, far from disliking him, Gloria had always harboured a little *tendresse* for him, resenting what she knew to have been Jean's easy conquest. On the surface all was well between the two sisters, but deeply buried, and almost always out of sight, there was a bitter jealousy which dated back to nursery days.

Gloria had been vastly curious to know why Jonathan had sought out her mother for this private talk and, being a member of a most practical family, had satisfied her curiosity by eavesdropping. She had often wondered about Jonathan and now she knew. If Jean, whom she knew to be pregnant, were about to be landed with an impotent husband, which seemed likely, then it served her right. Let her talk her way out of that one!

But – Gloria paused in her thoughts – was he impotent? Was he? Well, as her mother had told him so crudely, there was only one way to find out.

Gloria came back into the room wearing skin-tight pale-blue slacks and a cerise cashmere sweater which made Jonathan's eyes pop. Having glimpsed the 'goodies' unadorned, he found them even more entrancing thus.

'How was I to know Mummy had left you all alone?' she

20

asked prettily. 'Waiting for Jean, I suppose. Was that it?'

Jonathan could only nod.

'Well, it's lucky I was here then, because I happen to know for a fact that she won't be back for hours ... don't look so crestfallen, Jonathan. I'm here and, if you'd only take the trouble to know me, I'm just as nice as Jean. Please, please talk to me ... it will be such a treat to talk to someone intelligent for a change. Tell me about yourself ...'

'There isn't much to tell. You see, I went straight from school into the R.A.F.'

'Most of the boys I know bore me to tears. They have only one thing on their minds. ...'

'And what is that?'

'Now you're making fun of me, pretending you don't know. What's on *your* mind, right now this very minute?' She thrust her rounded breasts at him provocatively. 'Go on, don't be shy. Say what's on your mind. I won't tell anyone ... promise.'

'I think you'd be shocked if I told you,' said Jonathan.

'Try me and see. You couldn't shock me if you tried.'

'I don't quite know how to put it into words,' said Jonathan, blushing furiously.

'Words! Who cares about words? In this world it's deeds that count. ...'

He never did know quite how it happened, but a moment later Gloria was in his arms, Jean forgotten.

An hour later, putting on his clothes in her bedroom, Jonathan realized the enormity of his conduct. What made it seem worse was that he was out of love with Jean and madly, recklessly in love with Gloria who, sitting on the edge of the bed with nothing on, was laughing at him. 'Well,' she said, 'now you know, don't you?'

'Know what?'

'That you're not impotent, of course. Would you like me to give it to you in writing?'

'How did you know that?'

'I was listening behind the door when you told mother. Now you've nothing to worry about. But it took little Gloria to teach you the facts of life, didn't it?'

'Now what are we going to do?' he asked, as the customary depression settled upon him. 'About Jean and your mother, I mean.'

'*You* are going to do nothing, do you hear me, nothing except go away somewhere for a few days without telling anyone ... and anyone means Jean ... where you've gone. Then 'phone me. I've my own number here. I'll tell you what to do ... specially what not to do. Leave everything to me.'

'Above all things, darling, I don't want to hurt Jean's feelings ...'

'You won't hurt them ... you can't, 'cos why, she hasn't got any feelings, that's why. Now get out of here ... quickly, before someone finds us together.'

As Jonathan stepped out of one lift in the hall below, he saw out of the tail of his eye Jean stepping into the other. He did not think she saw him. Once outside, without turning round, he walked at furious speed the length of Curzon Street as far as Berkeley Square. Then, because it was beginning to rain, he hailed a taxi and returned to the Bayswater boarding house where he was staying. Hastily packing a bag while the taxi waited, he went to Victoria, taking the first available train to Brighton. Only then did his panic subside.

All things considered, it had turned out to be a memorable day, especially since it had begun so badly.

* * *

Three days of solitude and boredom spent looking out of his hotel window at umbrellas being turned inside out by squalls and occasional forays on to the promenade did little if anything to lift the load of worry which was crushing Jonathan. He was conscious of behaving – his word for himself – like a cad. He had betrayed the trust of an innocent and lovely girl and for as long as he lived he would never forgive himself for it.

But Jonathan need not have worried, need not have blamed himself so bitterly, for his fate was in sure and competent hands. Gloria, like her mother and sister, was a most practical young woman. When he telephoned her on the evening of the third day, she said gaily: 'Come home, all is forgiven!'

While this was not strictly accurate, it was nearer to the truth than might have been imagined in the circumstances. When Jonathan returned to the Park Lane flat, he was greeted affectionately by Gloria. Neither Doris nor Jean was in evidence. They were, it emerged later, visiting an eminent Harley Street abortionist with a view to getting rid of Jean's unwanted infant. Since under great pressure Jean had admitted Jonathan's complete innocence in the matter and since he, however green he might be, could hardly be expected to father another man's child, the sooner this embarrassment was removed the better. Without waiting to consult Jonathan, Doris had cancelled the wedding arrangements, withdrawn some four hundred invitations, accepting the situation philosophically and dealing with it as she saw best. She had yet to learn of the new complications. Wisely, Gloria decided not to burden her with these until an appropriate time arrived.

A romp between the sheets was, as Gloria knew only too well, a long way from a serious proposal of marriage. She was not even sure whether, if he proposed, she wanted to marry Jonathan.

It became apparent during the days which followed that he was nursing a guilty conscience where Jean was concerned. Jean, he was told, had broken the engagement. Why? She had changed her mind, which surely was every young woman's unquestioned privilege.

'But what happened to make her change her mind?' he asked Doris out of Gloria's hearing.

'Who knows what the true reasons ever are for a girl changing her mind?' replied Doris evasively.

'Did you tell her what I told you here in this room ... in confidence?'

'About you being impotent ... is that what you mean? No, I did not, so you can forget it.'

'I told you,' he went on reproachfully, 'because it seemed to me the only honourable thing to do....'

Doris sat bolt upright in alarm. Life had taught her that when men started talking about honour, honour was the last thing they had on their minds. 'I didn't tell her, Jonathan. I promise you that. But even if I had, it couldn't really have affected the issue ... could it now? You are, or you're not. Talking doesn't change anything. But talking as an older woman, I would advise you to set all doubts in the matter at rest. Get the best possible advice on the subject. It's important ... very important for you to know because knowing one way or the other can affect the whole course of your life ...'

'I do know ... now,' he said, looking up into a candidly appraising pair of blue eyes. 'I was worrying myself without need. I'm *not* impotent.'

'So that's where you've been for the last day or so. I wondered what you were up to. Took a nice little bit of stuff away for a trial run, eh!' Doris allowed her not very convincing upper-class diction to slip away from her, becoming again her natural earthy self. 'How was it? Up to expectations, eh? Go on, don't be shy ... tell Doris.'

This was too much for Jonathan. This was the way men talked, but to hear it from a woman's lips did not sound right. He knew if he remained under cross-examination any longer, she would manage somehow to worm the truth out of him and that he simply could not face. Looking at his watch, he fled.

*   *   *

When he contemplated the predicament in which he found himself, Jonathan panicked. Whatever he did seemed likely to be wrong. If, regardless of consequences, he had followed his inclinations, he would, as he viewed things, repair the wrong he had done to Gloria by a proposal of marriage. If he could have believed Doris, he would have felt better about things. Jean, he felt sure, had broken off the engagement, having been told by her mother of Jonathan's disability. How would Jean regard him when, as it would seem to her, having extricated himself from his entanglement with her by pleading impotence, he used her younger sister as a means of proving that he was nothing of the kind?

It was an impossible situation in which, wisely, he sat back and did nothing.

Then Fate, as so often happens when human perplexities seem insoluble, took a hand. There came from home a cablegram to say that his father was critically ill and asking to see him.

Jonathan had not seen his father since his last trip home in 1938, when he was sixteen years of age. Since then war had intervened and even if it had not, Dabney *père* had been in such straitened financial circumstances that, after paying for Jonathan's schooling, he would have been unable to pay the expensive return fare. The chief sufferer had been the father, for in the nearly eight years which had elapsed since their last meeting, Jonathan's memories of the other had grown somewhat vague and shadowy. They had corresponded regularly, for there was a very real bond of affection between them. But as they grew apart, the bond had become more tenuous. Jonathan had been made aware indirectly of his father's difficulties, but only indirectly. It had not escaped his notice either that the substance of the letters and the quality of the handwriting had deteriorated.

Ocean passages in 1945 were difficult to obtain. Jonathan was turned down everywhere he went until he had the bright idea of appealing for help from Grimsditch and Co., the City agents who had represented the Dabney interests in London for more than a hundred years. Harold Grimsditch, the head of the firm, in remembrance of the long association, found a passage for Jonathan in a ship loading for Port of Spain, Trinidad, whence he could obtain a schooner passage to Port Lewis. Although there were no longer any Dabney interests to represent, Grimsditch pretended to debit the cost of the passage to the non-existent Dabney account. The Grimsditch family had grown rich largely on Dabney business and, although the slick and impersonal attitude seemed to dominate business in most places, here was a happy exception.

4

Never go back! As a generality, it is a sound rule. There seems to be a physical law which says that things shrink in direct ratio to the time of separation. Port Lewis, seen from the careenage as the schooner *Sea Fox* dropped anchor after a rough forty-eight hour crossing from Port of Spain, seemed to Jonathan an even more squalid little slum than memory had painted it. The Tucker House, apart from the Customs House and other Government buildings, was the only edifice worthy of the name and then it wasn't much. The commercial centre was little more than a shantytown straggling around the small harbour and along the waterfront, where it gave way to pleasant little red-tiled houses set in gay gardens. On the two hills immediately above all this were Government House on the one and on the other the lighthouse, which flashed an unnecessary warning to deep draught vessels to give the place a wide berth. For the rest, undulating low hills were clothed in sugarcane, which, as it reflected no light, gave the landscape a sombre monotony. In folds of the hills, invisible from the sea, were even more squalid little villages, essentially unchanged for 150 years.

On the high point three miles or so from the town was La Bastide, standing in bold silhouette against the skyline, built of Brittany granite brought out to the island as ballast during the eighteenth century.

This, mused Jonathan grimly, is home. For this all these years I have been homesick.

'Dabney,' said the official at the immigration desk, reading from Jonathan's passport. 'Lots of that name here.'

'Now there's one more,' was the sour reply.

'Born here, too, I see.'

26

'Where were you born?'

'Barbados.'

'Well, you couldn't help that either, could you?'

'Staying here long?'

'Please God, no.'

One of the island's taxis was in for repairs, while the other had a flat tyre. Leaving his bags at the Tucker House, Jonathan set out on foot for La Bastide, glad of the chance to stretch his legs.

Dabney *père* was in a very low state. Ever since receiving the cable announcing Jonathan's imminent return, he had clung to life with a fierce determination to see his hero son again. The latter's modest exploits during the war had, seen from this sheltered backwater, assumed legendary proportions.

Dr Elias Daubeny, a cousin of the dying man, having a common great-grandfather, warned Jonathan that there was no hope and that the end could not be far off. 'If you want me during the day, hoist a flag,' he told Jonathan. 'At night, light the storm lanterns on the gallery. Edouard was always a good friend to me. Thanks to him paying for my education, I am a doctor today. I shall miss him as much as you will. The era ends with him. God knows what is coming in its place.'

Jonathan, his ears long out of tune with the sing-song speech of the island and its mixture of French patois and archaic English, could only with difficulty communicate with the two aged retainers, who shuffled gloomily around the big house, eyes fixed on the ground or focused on blank infinity ahead of them.

'There's a lot I want to say to you, my boy,' said his old father who was not really old, but worn out. 'I've been saving it for years, hoping you were coming back. But now you are here, I'm wondering whether any of it is worth saying. We Dabneys have been here a long time. We've left our mark here, but now our hand lies very lightly on the island. The story is nearly told. We are people with a past and no future. When I am gone, Jonathan, will you stay?'

'No, Father, I don't think so. What will there be to stay for?'

There followed a long silence.

'In your place,' the old man went on, 'I doubt whether I would stay either. We have been big frogs in a small pond and there isn't much fun in reverting to small frogs. It's hard on one's pride.

'There won't be much coming to you, Jonathan. I think you know that, but everything ... such as it is ... is in apple-pie order. Go to see Zachary. Everything is in his hands ... has been for a long time in case I went before you came back, or you went before I did. This old house, despite its story and associations, isn't worth keeping. It's a dismal place at best and the kind of life once lived here has been swept away. Let it go, boy, let it go. There's only one thing worth holding on to ... only one, and that is the Reef. Go down there before you leave. Fix everything in your mind's eye and hold on to it. The Dabney future, if there is a future, lies there. Hold on, boy. Tell me you'll hold on.'

'Yes, Father, I'll hold on. I promise you.'

All through that day and the night which followed, Jonathan sat beside his father's bed, letting him do the talking. His voice was weak and the silences long.

'Would you like me to hang out the lanterns for the doctor, Father? He'll come straight away ...'

'No, Jonathan, let the poor man sleep while he may. Why let him climb the hill just to wave goodbye ...'

Edouard St Laurent Dabney died as he had lived, without what the world calls greatness, a kind, considerate gentleman to the end.

Dr Elias Daubeny came soon after dawn and when he heard the news tears coursed down his honest brown cheeks. 'He was the best friend I ever had,' he said sadly.

When the funeral cortège wound its way to the cemetery, uncounted hundreds turned out to pay their last respects. Among them more than a hundred bore the name of Dabney, or one of its many variations. Five of them were the dead man's half brothers, all born on the wrong side of the blanket. Four of them were his own sons in like case. And there were cousins of every conceivable degree who claimed kinship traced back as far as the slave days, added to whom were the descendants of former Dabney slaves many of whom, as was the custom, adopted the Dabney name. Of them all only Jonathan could claim undiluted white blood back to 1781 when the first d'Aubigny arrived.

After the funeral, in the ornate salon of La Bastide prettied up for the occasion and for the last time, Jonathan stood for three hours while Dabneys of every hue came to shake his hand and offer their condolences, and there was hardly a dry eye among them. 'I am your great-aunt Tabitha,' said one old crone who came painfully on crutches. 'I am your cousin Walter Dabney,' said a man of his own age, 'and these are my children, Amanda and Peter. Your daddy was their godfather. God rest his soul.'

What impressed Jonathan most was the way these people brushed mere questions of legitimacy aside as not worth consideration. They were Dabney kin and nothing else seemed to matter. The only European equivalent, equally hard to understand, are the eager claims of people with nothing else to commend them than descent from royal bastards.

Zachary Daubney, whom Jonathan had been told by his father to visit, was a solicitor, one of the island's only two men of law. He was a handsome, brown-skinned man in his forties who had inherited from his father the practice whose mainstay since the turn of the century had been Dabney business. He and Jonathan were cousins ... of a kind. The fact that he spelled his name as he did indicated descent from the main stem of the Dabney tree dating from a time before 1880 when the name became so to speak stabilized as Dabney. Aside from his dark pigmentation, Zachary had an entirely Caucasian appearance. He closely resembled a distinguished English barrister whom as an articled clerk in London he had often met, admiring him enough to adopt the same mannerisms and affectations. But Zachary was his own man in all other ways, with an enviable reputation for probity.

'Well, it had to come,' said Zachary sadly to Jonathan, who sat opposite to him in the client's chair, 'but it was good that you were able to be with him at the end and comfort him in his last hours. As you well know, he was not a great man. Perhaps it was on account of that lack of greatness that he was so well loved. Greatness makes a poor bedfellow with kindness and modesty ... but I don't need to sing his praises to you of all people, so I'll come to the point....

'Your father's Will is simple enough. He left everything to you. Everything! I estimate if everything he possessed were to be sold right now, the proceeds would cover his debts and perhaps two to three hundred pounds. The chief asset is La Bastide, which is mortgaged to the hilt. So long as he gets his interest, the mortgagee is in no hurry to foreclose. Prices in the Caribbean are rising, so you need be in no hurry to sell ... if you can pay the interest. Then there is, of course, the contents of the house, all free of encumbrance. There is also a piece of land beyond the town and below the lighthouse. It is worth about £300 and is mortgaged for about that. But it has some 200 yards of sea frontage, which makes it worth holding on to. Have you any money?'

'I dare say I'm worth all told about £800. Being in hospital for so long, I haven't spent much for a long time. Perhaps some back pay due to me would bring it up to a thousand pounds....'

'Splendid! Then if you will take my advice you have a good chance of being a rich man before you are my age. Let us go together now to inspect your most important asset ... the Reef.'

At the southern tip of the island the rich sugar land petered out giving way to a barren rocky tract where goats eked out a bare existence from the mean herbage which grew amongst the palmetto scrub. It ended on a beach half a mile in length along which grew a few score of coconut palms. A quarter-mile offshore, roughly following the contour of the beach, was a coral reef, part of which was above water. The reef enclosed a lagoon making a safe harbour for small craft. Jonathan remembered the place vaguely from childhood. Somewhere along the beach, hidden under a tangle of creepers, purple and scarlet bougainvillaea, was a small house built of sawn coral blocks. Here at least three generations of Dabneys had come for occasional swimming and fishing weekends. His father had brought him there often. The worst feature of the place had been the sea eggs* found in abundance along the

* Sea urchins.

30

beach, their spines causing painful and sometimes poisonous punctures.

'All this is yours, Jonathan, entirely without encumbrance. At least twenty years ago your father tried to borrow money on it, but nobody was interested. Be grateful for that.'

'It doesn't look to me to be worth anything,' said Jonathan, 'and even if it isn't, I'm glad it's mine. It's truly beautiful and it's good to know that if it ever becomes necessary I can come back here to lead a Robinson Crusoe existence. But tell me, what makes you think it will ever be worth anything?'

'Things are moving in the Caribbean. It may all end in smoke. Jamaica was where it all started. Soon after the First World War the rich playboys bought land there ... mostly Canadians to begin with, coming down to escape the brutal winters. Land values leaped and fortunes were made overnight. The same thing is happening in Puerto Rico and the Virgin Islands. Next on the list is Barbados, where already there are signs of change.

'You see, Jonathan, the Caribbean is to North America what the French Riviera is to Europe ... winter sunshine, and those who want it will have to pay for it. So, I say to you, hold on, even if it means going without a lot of things you need ... or think you do. We can't influence the course of events. All we can do is sit back and wait for them to happen and until they happen there's nothing for you here, so don't think of staying. I'll hold the fort for you and tell you when to come back.'

During the next days, exploring the island where he had been born and where his roots were so deep, Jonathan was aware of conflicting influences at work on him. The sheer squalor of Port Lewis appalled him, while the warmth of his welcome at the hands of people he assumed would have forgotten him had been a wonderful experience. Perhaps after all it was something to be a Dabney. The great disappointment was to meet the seven or eight families which, claiming undiluted white blood, constituted themselves the aristocracy of the island. None had been there as long as the Dabneys but several could boast a hundred years or more of knowing no other home.

31

Nordic stock tends to deteriorate in the tropics, especially where life is too easy. Chattel slavery followed by the even more vicious economic slavery created a race of privileged white people unable or unwilling to perform the smallest task for themselves. Their stature dwindled until the only source of pride was the white blood itself. Malaria, rum punch, intestinal parasite diseases, in-breeding, rice eating, hot peppers on jaded palates and the false life of a mutual admiration society played havoc with the descendants of people who had been bold pioneers.

Jonathan accepted the hospitality of several of these families, people he had known from childhood. He had neither liked nor disliked them particularly, but had just accepted them as part of the scene because, until he went away, he had never known a world without them. Now on his return it was only the older generation which remained: the young had escaped, some to be educated in England, Canada or the United States, others of age into the services. Their only common denominator now was a determination never if humanly possible to return.

Jonathan, sensitive to atmosphere, had felt a certain patronage in the manner of his reception and found time to wonder whether, when the Dabneys were firmly in the saddle as the richest people in the island, they too had been guilty of patronizing. He hoped not, but feared that it was so.

Determined not to accept hospitality without returning it, he organized a dinner party for twenty-two covers at the Tucker House on the eve of his departure by schooner for Trinidad and England. He did it, not as a pleasure, but as a duty to the name of Dabney. Four white couples accepted. The rest of the guests were Dabneys, or one of the variants of the name, ranging in colour from the palest café-au-lait to dark brown. These two groups, affable enough when they met in the street or in the course of business, surveyed each other in silence from opposite sides of the room and, when it became apparent that the intention was to seat them all at the same table, the white group filed out with grimly set lips and did not return.

'If you had only asked me,' said Zachary the lawyer, 'I

could have told you that would happen.'

'It's of no consequence,' said Jonathan. 'Now I know where I stand. Isn't blood supposed to be thicker than water?'

'Not mixed blood, not here.'

'Now let's enjoy ourselves!' said Jonathan, becoming the cheerful host.

Enjoy themselves they did, and it was after midnight when the party broke up and the stalwarts escorted Jonathan down to the harbour where the schooner *Sea Fox* was lying ready for a dawn sailing. He was choked with emotion. These coloured Dabneys, who hitherto had given rise to feelings of guilt in him, an inherited guilt which was quite illogical, had shown him a warmth and sympathetic understanding which, unexpected as it had been, had moved him, causing him to regard them in new ways. They were members of a family of which he was an integral part. All feelings of his own superiority had vanished in the warmth of the meeting. Jonathan knew then, without knowing how or when, that he would come back. This was home.

*   *   *

Four months almost to the day after giving up his room in the Inverness Terrace boarding house in London he was back again. On the board addressed to him were four letters in the same handwriting. 'She must have telephoned a dozen times,' said the proprietress with a sniff of disapproval, 'and she made it quite clear that she didn't believe me when I said I didn't know where you were or when you would be back. I knew you weren't the kind to be running away from any young women ... or needing to.'

That's all you know, he was inclined to say.

Back in the privacy of his old room, Jonathan could not bring himself to open the letters. His reluctance to do so was so strong as almost to be a form of paralysis. He guessed that they were from Gloria. It certainly was not Jean's handwriting, which he remembered only too well. He was uncomfortably aware of his jobless condition and lack of prospects.

33

The thought of meeting either of the ffoulkes girls or their mother appalled him. He must keep out of their way at all costs until he knew better what he was going to do.

5

'It's all very well saying that you're willing to tackle any job, but what kind of job have you in mind? More to the point, what kind of job do you consider yourself capable of filling? What do you know? What specialized qualifications have you for *anything*? Which way do your inclinations lie? In short, put yourself in the position of a prospective employer who must of necessity be completely in the dark about you. I'd like to help you. I'm willing to help you, but the truth is,' Harold Grimsditch concluded, 'you are not an easy man to help.'

As Jonathan watched thousands of people surging into Underground stations and queueing for buses, all of them presumably with jobs and homes to go to, a cloud of despair settled on him with a realization of his own inadequacy. If the fire of genius burned behind those nondescript uninspiring faces, he mused, its brightness was well concealed.

Back in the privacy of his little room, barely more than a cubicle, his reluctant fingers began opening the letters. There was no postmark to put them in date order, for they had all had been delivered by hand. Although he had never seen Gloria ffoulkes's handwriting, he believed that they were from her. It had been a delightful interlude, fun while it lasted. Now the bill was being presented. There was no date on any of them, but the order in which they were written became obvious. They were commendably brief:

(1) Please 'phone me. I must see you.
(2) You haven't 'phoned me. The dragon in the office says she doesn't know where you are, the lying bitch. Why are you dodging me?

35

(3) You don't seem to care a bit what happens to me, you unfeeling bastard. I *think* I have some bad news for you.

(4) I don't *think* any more. Now I'm *sure*. What are you going to do about it? We must talk ... soon. Mother is away on the Riviera, buying a house, so the coast is clear.

They were all signed Gloria. Examination of the flaps of the envelopes showed quite plainly that they had been steamed open. The proprietress evidently did not appreciate being called a lying bitch. A curious woman.

It was now Jonathan's turn to write notes which were not answered and to be told over the 'phone that Gloria was not available. Leaving word that he was back at Inverness Terrace, he resumed his fruitless job-hunting. Returning one evening tired and dispirited, he was told that *the* – not *a* – young lady was waiting for him in the lounge. Judging from her demeanour, it was not going to be an easy interview. It was left to Jonathan to break the brittle silence. 'You're looking very well, Gloria,' he began. 'Put on a bit of weight, too, if you ask me.'

'You callous, purple-trimmed sly bastard!' she roared in a voice which caused the chandelier to tinkle. 'You put a girl in pod, run away and hide yourself for five months and then wonder why she's put on a bit of weight....'

There was a lot more, all of which was heard distinctly in the entrance hall, where the eminently respectable residents listened avidly while pretending to close their ears.

She concluded with, 'Well, what do you propose doing about it?'

'There doesn't seem much I can do,' he replied, 'but if you want me to, I suppose I can marry you.'

'This is my cue to swoon with joy, is it? The romantic hero returns, falls on his knees and implores the beautiful princess to smile on him, give him some small ray of hope. In a pig's eye he does! What do you take me for ... a dose of castor oil?'

Gloria was nothing like as angry as she pretended to be, being more than anything relieved to see Jonathan.

At this juncture the proprietress interrupted the dialogue.

'We cannot permit such appalling language in this house, Mr Dabney, so I must ask you to vacate your room in the morning ...'

'Come on Johnny,' said Gloria. 'I'll help you pack your bags and let's get out of this prissy slum now. Mother's still away and you can move in with me.'

Ten minutes later, white-lipped with fury, the proprietress watched them leave. She was unconcerned about the bad language, but it was the 'prissy slum' which had got under her skin.

As the taxi bore them to Park Lane, his arm firmly in Gloria's clutch, Jonathan felt himself in the grip of a force which it was hopeless to resist.

It was three days, three very pleasant days and nights, before they got round to any serious discussion of future plans. 'Does your mother know about ...?' asked Jonathan, completing the question with a nod in the direction of Gloria's swelling ripeness.

'Does she know? D'you think mother's blind, or something? Of course she knows! So does the milkman, the hall porter and the liftman. It wouldn't surprise me to hear that they are running a sweepstake on the day....'

'All this has come as a bit of a shock to me,' Jonathan mumbled.

'It came as a bit of a shock to me, too, but my shock came months ago. So what are we going to do about it? That's the first question mother's going to ask when she gets back here at the end of the week. What do we tell her? With both her little daughters up the spout and no husbands in sight, she wasn't best pleased last time I saw her. In Jean's case, of course, she took it for granted that it was you until you spun her that tale about being no good for a girl, and even then she didn't properly believe you, not until she got it out of Jean under pressure....'

'Who was it?'

'How the hell would I know? I doubt whether Jean knows for sure.'

Lacking standards of comparison, Jonathan did not find

all this as strange as a more experienced man might have found it. All the same, he found it highly embarrassing. What amazed him was to learn how glad he was to be finished with Jean. Gloria, he was beginning to believe, was a much nicer girl. Her eyes weren't so closely set. That had always troubled him a little about Jean. Added to which, on looking back, she had been such a liar, even over small, unimportant things. The crowning insult, of course, had been her readiness to foist another man's child on to him. But then, as an uneasy thought crossed his mind, was Gloria doing the same thing? No, he decided, that was not Gloria's way. She was too outspoken, appallingly so at times, to be like her devious sister.

While re-visiting the scenes of his childhood, Jonathan was ashamed to recall, he had hardly given Gloria a thought. There had been nothing about their encounter to lead him to suppose that she had regarded it as more than a light interlude. But, as he was learning, it was the biological consequences of light interludes which assumed such importance.

Doris MacNiven, as has been made apparent, was a most sensible woman. When told that Jonathan had returned to the fold, she made everything pleasant and easy. Her attitude was now let's see what's best to be done for everyone concerned, and at the end of their talk Jonathan found himself agreeing that marriage was the best way out of the difficulty. '. . . and as we don't want it born in the vestry,' she concluded, 'there isn't any time to waste.'

'But there's a snag . . . a big one,' he said. 'I've no job and soon I won't have any money . . . and it isn't for want of trying either. I was even turned down for a job as night watchman on a building site because I'm too young. Gloria is used to living in luxury. What can I offer her?'

'If that's your only worry, Johnny, you can forget it. I own a controlling interest in Bookbinder's . . . they're wine and spirit merchants, beer bottlers and so on. I'll give you a note to my manager and he'll fix you up with a job. It's the job I had in mind for you if you and Jean had married, so it comes to the same thing. A man should be independent of his mother-in-law, don't you think?'

It occurred to Jonathan that there would be little independence in the arrangement, but wisely or weakly, he remained silent.

'So that's settled,' said Doris briskly.

Bookbinder's office and warehouse was in Fulham, a part of London new to Jonathan. The building backed on to the river. Behind the door marked 'Managing Director' sat a surprisingly young man named Allardyce, who was alarmingly offhand. 'Yes, I remember,' he said when Jonathan had explained his errand. 'Doris told me all about you. You'll be elected to the board at the next meeting. How would it be if we called you "export manager"? It has a good solid sound to it. Suit you?'

'Well, yes, I suppose so. But I may as well tell you here and now that I don't know anything about exports. . . .'

'Don't let that bother you, my dear chap, because there aren't any exports anyway. It's more than we can do to supply our old customers.'

'I see. Then what do I do?'

'You endorse your salary cheque every month . . . unless, of course, you'd rather have it sent direct to your bank, and . . . well, just wait for instructions.'

'So what you're really saying,' said Jonathan shamefacedly, 'is that there isn't any job . . . I'm to be just an ornament.'

'Put it that way if you want to, my dear chap, but I wish I had half your luck. Marry the boss's daughter and so long as you don't blot your copybook, you're set for life. But don't imagine it's all going to be a bed of roses. Watch Doris. As a mother-in-law she may turn out to be rather high octane. Any idea of where you're going to make your home?'

Jonathan shook his head.

'Why not try Australia? Just about the right distance. Well, good luck, old chap. It's been nice meeting you. Now, I'm afraid you'll have to excuse me . . . love to Gloria. Nice girl that, you lucky dog.'

When, in the bus taking him back to the West End, Jonathan recalled the interview and all its shaming implications, he knew that in his entire life to date he had never felt so crushed by humiliation. Unless it had been Doris's intention to humiliate him, surely it would have been possible to have it all wrapped up a little more delicately? But then, in a moment of crystal clarity, he asked himself whether that would have made an essential difference. At most it would have been a sop to his vanity to go through the farce of pretending that he was going to earn his salary. If he accepted the situation, nothing could alter the degrading fact that acceptance made him – he winced at the word, which was not then quite outmoded – a gigolo.

Entering Hyde Park by the Knightsbridge gate, he made two complete circuits on foot and would have made a third if his limping gait had not become so painful. How, he asked himself, would his father have reacted if similarly situated? Poor as he had been during those last years, Jonathan believed, pride would have compelled the old man to throw it all back in Doris's face. But that, he argued, clutching eagerly at the face-saving formula, would not help to solve Gloria's problem, which in its way was even more pressing than his own. By the time he reached the Park Lane flat he had managed by some acrobatics of conscience to persuade himself that what he was about to do was for Gloria's sake.

'Well, how did you get on with Allardyce?' asked Doris when they met.

'Splendidly,' replied Jonathan. 'I must have made a good impression because he's put me in sole charge of the export department. I hope you're proud of me.'

Doris guffawed and they dropped the subject.

'By the way,' she said, 'has Gloria told you that we're moving down to the Riviera next week? I've been able to come to terms with the people who are selling the villa. You'll love it.'

'Where is it?' he asked out of politeness.

'On Cap d'Antibes ... with its own private beach and yacht harbour. By the way, Johnny, can you speak French?'

'I learned French before I spoke English.'

'Then you'll be invaluable because none of us speaks a word. Which reminds me' – there didn't seem much connection – 'you're going to need a lot of new clothes. Who's your tailor?'

'I buy my clothes off the peg.'

'If you don't mind my saying so, they look like it. We'll go to see Trimble's in Savile Row in the morning. Sir Eustace went to them for years. Until he began spilling food and drink down his front, he was always very smartly turned out. He owed them for fourteen suits when he died.'

'I'll try my best to be a credit to you,' said Jonathan sourly.

Because of Gloria's condition, a circus wedding was ruled out. She had to content herself with a simple Caxton Hall affair with the minimum of fuss. Doris, who had by then despaired of making any headway in the social life of Mayfair, was glad rather than otherwise. Even her not over-acute social sense detected for what they were the shabby spongers who had attached themselves to her, and she was determined not to give them the opportunity of amusing themselves maliciously when they saw Gloria. There was the further fact that the invitations had once gone out for the marriage of Jonathan and Jean. The latter's whereabouts was a closely held secret.

'Is there anyone you would like to invite?' Doris asked Jonathan.

'Yes, I'd like my half-brother Lawrence. He has just qualified as a doctor in Edinburgh and he'll be in London for a few days before returning home.'

'I didn't know you had a half-brother,' said Doris. 'You've never mentioned him.'

'Well, I suppose that's because we're not very close.'

Doris did not give the matter another thought until the wedding party was joined on the pavement outside Caxton Hall by a splendidly handsome coloured man, who greeted Jonathan warmly.

'Who's the coon?' asked Doris in a stage whisper.

'Let me present my half-brother, Dr Lawrence Dabney,' said Jonathan. Not tactful at the best of times, Doris swallowed hard and said: 'How come? Did they leave you out in the sun and take Johnny into the house?'

'Not exactly that,' replied Lawrence, laughing and not at

41

all taken aback. 'I'm from the sunburned branch of the Dabney tree.'

Doris and he got on like the proverbial house on fire and at the wedding breakfast she insisted on him sitting next to her. 'When I first met you,' she was heard to say after the champagne had been circulated a few times, 'I thought to myself I'd sooner have a bastard in the family than a coon but now, by God! I'm not so sure. I like you, Lawrence, damned if I don't.'

Most men of colour, being on the receiving end of such unaffected frankness, would have been angry, or at least embarrassed. But Lawrence had far too much poise and self-assurance to give way to any such weakness. He merely roared with laughter.

6

Peace had descended on the lovely garden of the Villa
Leonora. The buffet luncheon, starting at one o'clock and
lasting until after four, had just ended. Twenty guests had
been invited. Thirty-one had arrived and the last stragglers
had just left, cutting up the gravel drive with their incon-
siderate acceleration. One driver, too impatient to wait his
turn, had driven across the lawn and destroyed a bed of
cannas in full flower.

Doris, exhausted, had retired to the splendid master suite
she had pre-empted. The English nanny had gone for a
walk up to the Cap d'Antibes lighthouse, leaving Jean to
pacify her fretful son Stephen, who still lacked an official
father. The eminent abortionist whom she and Doris had
consulted in London had refused flatly to end Jean's preg-
nancy. Having been left too long, the risks were too great.
Across on the other side of the lawn, Gloria was looking
happy as she gazed into the cradle where her son Edouard,
aged only two weeks, was blowing bubbles and crooning.

The sight enraged Jean, whose plan to foist her son on to
Jonathan had gone astray. Jean had never been in love with
Jonathan, but he would have served her purposes very con-
veniently. And then Gloria, the sly little bitch, had stolen
him under her nose. Just how it had been managed she did
not know, but she could guess. It had all worked out so well
for everyone but Jean, who bit her nails with vexation.

Jonathan, lost in reverie, stood gazing intently into the
large goldfish pond where life, if not exciting, seemed very
peaceful. Sunburned and fit, he carried his natural good looks
with distinction. Surveying himself in a full-length mirror
a few hours earlier, he had been offended by the sleek elegance
of his attire.

'What's got into you these last days?' asked Gloria. 'Something wrong?'

'Nothing. Just looking at the goldfish, that's all. Anything wrong with that?'

'There *is* something wrong. I'm sure of it. Why don't you tell me what it is?'

'Because it isn't your fault and you wouldn't care to hear it. I'm going for a walk. Coming?'

'No, it's too hot. But don't be late. The Prince is coming to dinner. Remember?'

'I'd sooner forget it. . . .'

'Mind you're not rude to him again.'

'Let him mind he's not rude to me.'

To Gloria the life they were living was not far short of perfection. Indeed, the only way it could be improved for her would be if Jonathan were a little more appreciative of the good things being showered upon them. She liked him. She was inclined to be in love with him, but when and if that passed, she believed the liking would remain and grow deeper. At one time she had thought she understood him, but no longer. Discontent was gnawing at him. Why?

Doris had noticed it, too, but since it was not her way to wonder in silence, she was only waiting for a favourable moment to broach the subject.

Protocol in the make-believe world of phonies is very strict. It has to be when one reflects upon the matter, for otherwise the whole flimsy edifice would collapse. Observance of the order of precedence is vastly more important to the pseudo-aristocrat than it is to the real one. Prince Fattoccioli had the misfortune to be a tubby, undistinguished little man with long greasy sideburns and the trembling jowls of an Italian tenor. He strutted, even when sitting down. Most men of his ilk find it expedient to cultivate good manners, but he did not. As bartender at an exclusive club in Milan, he had ample opportunity to observe and cultivate atrocious manners and, having suffered them from his aristocratic customers, it delighted him to inflict them on others.

'Be a good chap and get me a very dry martini, Dabney,' he said before dinner.

44

'Help yourself Fatso,' replied Jonathan coolly and turned away.

Doris was so scandalized that the petals of her stephanotis corsage drooped and fell.

The beautiful Villa Leonora and its even more beautiful setting, the envy of all who saw it, was not a happy house. There was no home life, only brief, too brief, intervals between parties. Even to Jonathan, new to the hectic life of the Riviera, and not at any time over-sophisticated, it was plain that the shrill crowd entertained there so lavishly had nothing behind its absurd pretensions. He liked Doris despite her shams, realizing that underneath all the flimflam was a solid person with her feet on the ground. But it hurt him to see her demeaning herself by according this ill-mannered lackey the place of honour at table, bowing to his transparently ridiculous pretensions to princely rank. How the fellow squirmed when addressed as Fatso!

'Look at Doris,' said Jonathan later in the evening, 'gazing so soulfully at that fat clown and hanging on every word he utters. She's making an awful fool of herself ...'

'M'm, I'm afraid she is,' replied Gloria, 'but as you can see for yourself, she's having such wonderful fun that it would be a shame to spoil it. After all, what does it matter? And you mustn't forget that this is her house and her money that she's spending. Surely, Johnny, she's entitled to do what pleases her best? With all her little peculiarities, you must admit that Doris is kind and generous. ...'

'I do admit it and, since you raise the matter, I'm duly grateful for her ... bounty.'

'That's a horrid thing to say.'

'The truth often is horrid, darling, but bounty is the *mot juste* and we both know it. Look at the beautiful suite of rooms she has given us, servants everywhere, wonderful food and drink. ...'

'Well, what's wrong with it?'

'Nothing's wrong with it. It's what's wrong with *me* that I'm complaining about. I ought not to be accepting it all. I'm becoming like the bird in a gilded cage ... just another Riviera kept man, a poodle being led around on a silk ribbon.

45

Can't you understand? I'm seeing a picture of myself and I don't like it.'

'All right, Johnny, what's the alternative?'

'I've got to stand on my own feet, stop living like this and begin to earn some money before I grow so soft that I'll never climb out of this silk-lined trap. I've got to do it soon ... or never.'

'I'll help you, Johnny, but how do we set about it? You tried to get a job in London, but couldn't find one ...'

'Bookbinder's, which means your mother really, pay me £2,000 a year for doing nothing. I'd infinitely rather take much less and do something to earn it. I'm not a fool. I can learn the trade....'

'How much do you think you would earn that way?' asked Gloria.

'I'd be willing to start in at £400 a year and I'd see that I was worth it ...'

'That's real poverty, Johnny. Would you want me to share it?'

'You're my wife and if you love me you'll be willing to share anything....'

'Think, Johnny, just think what you're asking. Mother is rich and, as you say, generous. Jean and I have always lived in luxury as long as we can remember. I love luxury and I don't think I've got the guts to face poverty. Why should I ... just to satisfy your whims and bolster your ego? No, not for little Gloria. Tell me, Johnny, would it make you feel any better if I can persuade mother to give me now some of what she will presumably be leaving me some day? Would that help you lose the feeling of being what you call a kept man?'

'No, darling, it wouldn't. Instead of being a dependant in your mother's house, I'd become one in yours, and I wouldn't like that either....'

'If mother were willing, would you let me persuade her to lend you enough money to start some business of your own?'

'If I'd learned something about the business beforehand, yes, I might do that. But putting money into a business I didn't understand would be like pouring it down a drain.'

As Gloria saw things, Jonathan was a most satisfactory

husband. He was good-looking, pleasant-mannered, easy to live with and, despite early misgivings on the subject, sexually adequate. His only major defect in her eyes was his blindness in not recognizing a good thing when he had it. Bound up with it was a kind of obstinate pride which, if she had known his father, she would have understood better.

Realizing that their talk was in danger of becoming bitter, Gloria said soothingly: 'Let's both think it over and talk about it some other time.' The last thing she wanted was a quarrel. She understood his viewpoint completely, even if she did not sympathize with it. She was selfish and, unlike many selfish people, knew it. She was, even if she did not put it into the exact words, actuated by what she saw as intelligent self-interest. Only his tiresome pride prevented him from seeing things in the same way.

There followed over the next weeks other talks of a similar nature, none of which helped to bridge their differences. But with the end of the summer season in early September and the disappearance of the clamouring throng from the scene, the Riviera reverted to the delightful strip of coast it had been before it became a strident playground.

Gloria and Jonathan both loved walking. The latter still walked with a slight limp, but together they 'discovered' the hinterland of the Riviera, still unspoiled by crowds. Once on a precipitous eminence overlooking the slender thread of the Loup which ran swiftly past the northern limits of Roquefort-les-Pins and on to La Colle and the sea, they glimpsed a wild boar standing guard over a sow and a litter of piglets as they scuttled into a forest of scrub oak. On a golden autumn day, starting at Pont-du-Loup, they climbed by way of the almost vertical *Chemin du Paradis* to the village of Gourdon perched high above the foothills and the coastal plain. Amid these peaceful and beautiful scenes, despite their differences, these two became closer than they had ever been.

Even the Villa Leonora became peaceful. Calls were exchanged with 'nice' neighbours around the Cap. Jean, as might be expected, found them boring and made no secret of it. Gloria also found them boring, but was better mannered about it. Doris turned out to be the misfit. Someone from her bar-

47

maid days had recognized her and, just possibly without malicious intent, had spread the word. When one day Doris was heard to cut loose with a torrent of pure Billingsgate in an unguarded moment of annoyance, the Villa Leonora ceased to exist as far as its respectable neighbours were concerned.

'It's like living in a bloody cemetery,' she said when the penny dropped. 'I'm going back to London.'

The servants being 'temporaries' were quite happy to return to hibernate elsewhere. Jean and Stephen left in an Italian ship for New York and thence down to Nassau. There was no central heating in the house. Coal for open fires was wellnigh unobtainable and what little there was had to be kept for the huge kitchen range.

'Even if it's your idea of fun,' said Gloria tartly on the morning when there was no hot bath, 'it isn't mine. So, what next?'

Seeing problems through different eyes, each envisaging a different way of life, Jonathan and Gloria failed to reach a meeting of the minds. To Gloria it was all quite simple. She had no high ambitions for Jonathan. If only he had the sense to know on which side his bread was buttered, she believed, they could have a very pleasant life together on the £2,000 per annum allowance paid to him by her mother in the guise of a salary from Bookbinder's. Given a reasonable degree of conformity to her mother's wishes, other perquisites were to be expected. Any other way of looking at things was to Gloria absurd and, her own comfort, convenience and amusement being the paramount considerations, appallingly selfish.

Jonathan for his part had no wish to lead the kind of parasitical life which Gloria had mapped out for him. He had not mentally or in fact cut the ties which bound him to his birthplace. His ideas were vague and imprecise, but as the last of the Dabneys, strictly speaking the last but one of the white Dabneys, he felt the pull of twin duties: first to the name of Dabney and second to the island which had been their home for so long. He did not, because he could not, particularize.

Gloria, sensing Jonathan's determination and realizing that

48

this was a rock on which their marriage could founder, agreed much against her inclinations to fall in with his wishes.

Ten days later they sailed from Le Havre in a French ship calling at Port of Spain en route for South American ports. The accommodation was adequate, the food excellent, the six other passengers depressingly dull. Gloria and little Edouard developed bad cases of prickly heat. There was as yet no airfield on Newcastle Island. There were several schooners soon to leave for Port Lewis, but either they were full or would not take passengers, and until passages were available they had to hole up in the Queen's Park Hotel overlooking the Savannah.

In the schooner *Albatross III*, by the time Gloria learned that their accommodation was merely two bunks curtained off in an alcove of the captain's cabin, with rather frightening sanitary arrangements which had to be shared with the captain and two coloured mates, the schooner was battling head winds in the Gulf of Paria.

There are moments in life when silence can be far more eloquent than anything expressed within the limits of mere words. During the seventy-two hours between leaving Port of Spain and dropping anchor in the careenage at Port Lewis, Gloria maintained a tight-lipped silence. Jonathan braced himself in anticipation of the storm which would soon break over him.

They walked the quarter-mile from the waterfront to the Tucker House, their baggage on a handcart.

Zachary, who had heard of their coming by the grapevine, was the first caller. With his help a part of La Bastide was cleaned and made fairly habitable. It was here that the storm finally burst. Observing an old man with dustpan and brush at work on the stairs, Gloria asked: 'What is he sweeping up?'

'Only rat dirts,' replied Jonathan.

'Only rat dirts? Is that all? There must be at least five hundred rats in residence, allowing for a generous ration of twenty dirts per rat per day. . . .'

'There isn't food for as many rats as that here,' said Jonathan evenly, 'so don't let's make it worse than it is.

49

That panful of dirts represents more than a year's accumulation. In fact, I don't expect the place has been swept since I was here last. . . .'

'La Bastide you call the bloody place! Why not La Bastille? If you think Edouard and I are going to live in this rat-infested dungeon, Jonathan Dabney, you're very much mistaken. . . .'

Then she removed the cork and let rip the rage she had been bottling up for days. They were back in the Tucker House and in the room they had just vacated before she finally ran down and resorted to tears. What she said was unanswerable. Some of it, Jonathan was ready to admit, was even justifiable in the light of events. Wisely, he said nothing and went to sleep. The sound of his gentle snoring enraged Gloria all over again, giving her an excuse to repair any omissions from her previous outburst.

*   *   *

'It's beautiful. I have to admit that,' said Gloria after they had walked the length of the beach and bathed in the limpid water of the lagoon at Dabney's Reef. 'But when all's said and done, it's only scenery and scenery won't keep the rain out. We can't live here. . . .'

'Just wait until you see what it will look like. . . .'

'Wait how long, Johnny, and more particularly where?'

'I'd planned for us to move into La Bastide, but you don't seem to care for it. . . .'

'No, Johnny, I don't care for it and unless I'm bound hand and foot and carried there forcibly, I don't intend ever again to set foot in the bloody place, so let's just forget it. What other ideas have you got?'

'Well, my half-brother Hugh ... you haven't met him yet ... has a nice house on the other side of the island. He'd let us have a couple of rooms with a lovely view out to sea ...'

'Your father seems to have been very active after dark. What did he do in the daytime? And, if I'm not being indiscreet, what colour is he? Don't get the idea that I have any violent colour prejudice, because really I have very little. I liked the one who was at our wedding. He was charming. But it's a little overwhelming, you must admit, for me to find myself suddenly plunged into the midst of so many dusky in-laws. Would you think me unreasonable if I say that, all things considered, my preference is for people of my own colour?'

'I quite understand, darling, but you see I grew up with it and I'm used to it. . . .'

'You also apparently grew up to accept hordes of rats as part of the scenery and . . . hell's bells, something has stung my left foot and it hurts like bloody hell. Do something about it, can't you?'

'I'll fix it when we get back to the Tucker House. You just trod on a sea egg . . . urchin to you. You have to watch where you tread here, but you'll soon get used to it . . .'

By pouring hot candle grease on to the foot and peeling it off when cold, the spines of the sea egg were quickly removed, but they left a nasty inflamed area behind them.

The next morning, when Port Lewis came to life, a ship lay about a mile offshore. It was one of the *Lady* boats, as they were called, owned by the Canadian National Railways, and bound for St John, New Brunswick, via Boston. When some cargo had been lightered ashore, she sailed with one more passenger and an infant than she arrived with. 'I'm sorry, Johnny, truly sorry, but there are too many things here to get used to and I just can't take it. When you've got all this nonsense out of your system, come on back home, and I'll be waiting for you. But don't leave it too long, Johnny, because . . . well, things happen.'

Being a reasonable person, perhaps too reasonable for his own good, Jonathan was able to view things through Gloria's eyes and to understand some of her revulsion from the discomfort, fifth-rate food, flies and mosquitoes, together with a social system utterly foreign to her. Dabneys of various hues had received her with warmth, delighted that in little Edouard there was a white grandson as namesake for Jonathan's father. Little Edouard represented continuity which, seen as they all saw it, was more important than feelings of affection for any individual. Affection had to be earned and Jonathan had not yet earned it. That he would do so these other Dabneys did not doubt, but in the meantime he was owed some vaguely defined allegiance much in the manner of members of a Scottish clan towards their chieftain. Gloria being his wife, they had been prepared to give her a measure of their affection.

She was now a Dabney. The question of colour did not enter into the matter ... unless on her side. Much of what passes for colour prejudice and discrimination is nothing of the kind. The key to it is strangeness. Like clings to like and questions of superiority or inferiority do not of necessity obtrude themselves. People of white blood tend to forget that racial discrimination is by no means one-sided.

Gloria had resolved matters by departing. Jonathan had hated to see her go but, being unable to stop her and realizing how little he had to offer, had tried to be philosophical about it. Their marriage was suspended rather than broken. Meanwhile, there was work to be done.

7

Even to Jonathan who had been born there, the gloom of
La Bastide was intolerable now that he was alone. Through
Zachary's good offices he lodged with an elderly widow, not
a Dabney this time, who lived on the outskirts of Port Lewis.
Martha Galante had once been cook at Government House
where she had learned how to make even the local meat
edible. Jonathan lived well and cheaply.

From the widow's house to Dabney's Reef was seven miles,
the last two of which were no more than a narrow goat
track. Every morning after a hasty dawn breakfast Jonathan
set out on a bicycle. The early start was in order to be able to
get in a few hours of manual labour before the sun rose too
high to make it practicable. The little beach house where he
and his father had spent happy weekends had been abandoned
for more than ten years. It was completely hidden in a dense
thicket of vegetation some twenty feet in depth before it was
possible to see it. Many of the vines and creepers were too
thick to be slashed with a machete. Some had to be cut with
an axe and others with a saw. The stems of the bougainvillaea were as thick as a man's leg. When it was all cleared
and three immense piles of vegetation were drying in the hot
sun, roots had to be dug out to prevent it all growing again.

The whole task involved five weeks of agonizing labour
and rivers of sweat before there emerged the little house
Jonathan remembered. The roof had vanished. So had the
doors and windows. But the walls, built of sawn coral blocks,
remained intact. There was a lot to be done, but when it was
done it would be a place he could call home. Surveying the
little house and the huge bonfires sending pillars of lazy
smoke up into the peerless Caribbean blue sky, he knew
a deep satisfaction.

There was unemployment on the island, especially among unskilled labourers who were trying to win better conditions from the sugar planters. It would have been easy enough to have employed men to do what he had done single-handed. He could have afforded the small wages. But there was in Jonathan an urge which he himself did not fully understand, to wipe away the shame of months of pampered ease in the Park Lane flat and the Villa Leonora, prettied up like a dancing boy, lying in the soft beds, eating rich foods and drinking wines, none of which he had earned, pretending to earn his keep by tolerating the worthless riffraff battening like leeches on the fortune Doris had inherited and increased. Somewhere deeply buried in Jonathan, and not seemingly inherited, was a puritan streak which rebelled at the thought of reaping where he had not sown. Added to this was the galling knowledge that he was the last (Edouard did not enter into his calculations for some reason) of a long line which had been destroyed by easy living, running steadily downhill from the great wealth, power and prestige to the barely genteel poverty in which he had last seen his father. He was determined if it lay within his power to restore the good name and prestige of the Dabneys in the island across which they had scattered their seed so prodigally.

Running across the beach and plunging into the limpid water of the lagoon, Jonathan swam a mile, at the end of which his breath would not have extinguished the proverbial candle. Purged of easy living, flabby muscles had grown hard. He exulted in the sense of well-being which had returned to him. For the first time since he had been wounded he felt fit to tackle what lay ahead of him.

The reef was an unfrequented part of the island, visited only by the odd goatherd or an occasional fisherman. It was a surprise, therefore, to see a tall, gangling man prop his bicycle against a tree a hundred or so yards away and begin to pick his way carefully down to the beach. The newcomer, a man of forty to fifty years of age, had a craggy, pleasingly ugly face from which watery blue eyes surveyed Jonathan quizzically.

'I know who you are,' he said. 'I'm Robbie McAlister. We

54

met years ago when your father packed you off to school in England, but I expect you've forgotten me.'

'To be truthful, I have, but I remember your name from Father's letters. He liked you.'

'I liked him, both for himself and his curiosity value as one of the last surviving members of a dying species ... anyway in these waters. In short, he was a gentleman who exemplified the truth of Confucius's dictum that it is harder to be poor without murmuring than to be rich without arrogance. He had much to complain of, but I never heard him complain. Glad to meet you again, Jonathan.

'What, may I ask, is a man with a rich wife doing in this Man-forgotten corner of a God-forgotten island, cheating an African day labourer of his pittance?'

'How did you know I was here and what I was doing?'

'My friend, everyone knows. It is the talk of the town, or at any rate that thirsty part of it which congregates nightly in the bar of the Tucker House. Toil such as you have been at is not for Dabneys, not even for the uncounted multitude of sunburned Dabneys, least of all for the last surviving Caucasian member of the clan. My not very acute news sense, therefore, tells me that somewhere in all this' – he gazed at the three pillars of smoke from the bonfires – 'deeply buried perhaps, is some journalistic grist, to wit a story. Today is Wednesday. The *Novocastrian*, God willing, goes to press tomorrow. The whole colony, or that modest percentage which is literate, is panting to know what you are up to. It may not be so in London, Paris and New York, but here, you may believe me, a Dabney is news....'

'Excuse me,' said Jonathan with a grin, 'but do you always talk as much as this?'

'Always, anyway to a fresh listener like yourself, who has not heard it all before many times....'

'Then, to reply to your question, I am planning to turn that' – he nodded towards the skeleton of the beach house – 'into a place where I can live in peace and solitude for as long as it takes me to discover what I am made of and what I am going to make of my life.'

'If you should decide that you wish to be a newspaper

55

proprietor or a journalist, I shall be happy to make you a present of the *Novocastrian*, free of all encumbrance, to do with as you will.'

'What would you do then?'

'Come and live here, contemplate the Infinite and write the Great Novel which lies just under the skin of every journalist only waiting to be written. Come! The shadows are lengthening. Let us cycle back sedately into the metropolis where, if you will allow me the pleasure, I will buy you a drink.'

'Thanks all the same, but let us postpone the pleasure until I can afford to buy you one in return.'

'Spoken like your lamented father. But I have an alternative suggestion. Unless someone has got at it, there is, or should be, in the ballroom of La Bastide, a cask of old – I repeat old – rum, such as exists nowhere else in this benighted island. There remained at the time your father became too ill to drink any more approximately sixty gallons of it. My suggestion, therefore, is that while there is still light we climb the hill to investigate, leaving our cycles at the bottom. Does that appeal to you?'

Darkness had fallen before they found a candle, washed a decanter and two glasses and tried a dozen keys before finding one that fitted the lock of the ballroom.

Pulling two long chairs out on to the gallery, where Jonathan's father had loved to spend the evenings, they relaxed into an easy intimacy as though they had been friends for years.

'I'll make an admission,' said Jonathan, sipping the third glass of the potent spirit, 'if the pleasant sensation that is making my toes tingle is a sign of being drunk, it will be for the first time in my life. Do you find that strange?'

'You are to be envied, laddie,' said McAlister sadly. 'It is a truly noble rum and if, as I hope and suspect may be so, your dear father's spirit hovers somewhere out there in the darkness, it will gladden him to know that his son and his old friend Robbie are drinking it.

'The raw rum of commerce,' McAlister went on, 'turns men into beasts, whereas this is a drink for gentlemen and sages. Not, let me say, that I am either, but it is a sign of grace that I would dearly like to be both. Nevertheless, I was wise enough to follow a trade which enables fools and failures to dignify their nonsense by the typesetter's art. . . .'

Lulled, as by the droning of bees, Jonathan fell asleep, and when he woke refreshed an hour or two later, the rum decanter was empty but McAlister was still talking.

A soft refreshing trade wind was blowing across the island, putting the mosquitoes to flight, so they stayed where they were until dawn told them it was time to go home. Jonathan, who knew that he did not make friends easily, believed that in this garrulous Scot he had found a friend.

8

Villa Leonora,
July 9th, 10th or maybe 11th.
1949, isn't it?

Dear Johnny.

I'm the woman you married. Remember? I have been
thinking of you a lot lately. Not languishing for you, but
just thinking. It may interest you to know that I have just
returned from having a baby in London. Yes, our baby, a
girl. I have held off having her christened in case you might
care to play some part in naming her. Except for Doris,
Mabel, Helen, May, Gloria and Jean, all of which I detest,
I will gladly fall in with your ideas if any.

I write this while there is still peace here. In a few days,
to be precise July 14th, mother's beloved phonies will begin
to descend on us like a flock of hungry vultures.

Before giving you all the news I should mention that
when our daughter's birth was registered in London, I had
to give her a name. So I called her Mary for that purpose
only. We can call her anything we please.

Jean is no longer here. It is a relief not to have her glower-
ering at me. She now calls herself the Countess Pitarescu on
the strength of having married an alleged Rumanian Count
of that name. I call him Picturesque, which he is. They had a
Hollywood wedding, photos in the shiny weeklies, the lot.
They sailed from Cannes for Buenos Aires. He has, or says
he has, a rich brother in Argentina. We shall see. Jean, she
always was careless, left little Stephen here with me. He
is a poor neglected little brat and I am sorry for him. There
is another English nanny – the first one left – and she looks
after Edouard and Stephen. I can't gush about Edouard or,
for that matter, any children. He is healthy, even-tempered

58

most of the time, but flies into occasional rages. So far I haven't discovered why, but it will emerge. He may for all I know to the contrary be intelligent. For more detailed information, I suggest you come and see for yourself.

Doris is positively blooming. She reminds me of the dog with a bone in his mouth who sees a bigger one reflected in a pond and drops the substance for the shadow. In her case the substance is that she really is Lady MacNiven, but she can't make up her mind whether she would be wise to drop this and become Princess Fatso. I have begged and implored her not to. Poor Doris! She loves to believe that all her shabby geese are swans. Which reminds me that, in case you don't know it already, she likes you. She has had a notary digging into your family history and he has convinced her that (for a few million francs, of course) you can be entitled to call yourself the Comte d'Aubigny or d'Aubigné. When I told her that even if entitled to you wouldn't do it, she said that there was nothing to prevent me from calling myself the Comtesse. You, she says, should be ashamed of yourself. He – that's you – is depriving his wife and his son of their rights.

Anyway, whether this is so or not, you are depriving me of rights which are far more important to me. I believe they are called conjugal rights in polite circles. It may surprise you to know that so far I have been faithful to you. Don't let me sound too virtuous about it. Frankly, I am ripe for some slap-and-tickle, but it will have to be a man, not some furtive little Riviera lounge lizard. How about it?

There has been time for me to consider your attitude towards life as it is lived at the Villa Leonora, and I don't blame you for it. I hope, likewise, that you understand my refusal to live in your ancestral dungeon. But somewhere between these two poles we ought to be able to find a compromise, a place where I can be comfortable, useless and elegant and where you can go through the motions of being useful in the way your puritanical conscience dictates. Edouard does not miss you yet, but he is surely entitled to a father?

I don't really want a divorce, because it always seems to me such a grubby affair. But if that is what we are heading for, then I say better sooner than later. So, regarding me as a pill and Doris's boodle as the sugar coating, in common fairness I want to know whether you intend to swallow me, or whether your island peopled by dusky Dabney is the greater attraction.

I am being as honest as I know how to be, so please be the same.

Love,
Gloria.

The tone of the letter was bewilderingly neutral, friendly enough, but putting the ball into Jonathan's court. Do whatever you please, but waste no time making up your mind, and don't expect any persuasion from me. Its immediate effect was to cause Gloria to rise in his estimation. Its honesty and candour merited a similar reply. He spent the whole of a long evening composing it.

P.O. Box 149,
Port Lewis.
July 30th, 1949.

Gloria my dear,

I have read and re-read your long letter. I understand how you feel about things, even if I don't sympathise. Perhaps I am being unfair and unreasonable in expecting you to give up the advantages which your mother's wealth can give you. But we both know enough about the world to know that a good part of love is respect, and you could not possibly respect me if I were content to sit back, all prettied up in clothes Doris had paid for, leading the aimless, contemptible life of a kept man amongst all her musical comedy acquaintances, whom I can't call friends. Bluntly, I won't even consider it.

Now let me tell you my small news such as it is. I expect you remember me pointing out to you a thicket on the beach at Dabney's Reef, hiding a small weekend house used by my family. Well, with these two lily-white hands I cleared it all. For many days I hacked and axed and sawed and dug until the house once again saw the sunlight. All the woodwork had rotted away and it is now being roofed, given doors and windows. I will admit to you that I did not really need to do all that hard labour, except that I needed to prove to myself that I could do it. I am glad now that I did for it has paid handsome dividends and in unexpected ways. First of all in health. I am lean, tanned and fit. I could fight my weight in wildcats. For a long time, as you know, my family has not been noted for anything much more than honest dealing and a certain languid elegance. The hardest work a Dabney has done for at least a century has been to mix rum punches. When I returned here I was regarded not exactly with contempt but with a sort of smiling tolerance. The whites were afraid that I would want to borrow money from them, while the dusky Dabneys, as you call them, had mixed feelings. They were glad to see me and welcomed me warmly, but it saddened them too, because without rich sugar land (our only real source of wealth) they were sure that I would fail to make a go of whatever it was in my mind to do. But a Dabney with his sleeves rolled up (in fact, I had no sleeves to roll up and have worked in minuscule swimming trunks) was such a novelty that they began to think again. Instead of being sure I would fall flat on my face, they now hope I will succeed. You may well ask what it is I am trying to do. I am trying to make the otherwise worthless land I inherited worth something. To some small degree I have succeeded. Twenty years ago my father could not find anyone who would lend him any money at all on the property. Let the land crabs have it, they said. Last week I received an offer via Zachary, the solicitor, for £2,000 from an unknown buyer. Naturally, I refused it.

My little house when it is finished will be cool and comfortable, four rooms including a kitchen. As I think I told you, it is built of coral sawn into big blocks. It could be mistaken for Carrara marble. The same kind of coral is available in almost limitless quantities. It has been building up from the sea bottom for millions of years. Blasting a wider and deeper entrance into the lagoon, which I intend to do, will provide enough rock to build fifty houses. The waters around here abound in the game fish which millionaires delight to catch. Dabney's Reef, with shore facilities and a safe anchorage, will make a perfect base. The winter climate is superb, even though the same can't be said for the rest of the year.

If I can bring this off, and I think I can, it will not only be my personal achievement, but it will mean that the name of Dabney once again amounts to something. I could even be the means of ushering in an era of prosperity such as the island has never known without slavery. That's the story. With you to help me (not financially, but by being here), we will not only succeed but have a happy life doing it.

I don't want to make this sound like a sermon, but a wife's place is with her husband.

As to our little daughter, I would like one of her names to be Esther after the mother I never knew.

Give my warmest wishes to your mother. I like her and am glad she likes me. Though why, I don't know. Tell her from me at all costs to avoid that scut Fatso. If you would like chapter and verse about him, the barman at the Casino, the one called Mario, can tell you the whole dirty story. I tried to tell her once, but she would not listen.

Kiss the children for me. Edouard, as you say, is entitled to a father. Then let him have one ... one he can respect.

If you and I can't work out some sort of a compromise, then divorce is the only answer. I will make it as painless as possible for you. But it will be a great pity and we may both live to regret it.

My love to you,
Johnny.

He purposely did not make the letter a passionate plea for her to come back to him. There was too much horse-sense in both their letters to make a passionate plea anything but ridiculous. But as Jonathan sealed his and dropped it in the box at Port Lewis, he knew that it was all over. Gloria would not surrender the fleshpots and nothing would tempt him back to them. It was easy to say at that late stage that they should never have married, or that he should have left the burning plane ten seconds later than he did, so that instead of dropping him in the grounds of Ashpole Manor he would have been carried a mile further on. But even if that had happened, another pair of soulful blue eyes with nothing much behind them might have sapped his reason. It was hopeless, he was beginning to realize, ever to try to anticipate the vagaries of Fate. Accidental meetings on a street corner, a flat tyre, a parachute that opened too soon or too late, these could be and often were the real turning-points in life, while carefully planned objectives came to nothing.

*   *   *

Dr Elias Daubeny, who had attended Jonathan's father in his last illness, was ready to retire. He was old and tired, and, because he had never aspired to be otherwise, poor. He had been the kind of doctor who combines his functions with a role akin to that of a parish priest. His practice took him all over the island. His patients paid him when they could, which often meant never. He was the safe repository of all their secrets, medical and otherwise.

There was an acute shortage of doctors on the island, while the standards of those in practice were not high. Fee-paying patients living in the town did not lack attention, but poor people living in remote villages were not so fortunate. There were no telephones out of the town and no way of getting medical aid in an emergency, except by walking or cycling, to appeal to Dr Elias Daubeny who hardly knew what it was to have an unbroken night's sleep. It came as a blessing to him when Dr Lawrence Dabney with a brand new degree backed by a year specializing in tropical medicine, returned home. Dr Elias could have sold his practice for a trifle, but he elected to give it to the younger man with his blessing, and there came a day when the older man walked out thankfully, leaving everything to his successor.

While, as Dr Elias would have been the first to admit, Dr Lawrence was the better qualified and more up-to-date physician, as well as being a more skilled surgeon, the patients made it clear that they thought otherwise. The old man in their eyes made up for his old-fashioned ways by the kindness of his heart. Dr Lawrence was kind, too, but kindness comes in many disguises, sometimes wearing the appearance of callousness. He was a good doctor, but he would not have made a good parish priest.

Lawrence, being the half-brother who had come to the Caxton Hall wedding, soon fell into an easy intimacy with Jonathan, but Jonathan saw far more of his father's old

63

friend and doctor, Elias. The latter, a widower, now and for the first time in his adult life with time on his hands, loved fishing. The small cabin cruiser aboard which he had spent all his leisure hours lay at moorings in the careenage at Port Lewis. At Jonathan's suggestion, he brought it round to Dabney's Reef and anchored in the lagoon where, free of the importunities of former patients, he was able to lead the kind of life of which he had dreamed for years. 'I've often suspected it,' he said, 'but now I know it's true. At heart I am a bum.'

For weeks he fished offshore in the early morning and late afternoon, when the sun was not too hot. With a two-hour siesta after lunch and ten hours' solid sleep at night, he caught up on his rest, shedding twenty years in appearance. He was a man bathed in contentment.

He watched while Jonathan, clumsily at first, but gathering a rude skill as he worked, fashioned window frames and doors for his small house. For the roof beams, which were beyond his capacity, he brought in two skilled wood-workers from the town. No tiles were available, but a ship from Canada had brought down a barge-load of corrugated plastic sheets with which Jonathan completed the roofing. Most of the furniture at La Bastide was built massively of mahogany. Some had been built in the rooms where it was used, too big to be moved and destined to stay there forever. But he was able to find two beds, kitchen chairs and a table, long cane chairs, crockery, cutlery and needlessly large copper pots and pans belonging to an age long past. Mice and moths had left blankets looking like lace, fit only to be burned, but in a vast linen press there were enough embroidered linen sheets and pillow cases for an hotel, together with some serviceable bath and hand towels. From what had once been his mother's bedroom, which had been kept locked since her death, Jonathan brought away a set of six fine cut-glass candlesticks, some dressing-table trays, two flower vases, a bedside table and an oval wall mirror. These last were totally unfitted for his new quarters, but he permitted himself the luxury of a little sentimentality. These, all things she had used, were a link with the mother he had not known.

When Elias Daubeny took it into his head to spend a few days at his house in Port Lewis, he would take advantage of an occasional lull in the trade wind and make the journey by sea round the island, returning with a stock of fresh provisions, reading matter and whisky. Like most men grown to manhood on well-matured rum, he would not drink the raw new spirit available in the shops.

Watching Elias returning from one of these trips, Jonathan saw, as the small cruiser was picking its gingerly way through the gap in the reef, that he had a passenger.

The newcomer was a gaunt middle-aged woman whose plainness was relieved by the warmest smile Jonathan ever remembered seeing. 'Alice McGraw and I are old friends,' said Elias, 'so old that when we first met I helped her mother change her diapers. So we have no secrets from one another....'

It transpired later that in his student days Elias had boarded with the McGraws in Montreal and they had been friends ever since. Alice was working in New York and the old folk were dead. Alice was the McGraw in the small Abbott-Hutchings-McGraw advertising agency. 'We specialize in travel advertising,' she said. 'We are the inventors of coral strands, sun-drenched tropic isles, palm-fringed beaches and cerulean blue skies, but we forgot to copyright them.'

Three is considered a bad number, but it was not so in this case. So easy was their intimacy that Jonathan felt he had known them both all his life.

'I come down here for a week or two every year,' Alice said. 'I call it my annual decompression. The pace in New York is killing. Elias here tells me I need this sort of thing. Now he's taking his own medicine and I'll help him do nothing.'

Elias turned over the cruiser to Alice, while he occupied the spare bedroom in the beach house. Alice at her own suggestion swam ashore in the mornings to make breakfast. While the other two lazed, swam and fished, Jonathan cleared a site for another beach house, for which two men were at work sawing coral blocks.

'What do you want two houses for?' asked Alice. 'Going to raise a family?'

'I plan to turn it into a store, club house, bar, perhaps even with a restaurant. Small pleasure craft are finding their way down here from the States and Canada, especially in the northern winter. Like you, they will come to laze and fish. When they see this place, they'll never want to see Port Lewis where they go now.'

'Smart idea, Johnny. When you're ready I can send you more people than you can cope with. This' – she took it all in with a wave of the hand – 'this is paradise. While you're at it, why not build a third house and let off the rooms?'

On the last night of Alice's stay, sitting round a driftwood fire on the beach, with the whisky bottle circulating slowly, they grilled freshly caught crayfish, split in halves and served with a piquant sauce. With a nearly full moon riding high overhead, the soughing trade wind rattling the palm fronds, the gentle lapping of the wavelets and the intoxicating scent of a *dama del noche*, almost certainly a survivor from the time when this had been the Dabney weekend beach house, the sheer beauty of the evening struck them speechless. 'Back in New York with the Third Avenue El shaking the apartment house to its foundations,' said Alice when they said good-night, 'I shall think of this evening and I shall cry like a baby. You lucky, lucky people!'

Her going left a void that was hard to fill.

'Why,' asked Jonathan when they had waved her aboard her ship, 'didn't some man sweep her off her feet and marry her long ago?'

'I've often asked myself the same question,' replied Elias. 'It always seems that it's the brainless little chippies with pretty legs who catch the men. Alice's standards, I fancy, were very high and she didn't meet anyone who measured up to them. Or, it could be, she valued her freedom and independence too highly. Or it could be one of a score of reasons. Who knows? Experience tells me that the obvious reason is never the real one.'

* * *

For the next many months the project at Dabney's Reef went ahead with agonizing slowness. Skilled workers were available only when they could not obtain better paid work elsewhere. By watching masons, joiners and plasterers closely, Jonathan managed to learn some of their skills after a fashion. Then came a period when plenty of men were available, but when he lacked the money to pay them.

In June 1950 Jonathan learned that Gloria had divorced him. To avoid brooding over this he took refuge in work and by nightfall he was fit only to eat a meal and fall into bed.

Zachary could not or would not raise money by borrowing on or selling the few remaining assets. 'Be patient,' he urged. 'Time is working for you if you will just hold on. If you need a little money for day-to-day living, I can let you have it, but your ambitious plans will have to wait. If you would only realize it, you are a very fortunate young man. You eat well. Between meals you can laze in the sun, swim or fish. There are millionaires who would envy you....'

All of this was probably true, but it was small comfort to a man in a hurry.

Then when it seemed that things could not be worse, they took a turn for the better. Jonathan seldom troubled these days to pick up his mail at the post office. Gloria no longer wrote. The bank in London sent statements, but knowing that his credit balance was next to nothing, he did not even trouble to open them.

One day in August a poisoned foot took Jonathan to see his half-brother Lawrence, who had at last begun to make a name for himself. On the way back to the Reef, he stopped at the post office to pick up his mail. There was a bank statement, a letter in the handwriting of an R.A.F. friend and a typewritten envelope from London which he did not recognize. That evening, by the light of a hurricane lantern, he opened the friend's letter, which contained little of interest. The bank's letter he threw into a drawer with the rest. The third letter was from the firm of Bookbinder's. His first thought was that Allardyce, the sarcastic so-and-so, was having a little fun at his expense. Out of the envelope dropped a cheque. The letter read:

Dear Mr Dabney:

I am instructed by our Chairman to inform you that as from December 31st this year the company will not require your services as it has been decided to suspend all export operations indefinitely.

At your convenience kindly acknowledge the enclosed cheque for the amount of your remuneration until the above date.

Yours faithfully,
(illegible)
Secretary.

The tears which fell on to the letter were compounded of mixed gratitude and relief. Doris, despite her rough tongue and foolish pretensions, had turned up trumps. It was her kind way of telling Jonathan that she understood his attitude and did not blame him for the broken marriage.

Opening the bank's last statement, Jonathan found that his salary from Bookbinder's had been paid to his credit since leaving Europe. This, added to the cheque on the table, meant that he could dispose of nearly £3,000, more than enough to complete the first stage of his plans for Dabney's Reef.

9

Jonathan, seeing but unseen, standing in the pool of darkness below a big mango, surveyed the busy scene with quiet satisfaction. Four motor-cruisers lay moored in the lagoon, their deck lights reflected in the still water like moon paths. In the dining-room of the Dabney's Reef Club, as it was called, twenty odd diners were eating *bouillabaisse*, served from an immense copper cauldron by Graziella the beaming Martiniquaise cook who, standing well over six feet without socks, had been nicknamed Skyscraper. Her velvety black skin gleaming with sweat from her exertions in the hot kitchen, she was in her element. She loved good food herself and much of her pleasure was derived from watching others enjoy the food she put before them.

Adjoining the dining-room was a well-stocked bar. Here, dispensing drinks and incandescent smiles, was Graziella's daughter, Chantal. Where her mother was tall, built like a beanpole and a warm brown in colour, Chantal, a little over average height, was built on voluptuous lines. She would have passed without notice in the streets of Naples or Palermo as a true Mediterranean beauty with a hint of Saracen ancestry.

'A pretty scene, isn't it?' said Dr Elias, coming silently to join Jonathan, who had moved to the deep shade cast by a casuarina, surveying his little kingdom with satisfaction. 'You should be a part of it,' the old man went on, 'not standing here like a policeman. They're all enjoying themselves ... that's what life is for. You, Johnny, you take life too seriously. How old are you? Nearly thirty, eh? Then you've let your youth slip past you and, if you *don't* wake up soon, you'll find yourself a middle-aged man who's never had any fun. Work is all very well in its way but, like whisky, it needs to be diluted, whatever the Scots may say. You have every right to be proud of what you've achieved here, so be proud, sit back and enjoy it for a while.'

'I can't sit back, not yet anyway. There's too much to be done.'

'To what end? What do you hope to achieve? This venture maybe won't make you rich, but it will keep you in comfort and in the long run, you may believe me, a good digestion is worth more than a big bank balance. Come along to the bar and buy me a drink. I can't afford your prices. . . .'

'What do I hope to achieve?' Jonathan echoed. 'Do you know, Elias, I'm not sure I know the answer to that. It's all muddled in my mind, but it has something to do with my father, with the name of Dabney, which used to be a proud name . . .'

'I know, Johnny, you've developed a conscience on account of the sins of your ancestors. I'm descended from one of their by-blows . . . what of it? I don't bear anyone a grudge about it. I'm a happy and reasonably successful brown-skinned man who, if a Dabney hadn't taken a brief fancy to my great-great-grandmother, might still be living in black ignorance in one of those squalid little villages. His intentions weren't good or, for that matter, bad. He was a randy young reprobate out for a little fun. But whatever his intentions, it turned out well for me.

'D'you know something Johnny, as a doctor I dare say I've had a hundred Dabneys, or thereabouts, as patients, and I never heard a word from one of them suggesting resentment. They were proud rather than otherwise of their origins. . . .'

'What are you trying to tell me, Elias?'

'That no burden of responsibility for the sins of your ancestors, or what would be called sins in the north temperate zone, rests on your shoulders. Most morality, certainly sexual morality, is a matter of latitude, and the nearer to the Equator the less censorious people tend to be. Nordic morality is essentially no better than ours, for it is the appearance of morality that counts for more than the morality itself. You, dear boy, are a hybrid. If you feel as I believe you do, you should take your misgivings back to the latitude where they belong. You'll not be a better man for it, of course, but you'll be more respectable ... if that is what you want.'

Jonathan seldom drank more than just to be polite, but on this enchanted evening, sweet with the scent from the lady-of-the-night, gay with the sounds of dishes clattering, corks being pulled and the tinkle of women's laughter, his two whiskies went pleasantly to his head. It all added up to success, but what was success unless the cup were drained?

Twice Jonathan found his eyes locked with Chantal's, who looked too incredibly beautiful to be serving behind a bar. When she pushed the drink chit across for him to sign their hands touched briefly. He shivered as an electric shock seemed to run up his arm.

'See what I mean?' said Dr Elias with a chuckle.

The conversation might have developed but for a digression when, from a yacht registered in Fort Lauderdale, Florida, a party of four came ashore to claim the table they had reserved. The swaggering little man who was the host glared rudely at Elias standing by the bar and two men of colour who were eating dinner at a near-by table.

'Hell, if ah'd known niggers was served here, we'd have stayed on board t' eat,' said the newcomer in gooey Florida cracker accents.

Talk, laughter, the rattle of knives and forks stopped abruptly. Nobody spoke, or moved. The silence became oppressive. Jonathan, aware that this was a crisis to be met head on, took a deep breath. The party was taking its seats at the reserved table. Signalling to the outraged waiter to clear the table, he said quietly, but in tones which carried throughout the dining-room, addressing the offender: 'You have just used a word which we do not tolerate here. You will not be served ... now or at any other time.'

A ripple of applause ran round the room as the party filed out. An elderly American, in a voice trembling with indignation, said: 'Trash like that should have their passports withdrawn.' Turning to Jonathan, he added, 'Permit me to congratulate you on that little speech, sir. It isn't for me to offer advice, but I fear that others like him will have to be put in their places. You gentlemen' – he bowed in turn to the three men of colour – 'should be flattered. If the little man were not so conscious of his own inferiority, he would not have had to assert himself so loudly.'

With the exception of one Canadian party, the rest of the diners were Americans. Although they were all indignant about the offender's behaviour, it was plain that for the future some clearly defined policy would have to be formulated. Jonathan himself might not always be on hand to deal with such a situation, and the coloured staff could not fairly be expected to take the initiative.

Elias, when consulted on the subject, was appreciative of Jonathan's attitude, but not enthusiastic about it. 'In principle, of course,' he said, 'there can be no question about your rightness. But what really did you accomplish? Your gesture, I expect, made you feel better. But I and the other two chiefly concerned weren't made to feel better. Speaking for myself, I was acutely embarrassed. Racial discrimination exists. It is one of the facts of life which it is better to live with than start a war....

'A man, a highly qualified doctor, was recently driven out of Port Lewis because he was "a bloody Jew". Who drove him out? Not the white community, but the black, which in all my lifetime has only known one Jewish family, owners of a small general store which never flourished. "Here is a Jew, a strange creature," they said in effect, "let us persecute him." The black man, who has known oppression, delights to find someone he can oppress. It makes him feel important. But, Johnny, that isn't a black attribute: it is a general human attribute. So the remedy seems to be to abolish humanity. The nuclear physicists may do so yet, but not as a matter of policy. So walk very carefully, Johnny, for the ice is thin.'

Robbie McAlister counselled moderation. 'Watch how the situation develops before starting a crusade, my lad. If Dabney's Reef turns out to be a successful venture, and I believe it will, the people of this island, quite regardless of colour, are going to be a negligible source of your takings.

It's the almighty dollar that's going to produce the sweet music from your cash register, so don't forget that although Americans as a whole don't condone that chap's conduct, many of them feel strongly on the colour question. So, you will have to ask yourself, are you going to risk antagonizing an unknown majority in order to spare the feelings of a negligible minority?'

'In common decency, I don't see that I have any choice in the matter,' said Jonathan. 'This island is full of Dabneys of all shades of colour, four of them my half-brothers, and cousins of every degree. How can I stand by doing nothing when they are insulted?'

'My dear Johnny, a businessman takes little things like that in his stride, so make up your mind if you are a businessman or a Boy Scout?'

'If you were in my place, what would you do?'

'I'd most likely drink the bar dry and go broke. But if I were to tackle the problem in a practical way, I would be inclined to buttonhole the odd dusky customer on arrival and explain the situation to him as nicely as possible. Then, if in the face of that he cared to stay, you would have to hope that he wouldn't be insulted.'

'That's a coward's way out of it....'

'Of course it is, but take my word for it that the hero's way won't be very comfortable ... or profitable. Take a leaf from my book and learn. In order to keep afloat financially, I must have a certain minimum amount of paid advertising. These and job-printing come from the same people ... more or less. If my editorial columns offend those people by running counter to their interests, or for any other reason, they are not going to give me their support. Why should they? To them I am a convenience, not a necessity. To me they are a necessity and they know it. So what do I do? I compromise. I won't write lies to placate them, so when I am given the choice between telling lies and remaining silent, I remain silent and survive.

'You, my dear Johnny, are situated much as I am. Your future depends on the support of tourists, some eighty per cent of whom will be Americans. Of these, shall we say conservatively, twenty per cent feel strongly on the colour question. Some of these, admittedly the extremists, draw a distinction between Negroes and human beings, as was the widely held view in the days of slavery. Don't let's concern ourselves with the rights and wrongs of the matter for the moment, but confine ourselves to the practical issues. If you want American tourists, and unless you want Dabney's Reef turned into a battleground, you must compromise by making some concession to their prejudices ... however distasteful to you they may be. Those are the facts of the case, Johnny, and you cannot escape from them. Go back and think about it and when you've done that, think some more.'

Alice McGraw came down for a couple of weeks that winter, needing a quiet rest. While she and Jonathan were standing at the bar, an American couple arrived from one of the pleasure craft in the lagoon. They ordered a drink at the bar, looked around the dining-room, saw Lawrence Dabney and another man of colour at a table, drank their drinks and left without allowing their reason for leaving to be apparent to anyone.

'Now there's a case of pleasant, well-behaved people who have honest feelings about the colour question,' said Alice McGraw. 'You may not agree with them, but you can't complain about their behaviour. Nobody was offended. I've more than once walked out of a place because I didn't like the looks of the people I saw there, once because of two drunken black men. It was because they were drunk, not because they were black....'

'Those people who just left,' said Jonathan, 'were the kind I want to attract ... quiet, well-britched without being blatantly rich ... an ornament to any resort. I'm truly sorry to see them go....'

'The way to avoid unpleasantness of any kind, Johnny, is to devise a way of letting people know in advance that the colour line is not drawn here. Then it would seem the trouble-makers would give the place a wide berth. Have you got a pencil and a piece of paper...?'

After several minutes' scribbling and deletions, she passed

74

the result across the table. 'How's this? Have it printed clearly on letters confirming bookings.'

We are not responsible for the colour of our skins – only for the way in which we wear them. At DABNEY'S REEF there is *no racial discrimination*.

'It may cost you some cancellations,' she went on, 'but let's hope the people who do come will be more pleasant.'

After due deliberation Jonathan adopted this suggestion, whose first fruits were unexpected. A note, written on Government House notepaper, arrived one morning by messenger. It was to the effect that Captain Slingsby-Nethercott required a table at dinner that evening for himself and a guest and would appreciate the opportunity of a few minutes' conversation with Mr Dabney.

Slingsby-Nethercott, who turned out to be an A.D.C., arrived alone, saying that his guest would arrive later. Would it be convenient if they had their little chat before he came? He was expensively tailored. Flaxen hair, blue eyes and a rather toothy smile made him appear as a slightly, very slightly, malicious foreign cartoonist sees an upper-class Englishman. These and the good manners mandatory for the job of A.D.C. completed the picture. It was evident to Jonathan that the errand which had brought him was somewhat distasteful. Seeing the other surveying the people at the bar nervously and sensing the reason, Jonathan said: 'Why don't we take our drinks into my office? It's pokey but private.'

'Jolly good idea! Splendid!'

When they were seated out of earshot of the others, the A.D.C. began: 'His Excellency regards you as a very important person ... a dollar earner, what!'

'I earn a few, but not as many as I'd like to, of course ...'

'Quite!'

The ball was in Jonathan's court, but he waited.

'Jolly good drink this; what is it?'

'It's a Martinique rum punch. Very popular over there I'm told. The girl behind the bar comes from there.'

'Does she, by Jove! And what a smasher she is! No relation of Napoleon's Josephine by any chance? From all accounts she was easy on the eyes, too.'

'No, not that I know of.'

'Delightful place you have here! I must come here often. I've only just come to the island ... don't know my way around yet. Has His Excellency been here?'

'Not that I know of. But that doesn't signify because, not knowing what he looks like, I might easily not have recognized him ...'

'That's a good one, that is!' guffawed the A.D.C. 'Might not have recognized him. You know, Dabney, you're a bit of a wag. Might not have recognized him, eh? Fat chance! ... But your idea that he could have come here unrecognized gives me a good laugh. Does the Royal Coach slide round Parliament Square unnoticed? It does not. H.E. doesn't run to outriders and trumpeters ... yet. But when his valet pours him into his uniform, let me tell you, he doesn't let anyone forget who he is. If you haven't got a red carpet here, he'll be glad to bring his own. I say, I hope you don't mind me calling you Dabney ...'

'Not at all. What shall I call you?'

'My friends call me Bertie ... surname's a bit of a mouthful. I hope we're friends.'

'I see your glass is empty, Bertie. Same again?'

'Thanks. I'll come with you ... I'd walk round the island to see that little filly again.'

They returned to the office with their drinks, Bertie reluctantly.

'You know, Dabney, you're being frightfully decent ... well, I mean making things so easy for me ...'

'What things?' asked Jonathan, introducing the first faintly sour note.

Bertie swallowed hard, his somewhat prominent adam's apple showing signs of distress.

'Perhaps I should have explained before ... the fact is that I'm here on H.E.'s business ... all a bit delicate, what!

'He's expecting an American admiral here shortly. At the moment the date is not quite sure. Well, realizing that

76

Government House isn't exactly famous for its gaiety ... H.E. thought it might be a good idea to have the admiral and his staff out here ... lunch or dinner. Give 'em somewhere to change perhaps and they might like a swim ... see what I mean?'

'I'll be only too delighted to do what I can and help make it a success. I'd need to know numbers of course, and if possible I'd like two or three days' notice ...'

'Quite, quite! I say, do you think I could have another of those delicious whatyoumaycallits? Seems to me it's time I pushed the boat out instead of sponging on you all the evening ...'

'Nonsense! You're my guest. Good, aren't they?'

'Tophole. Nothing like this at Government House ... local rum, sweet sherry and for gala occasions claret cup. Cheers!'

'Well, let me know the date and numbers as soon as you can and I'll do my stuff. American ships are dry, but they drink like fish when they come ashore. Now, if you'll forgive me, I have some people waiting to see me. Dollars, too. All in a good cause, eh?'

'Well, I won't keep you long, but there is just one more little matter which H.E. has asked me to clear with you. Some Americans, as you doubtless know, are just a wee bit touchy on the subject of colour. Something to do with the Constitution, I believe, although I haven't the foggiest idea of what the Constitution is, have you? Something about all men being brothers under their skin as long as some of them don't get too sunburned ...

'The fact is,' he floundered on, 'that H.E. wants to be assured that there won't be any ... shall we say ... awkward incidents, if you know what I mean. Being his guests, H.E. doesn't want their delicate susceptibilities offended in any way....'

'In what particular way, Bertie?' asked Jonathan, determined not to make it easy.

'This is the difficult part, which is why I wanted this little chat to be private. In short, when I go back can I assure H.E. that ... I won't beat about the bush, although I find it all most embarrassing ... that his American guests won't be offended by the sight of coloured people in the same room with them?'

'Ah!' There it was, about to be laid on the line.

'As Her Majesty's representative here, you understand, H.E. doesn't want any unpleasant incident....'

'I'm quite sure he doesn't, but we mustn't forget that around ninety-six per cent of the population of this island is coloured, all of whom are loyal subjects of the Queen he represents. His first duty surely is to them, to protect *them* from insult....'

'Now I don't like this any more than you do, Dabney, but I'm only an A.D.C. ... All the Dirty Chores that stands for ... and you can't expect me to go back to H.E. with that. He'd blow a gasket. What am I going to say to him?'

'Tell him the truth, which is that on any given day I can't anticipate the pigmentation of my guests. If the American party had come today and if their susceptibilities are as delicate as alleged, which I take leave to doubt, they would have been scandalized by the presence of a party from a Brazilian yacht ... all well-mannered, charming people, mark you ... but some of them were distinctly sunburned. Would he ... the Governor, that is ... expect me to eject them for fear of offending his guests? You want to know what to say to him, so tell him that if the Americans come they will be given the best food, drink and service we can possibly give them and made to feel most welcome. But more than that I will not promise and if that doesn't seem enough, I suggest that he entertains them at Government House where he can weed out undesirable fellow guests....'

'I'll tell him that, wrapped up a bit of course, but I'm afraid he won't like it.'

'Any more than I like being told to hand-pick my guests here.'

'But there is a difference,' said Bertie, not entirely convinced by his argument. 'He *is* the Governor.'

'Then, as I am sure you will agree, his first duty is to the people he came to govern....'

'You know, Dabney, you're being a wee bit uncompromising. Won't you try to make things a little easier for *me*.'

'Very well, Bertie, I'll try. Will you please convey my compliments to His Excellency, say that I am greatly honoured by being entrusted with the entertainment of his American guests and I will do everything in my power to make it a memorable occasion which will forge another link in the chain of Anglo-American amity. And if you think it will sound better, set it to music. ...'

'You're an awkward cuss, Dabney, and as my guest seems to have lost the way, why don't we have another of those splendid drinks. Let me buy them. It will give me an opportunity of whispering in that smashing girl's shell-like ear. What's her name, by the way?'

'Chantal. Pretty name, isn't it?'

Bertie was away for at least fifteen minutes, during which Jonathan tried vainly to analyse the sense of annoyance which swept over him. Chantal was a pretty name. Why hadn't he realized that before?

'Do you know what I prescribe for you, Bertie?' said Jonathan, noting that the other was looking a little pale. 'I prescribe some blotting paper before the kitchen closes for the night. How about some fish and chips? That's what I'm having.'

'When I get back to town I'm going to tell the old man you're not such a shit as I was led to believe. Damned good chap, Dabney, thass what I'm goin' to tell him, damned good chap. Bit hipped about our black brothers perhaps, but knows how to look after a guest. Leave it all to me ... maybe I will set it to music. I'll wrap it up a bit. The old man's not a bad chap really ... bit pompous ... has to be ... no brains ... that's self-evident, isn't it ... wouldn't have picked me as his A.D.C. if he'd had any brains. But don't cross him, Dabney, don't cross him. You'd be making great mistake ... Governor's got plenty of ways of putting the skids under you ... never forget it. Would it inconvenience you if I went for a walk along the beach ... don't want to be sick down the front of this jacket, so I'll leave it here if I may. Pity to spoil it ... specially because it isn't paid for yet. ...'

10

The Governor's party for the American admiral and his officers went with a bang and without the smallest unpleasant incident. Jonathan did not receive the party personally, leaving it to the coloured butler Newcombe, who had once buttled at Government House long before the present incumbent's time.

Bertie, who arrived at Dabney's Reef ahead of the party, presumably to see that all was well, gave Jonathan a huge wink when, in the flickering light of a driftwood bonfire on the beach, the Governor and the Admiral, flanked by two sweating policemen, appeared on the scene. The ludicrous aspect of the affair, which prompted Bertie's wink, was that one of the junior officers turned out to be a handsome, full-blooded Negro. All the preliminary fuss had been for nothing, serving only to prove what everyone in his entourage knew already, that the Governor was by way of being an ass.

The party was a great success. Most if not all of the guests were introduced to two new dishes, *bouillabaisse* and roast peacock. In point of fact the peacock was turkey, but the former sounded better. Even the Governor unbent under the influence of Martinique rum punch, a huge bowl of which was on the table for guests to serve themselves with a dipper.

When the party had left by water in the Governor's launch for Port Lewis, Jonathan heaved a sigh of relief that all had gone well. On a petty canvas it might have been called a triumph against great odds, but he somehow failed to see anything but that it was petty. Dabney's Reef was a success, he supposed, to the degree that it was giving him a comfortable living, if not riches. Starting from scratch, he had floundered to some success, partly because he owned far and away the most beautiful spot in an uninteresting island where everything else had been subordinated to sugar.

The income-producing part of Dabney's Reef was now twelve rooms, each with bath and verandah, or balcony, the moorings in the lagoon, the restaurant and the bar. All these commanded high prices during the northern winter season from November to the end of February, less at other times and closing down altogether from August to November when hurricanes were on the cards.

Thanks largely to Alice McGraw, who acted as the Dabney's Reef representative in New York, and her sister Kathleen, who handled all Canadian bookings from Montreal, the accommodation ashore and the lagoon moorings had a waiting list for most of the year.

The rest was his good fortune in finding Graziella. She had some French blood, but whether practical good sense and organizing ability was hereditary or acquired by contact with French women in Martinique was unimportant beside the fact that she had these qualities. She knew how to buy provisions, how to cook and serve up mouthwatering food such as the island had never known. A large part of the population spoke a French *patois*, a hangover from the days of French rule, and had little difficulty understanding the verbal bouquets she used to stimulate the laggards under her. Like all born disciplinarians, she had the knack of making her victims like it. Jonathan's salvation was that she liked him and, recognizing his incompetence, swept everything into her capable hands without robbing him more than moderately. Jonathan, naturally, handled all correspondence and bookings.

Bearing these things in mind, Jonathan, it might be supposed, was indulging in some self-congratulation. But this was far from true. The satisfying sense of achievement was not there. Although all the plans were ready, and a large sum available from the bank if required, with the contract for the builder lying on his desk unsigned, he hesitated. The contract was for the building of a total of forty small to medium self-contained apartments, comprising one or two bedrooms each, with bathroom, kitchen, living-room and

81

balcony, eight apartments a year for five years. But there was a snag. There is almost always a snag. A clause in the contract, never discussed but slipped in quietly when negotiations were complete, gave to the guarantor, a shadowy real-estate shark in Miami who had never appeared in person, the right to veto a sale to anyone if in the guarantor's opinion the buyer were an undesirable person, or likely to be uncongenial to the other residents.

Zachary, who in all other respects found the terms of the loan acceptable, told Jonathan that it was merely a protection against one buyer making the other apartments unsaleable.

'It looks to me as though it's thinly disguised racial discrimination,' said Jonathan unhappily.

'Undoubtedly it could be so interpreted,' Zachary agreed, 'but you may be sure that without this clause the other side won't sign.'

'Try them and see.'

'Very well, I'll try them, but I am not optimistic. I don't like this sort of thing any more than you do, Johnny, perhaps even less, because being a man with coloured blood myself, I should resent it bitterly. But I don't, Johnny, I don't. We ... by we I mean people in a like situation ... are used to it. That's the way the world is, not the way we would like it to be. A day will come perhaps when justice will prevail, but so far in the world's history social justice has always been bought at the cost of bloodshed, the remedy often worse than the injustice it sought to abolish. If as a man with a brown skin I'm debarred from living in one of your lovely apartments because my neighbours might not like me, then I tell myself I might not like them ...'

'See what they say,' said Jonathan with set jaws.

'Very well,' replied Zachary sighing, 'but let me tell you that in my experience a man who begins a one-man crusade is beaten before the start. Perhaps one of the reasons why so few people have principles is because they can't afford them.'

That was how matters stood on the evening of the Governor's party, which explains why Jonathan, who might well have been jubilant, was very much otherwise.

82

Elias, rowing ashore in his little dinghy, found him slumped at the bar, an untasted drink in front of him, looking thoroughly dejected. Pulling down Jonathan's lower eyelid, he pursed his lips. 'Let me take your pulse, Johnny,' he said, suiting action to the word. 'Now your tongue. Humph! How's your appetite?'

'It's too damned hot to eat much.'

'Most people eat too damned much anyway, so don't let that worry you. There's nothing much wrong with you ... nothing that can't be cured in short order. You've got what a former patient of mine used to call "the sufflications".'

'What in blazes is that?'

'I remember the Latin name, but for the moment I've forgotten what it's called in English. It will come to me. Before I go to bed I'll have the prescription made up and sent over to you. What time are you going to bed?'

'In ten or fifteen minutes. Why?'

'Be sure to leave your door unlocked. I won't forget. Sleep well. See you in the morning.'

'Thanks Elias. Good-night!'

The kitchen had closed down. The 'Skyscraper' was sitting outside fanning herself with a young palm frond, seemingly deep in thought and gazing out at the phosphorescence as small waves creamed over the reef. It was a glorious night, even if a little hot for comfort. Elias pulled up a chair to join her. These two had become good friends. Graziella was a wise, far-seeing woman.

'Johnny does not look well,' she said. 'I was watching him this evening. He is too serious ... maybe worried about business. He needs some medicine to make him laugh ... or a holiday.'

'A doctor cannot help him. A holiday would not help either,' said Elias. 'The cure is here ... at home.'

As he spoke he looked across meaningly to where Chantal was closing the bar. The beach was deserted. Chantal, throwing off the only garment she wore, walked slowly down to the water's edge. When it was up to her waist she plunged forward and with strong, clean strokes swam out along the silver path of the rising moon.

Graziella nodded understandingly, and when the girl swam back met her at the water's edge, where they exchanged a few words. Chantal went to the cottage which she shared with her mother, soon emerging wearing something shapeless which had the sheen of silk.

Elias and Graziella watched in silence as Chantal went across to Jonathan's room, pausing on the verandah before opening the door, entering and closing it behind her. The watchers maintained silence for a full half-hour.

'It is well,' said Elias in the island French he always used with Graziella.

'She is a good girl,' said her mother, 'and they will be happy together.'

*   *   *

Three days were allowed to pass before mother and daughter spoke of the matter.

'Are you happy?' asked the former.

Chantal's radiant smile told its own story.

'Is he happy?'

'He thinks he is not, but it will pass.'

'What is wrong?'

'He talks always of marriage. He is ashamed. He fears that he has taken unfair advantage of me. . . .'

Graziella chuckled. 'Let him think so always. That way you will hold him. Marriage will not hold an unwilling man. At all costs you must not marry him. Give him a child. That will hold him. . . .'

'I will give him many children. . . .'

'Don't talk like a fool! Give him one child, no more. Do you want to look like the old crones in the villages, worn out at thirty by too much child-bearing? Look at me! I had one child . . . you. I am forty-four years of age, still a young woman. Hardly a day passes that some man does not make me improper proposals or pinch my bottom. I do not encourage them, but it is most comforting to a woman of my age that it is so. Remember that. One child . . . one only, and you will live to thank me.'

84

'I do not want that he should feel guilty, Maman. If there is any guilt, it is mine. He did not invite me to his bed. . . .'

'Let him feel guilty if it pleases him. It is in his nature. He feels guilty for what he thinks are the sins of his father, his grandfather and others before them. The island is full of Dabneys but nobody cares ... nobody but your Johnny. Nothing will ever cure his sense of guilt. It is one of his few luxuries. Never try to deprive him of it.'

'But why, Maman, why should a man feel guilty?'

'I am not sure I know the answer to that, but some men, especially those of the white races, grow up to believe that the pleasures of the bed are for men only and that for women they are a painful duty.'

'How strange!'

'Indeed, how strange! But let that be as it may, and just remember that a sense of guilt will bind him to you with chains stronger than the mumbling of a priest. If he wishes to be free, let him be free. Only a foolish woman wants an unwilling man.'

*   *   *

It came to Jonathan slowly that his feelings first for Jean and then Gloria, which in turn he had thought of as love, had been somewhat less than that. Now it was altogether different, for Chantal completely absorbed him. If this were not love, then he was incapable of it.

Until now there had always been an uncomfortable sense of being a mere spectator looking at life from the outside. Now, miraculously, he was a part of it.

Another important change had taken place; this in his attitude towards Dabney's Reef and the grandiose plans he had been formulating. From being a place where he planned to make a great deal of money as a symbol of Dabney success, vindicating past failures, it became a home. A spacious bungalow, built as an investment for seasonal occupation by very rich people, suddenly seemed far too delightful for such base purposes. Jonathan and Chantal moved their small belongings into it and settled down to domesticity.

The beach had become a quiet, restful resort for mostly elderly people wanting to escape the northern winter. There was no dancing or orchestra. Calypso bands were barred when Carnival came around. Those who wanted to hear their hideous cacophony could go into Port Lewis to do so. It was an uncomfortable trip by road, but, weather permitting, a launch went there every day, sometimes twice.

When neither side would give way regarding the restrictive clause in the contract for building the apartments, the project was perforce dropped. It proved to be a turning-point in the affairs of Dabney's Reef. Since it ceased to go forward and grow in importance and since it is not in the nature of things to stand still, the only way left to go was backward. At first the process was imperceptible because so slow. Quiet-living elderly people are of necessity a wasting asset to a resort, and as their ranks thinned they were not replaced by the young and lively people who, despite the honkytonk atmosphere they brought with them, were spending money in amounts so huge that they were changing the face of the Caribbean. Dabney's Reef itself was still a delightful resort. Its deterioration, if it could be called that, was in the lessening of pressure for accommodation in the high season.

Tucker of the Tucker House in Port Lewis had built a beach hotel on the outskirts of the town and since it was not in a beautiful situation and the swimming was not good, there were times when Graziella's facilities were strained to the limit by the overflow from Tucker's guests. Graziella herself, after a holiday in her native Martinique, returned with a man in tow, one Maximilien Taitbout, who it transpired had been *maître d'hotel* at one of the Transatlantique hotels in Morocco. He brought some distinction to the restaurant. He was a handsome man of dignified bearing, something of a disciplinarian, who took much of the load of work from Graziella's shoulders.

Jonathan, who never questioned the amount of his monthly share in the catering profits, was well content with the arrangement. Not so Chantal who, despite her changed status, refused to relinquish control of the bar.

'Maximilien may not be a thief,' she declared judicially. 'I do not say he is one, Johnny, because I do not know. But even so, he would soon become one. All barmen – I have not met them all, of course – are thieves, bandits and assassins. The temptations are too great to be resisted. Ten per cent of the profits ... that is reasonable. Even I used to take that for myself, but they are not content with that for long.'

It was only when Chantal's belly was so big that she moved with difficulty in the confined space behind the bar that she could be persuaded to install a locum, and then it was only for a week before the August closing.

With the minimum of fuss, without even troubling to send for Elias, who was standing by for the event, Chantal gave birth to a fine healthy son. His birth was registered under the name of Nicolas St Laurent Dabney. Christening was postponed until it was decided whether it should be a Roman Catholic or Protestant ceremony. Jonathan's mild preference was for the latter, Chantal's for the former. In the end it was neither.

True to Graziella's prediction, the birth of Nico, as inevitably he was called in the family, brought his parents even closer together. Elias, whose 'prescription' had been in good part responsible for bringing about this happy conclusion, felt himself entitled to a large share of the credit.

11

The uneventful years were sliding by on greased wheels for Jonathan, Chantal and Nico, and because happy domesticity tends to be wearisome to all but the principals concerned, there is little to be said about it. Change, it seemed, was everywhere apparent except at Dabney's Reef, where life pursued its even tenor.

With the building of an airfield the isolation, which had been much of the island's charm, was ending. The big international jets could not yet be landed, but smaller planes belonging to the West Indian airline arrived regularly from Trinidad, Barbados and further north. Gushing travel writers, given lunch at Dabney's Reef by the equally gushing Miss O'Malley of the Tourist Bureau, so overworked 'unspoiled' as to make it certain that the island would be spoilt in short order, for Dabney's Reef was no more typical of the whole island than Kensington Gardens is of London. The view of Port Lewis from the lighthouse looking down on it dwarfed some of its squalor. After which flying tour there was just time to catch the afternoon plane out. The less these people were shown of the island, the more lyrical they were in their enthusiasms. Truth and accuracy play a negligible part in travel journalism, whose real function is to gloss over foul climates, tyrannical governments, insanitary conditions, inedible food, endemic diseases, phoney folklore and other delights waiting for unsuspecting tourists.

A part of the airfield was built upon some of the worthless scrub land owned by Jonathan who, as a public-spirited gesture, donated some thirty-odd acres for the purpose. He was only just in time to scotch the plan to name it Dabney Field.

One of the early fruits of this change was the arrival of retired people from North America and to a lesser degree Britain, who built comfortable but undistinguished villas, as well as a few rich people who built for winter occupation only. Some twenty odd of these new houses were built upon the piece of land below the lighthouse which Jonathan had inherited from his father. Advised by Zachary to do so, he had paid off the £300 mortgage and held on, finally selling it off at prices varying between £400 and £800 per building plot. Much of the value stemmed from the land's sea frontage. He was now delighted that he had resisted the temptation to 'develop' Dabney's Reef.

The newcomers injected some life into the island's white society, hitherto dominated by the tired, lack-lustre sugar-crat families, which had long been considered its aristocracy. These and the newcomers, having little in common, established few points of contact. Living behind their high hibiscus hedges, meeting only their own kind, they ceased to be a factor in the island's social life. In-breeding had dragged them down from their high estate: now it was leading them on to extinction.

Jonathan was on good terms with many of the new residents. These people did not exchange visits with Jonathan and Chantal, although they frequently came for lunch and a swim.

One day, after a big luncheon party had gone, Jonathan found Chantal in tears. The reason soon emerged.

'Those people like you, they laugh with you and make jokes. They are polite to me, but not in the same way. Why? What is wrong with me? To them I am just nothing?'

As Jonathan had known for a long while, this was bound to come. The wonder was that it had not happened long ago. Now nothing but the blunt and unpalatable truth would serve. Chantal was too elemental to be fobbed off with anything less.

'Why do they not invite us to their houses?' she stormed.

'Do you remember when I asked you to wear shoes ... it must have been two or three years ago?' he began.

'Of course I remember. There were none in Port Lewis big enough for me, so you made a pencil drawing round my feet and we sent to have them made in Trinidad. What has that to do with those people not asking us to visit them?'

'A lot, darling. You won't like it, but I'll tell you. You have never worn shoes in your life, have you?'

'No, I tried but they were uncomfortable. . . .'

'Well now, these people have worn shoes all their lives. It wouldn't occur to them to do anything else. Except when I'm on the beach or in bed, I always wear shoes. It's a custom and I'm used to it.'

'If that is the reason why they do not invite us, I will wear shoes even though they hurt like hell.'

'That is only one of the reasons,' said Jonathan, hating what he had to do. 'I have been asking you for years not to serve behind the bar. . . .'

'You know that if we employ someone, we shall be robbed,' Chantal said fiercely. 'Besides, I like my bar. It is fun. I mix good drinks and they pay a lot for them. . . .'

'That is not the point. . . .'

'Then what is the point?'

'I am supposed to be an important person here . . . anyway fairly important . . . and it isn't right that my wife should be serving behind a bar. . . .'

'I am not your wife. . . .'

'You are the mother of my son. I wish you were my wife and you are known as Mrs Dabney. Heaven knows I have asked you to marry me often enough. Why won't you?'

'Maman, who is a wise woman, says that if I marry you I shall lose you. . . .'

'What foolish nonsense!'

'It is not nonsense. Look what happened to that other woman you married. She lost you, didn't she?'

'She left me, which is not the same thing. But stick to the point. All this began with you asking me why people do not ask us to their houses. I am trying to tell you why, so keep quiet and let me tell you. You are known to most of these people as a barmaid. That is natural because whenever they see you you are behind the bar.'

'I told you, I like my bar.'

'I know you do. But people ask why I, the owner of Dabney's Reef, whom they think of as a rich man, allow my wife ... all right, you are not my wife, but let us call you that ... why I allow my wife to serve behind the bar? What kind of a man is that, they ask? He can have no pride.'

'Is it a bad thing to be a barmaid?'

'No, it is not exactly bad. But it is what is known as a menial job....'

'Menial ... what is that?'

'A servant's job, but not quite that. Ask Elias to explain it to you in French ... your French, not mine.'

'There is something else?'

'Yes, there is, and we may as well have it all out in the open. It is the way you speak. The French doesn't matter because none of the white people speaks Creole French, but the English does matter ... yours is not the kind of English spoken in those houses where you would like to be invited ...'

'What is wrong? I speak English good ... well.'

'You speak it well, darling, but you speak it as if you learned it from drunken American sailors.'

'You know why? Because I first learned it from American sailors and because almost always they were drunk, that is why.'

'I am not blaming you, but trying to answer your question....'

'First I must try to push my big feet into shoes, even if it kills me. Then I must give up my bar and watch while some thieving sonofabitch takes all the profits. After that I must start all over again to learn another kind of English. Who will learn me to speak that kind?'

'I will find someone for you if you would like me to. But *I'm* not asking you to change anything ... I love you as you are, big feet and all.'

Robbie McAlister's sister Margaret was staying with him for a few months. She was a B.A. and in every way a more cultured person than Robbie. She had a little money, but not enough for her needs. She knew and liked Chantal.

'I'll do it,' she said when it was put to her, 'but it is a crime to take someone as sweet as Chantal, so natural and unaffected, and perhaps spoil her by teaching her prunes and prisms. And to what end? To be patronized by people, nice enough in their way, who haven't an idea in their heads, not even a bad one. It is a pity. All they think about is bridge, gossip and cocktail parties. But the worst part will be hiding those glorious legs underneath long skirts, so as not to show people her beautiful feet, which are going to look like hell in shoes. It's a crime, Johnny, and I hope neither of you will regret it.'

For two hours daily over six months Margaret McAlister laboured to change Chantal from her charming self into a stilted and self-conscious young woman, insecure, in terror of making the mistakes which loomed ahead when she made her début in what passed for society.

'She's miserably unhappy, Johnny,' said Margaret, 'certain that people will laugh at her. What's more, she's not far wrong in that. People can be so damned cruel. How would it be if I talked her out of it?'

'It would be fine with me. This is all her idea, not mine.'

'But she's doing it for you, Johnny, or thinks she is, which is the same thing. She wants you to be proud of her ... instead of which a day is coming when you'll want the earth to swallow you for sheer embarrassment. . . .'

Margaret McAlister's assessment of human cruelty towards someone like Chantal in the circumstances she would have to face may have been and probably was accurate, but where she went wrong was in underestimating the girl's grit, determination and talent for survival.

Jonathan, in the belief that Chantal would feel less conspicuous in a large gathering than a small one, arranged for her social début to take place at what was called the Christmas Ball which, started by the newcomers (and, therefore, automatically boycotted by the old sugaristocracy), had become an annual event. Jonathan, who still owned La Bastide, lent the old ballroom for the purpose. The only other room large enough was in the new Tucker House, which Tucker was willing to lend on condition that tourists staying in the hotel might be admitted. The offer had been accepted the first year, but with deplorable results. Tourists had turned the ball into a rout. Some had appeared in beach attire and, asked to change into something more suitable for a formal occasion, had started something near a riot, and what had begun as a decorous assembly ended in a drunken brawl.

Chantal had chosen to wear a dress of turquoise-coloured cotton printed with splashes of scarlet, the long full skirt sitting low on her hips. Whether by luck or judgment, the hibiscus bloom in her black hair was a perfect match to the scarlet in the dress. Tall without them, the high-heeled shoes made her tower above any other woman in the room.

The Chairman of the Ball Committee, a Mrs Manwaring, a well-known 'organizer' in her native Toronto, was a kindly soul who took Chantal under her wing. She sensed the agonies of anticipation which the latter must be enduring.

If Chantal had not been the most conspicuous person in the room, it might have been easier for her. Only a couple of inches shorter than her mother, the Skyscraper, her graceful movement and sheer beauty, to say nothing of her attire, were breath-taking.

'They may hate me,' she said to Jonathan on the way to the ball, 'but they will know that I am there.'

Chantal's ability to laugh at her own *gaffes* was charming. So, instead of laughing at her, people laughed with her, and the warmth of her incandescent smile did the rest.

For the first hour she limped around the floor with her various dancing partners who, assuming from her grace that she would be the best dancer in the room, were disappointed. At one moment, while dancing with a tall young Canadian from Montreal, she was heard to utter a groan. Then a hushed silence fell as slowly, deliberately, one at a time, she kicked the shoes up into the gallery which ran round the ballroom high above the dancers. They landed with a soft plop clearly audible.

'Now let us really dance,' she said, falling into step with her partner, a first-rate dancer himself who, sensing something of her wild, reckless mood, came to life.

Most of the dancers left the floor, feeling their own inadequacy in face of the mad, joyous whirling performance these two gave. When it was over the young Canadian – from Canada's Sandhurst at Kingston – flushed and breathless, bowed profoundly as he thanked her. Chantal's reply was to

93

sink to the floor in a superbly graceful gesture which might have been taken from a ballet.

During the whole of this unrehearsed spectacle – his eyes glued to Chantal and her partner – Jonathan stood in frozen immobility. It was the kind of performance whose logical ending is in a bed. Without putting it into words, Jonathan knew this. The young Canadian knew it, too, and he had the wit to fade away into the night, not to be seen again that evening. Spectators with acute perceptions knew that he had done the wise thing.

On the drive back to Dabney's Reef after the ball, Jonathan and Chantal hardly spoke. Overheated after the exertions of the evening, they swam across the lagoon and back. Chantal broke the silence which was becoming brittle.

'He was a good dancer, that young man, hein?'

'Was he?'

'Johnny, I believe you are jealous.'

'Of course I am jealous. Any man would be.'

'That is good. I am glad.'

'I think we should be married. I would feel safer then.'

'No, Johnny, not for Chantal. If you feel safe then you will no longer be jealous ... and I like you to be jealous.'

'You little bitch!'

'Not so little!'

That evening was a landmark in their lives. Jonathan, whose rôle had always been that of the worldly-wise partner, worldly-wise only by comparison with Chantal, became aware that in some way he failed to understand their rôles had been reversed. Her refusal ever again to wear shoes symbolized a victory over narrow convention, giving her confidence in herself and in other people's willingness to accept her as she was without pretence.

The Christmas Ball brought Chantal's social education to an abrupt halt. What she had not learned, she had no wish to learn. She was not foolish enough to suppose that she could ever learn to be a *grande dame*, even if there were any likelihood that in the island's limited society she would ever be recognized as such. Her command of polite English was vastly improved, even if a trifle too 'refeened'. What had given her confidence in herself was that striking beauty, warm-heartedness, good humour and spontaneity had almost universal appeal. The choice flowers of speech from the Brooklyn Navy Yard, now thrust into the background, could be resuscitated when and if needed.

In the logical sequence of events Margaret McAlister, having nothing more for Chantal, took over the education of Nico, now aged seven. Chantal, only too well aware that the task was beyond her, was more than willing to surrender it.

Nico was a bright, lively child, reasonably sweet-tempered, and with a vast curiosity regarding everything he saw and, particularly, touched. It was evident from cradle days onward that he had brains in his fingers. He would spend long and happy hours taking mechanical toys to pieces, putting them together again, thereby acquiring a knowledge of first principles.

People meeting Chantal for the first time and knowing nothing of her background could, and occasionally did, assume her to be wholly Caucasian; not people who had lived any time in the West Indies, who would know that she was not. Jonathan had no other blood but Caucasian. But it was impossible to mistake their son Nico for anything but what he was, even though his colour was no darker than Mediterranean swarthiness. There was no suggestion of negroid features such as kinky hair and thick lips, but surveyed through half-closed eyes ... experienced eyes, he had what may be termed a negroid outline. His movements were African. He could cross his feet and squat, rising to his feet again without help from his arms. Certain kinds of music caused his body to dance, even when sitting down. Strangers did not think of such things: all they saw was the warmth and spontaneity and the incandescent smile he had inherited from his mother.

Two hours daily under Margaret's watchful eye, learning what seemed to be unnecessary lessons, made Nico's sunny disposition conspicuously less sunny. His lively curiosity caused him to want to know why such boring things were needed, and when he was fobbed off with evasive replies, thunder-squalls were not long in coming.

People said that Nico was like his father, but Jonathan failed to see it. They were temperamentally at poles apart, but a good father-son relationship was building. Nico found his father's placid nature easier to understand than his mother's volatility, which sometimes inexplicably exploded into screaming rage.

12

Returning from Port Lewis late one afternoon, Jonathan called at the airport, which was on his route, to see if the newspapers from Europe and the North had arrived. He parked his car behind a taxi driven by one of his half-brothers. The four half-brothers were by four different mothers and there were wide disparities between them. All four had been given equal opportunities in the matter of education, but only two had availed themselves of it. Lawrence, who had been at Jonathan's first wedding, was, as we know, a doctor. Hugh, who had studied law, was a real estate agent and doing well. Arthur, an amiable roughneck, was a fisherman out of season, who rented his boat and himself to wealthy deep-sea anglers in season. The last, Bill, was a taxi-driver. Jonathan was on good terms with all of them, but their widely differing interests and modes of life tended to be a barrier between him and the last two named.

'Hey! Johnny, long time no see!' called Bill when he saw Jonathan go to the news-stand. 'Be seeing you in a few minutes. I've got a fare out to your place. Buy me a drink, eh?'

Jonathan nodded. 'I'm not expecting anyone. I wonder who it is.'

'Dunno! She'll soon be through the Customs. I'll bring your papers ... which do you want? Can't have you hanging around and robbing me of a fare. So long!'

Thinking no more about it, Jonathan drove home. Lone women who came out of season were sometimes divorcees, wanting to lick their wounds in solitude. They could be a problem.

Night had dropped like a black velvet curtain when Bill arrived with his passenger.

'Please wait for me in case there is no room for me,' said a voice which was vaguely familiar to Jonathan.

'I'll wait, but there's no need. Likely as not you'll be the only guest. Johnny!' roared Bill. 'Lady wants a room.'

Going forward to meet the newcomer, Jonathan felt a pair of strong arms encircle him, and a kiss on either cheek. 'Don't you know me, Johnny?'

'No, not until you come into the light.'

'It's Doris, Johnny. Tell me that you're pleased to see me, or I shall cry.'

It was Doris, looking surprisingly little older, rumpled from travel, a trifle raddled, but evidently glad to see him.

'You'll want a bath and a change before anything....'

'And a drink, Johnny. At my advanced age I'm finding the bottle a great comfort....'

'Then you must dine ... with *us*. I've married again....'

'I know that. An old friend who winters here keeps tabs on you for me. Says your wife is as charming as she is lovely. I can't wait to meet her.'

Still chattering, Doris allowed herself to be shown to her room. Jonathan did not remember her as being so garrulous.

'Who is that woman?' demanded Chantal while they were waiting at the bar for Doris to return.

'She is Lady MacNiven, or was when I last knew her. She may easily have some other name now. She was once my mother-in-law....'

'What does she want here?' Chantal smelled mystery. The usual sweetness of her disposition was beginning to curdle.

'I don't know. She hasn't told me yet. But she will....'

'Do you like her?'

'Yes ... here she comes....'

When the two women were introduced, Doris was cordiality itself, but Chantal was polite and no more. They ordered rum punches. Doris had had two in her room already, but did not show it. Chantal, determined not to flatter Doris by putting on airs, went to the other extreme, on the somewhat involved theory that by these means she would show that she was not impressed by the other's title. She sipped her rum punch, rolled it round her mouth critically and said: 'It is not bad, but not as good as I used to make when this was *my* bar....'

'If it isn't a rude question, why did you give it up?'

'Johnny wanted me to. To be a barmaid was not dignified enough for him.'

'How strange! Johnny must have a real affinity with barmaids. Long ago I was one in England....'

'How did you meet?' asked Chantal, taken aback.

'He arrived in my garden by parachute. Has he not told you the story?'

'What is this about parachutes?' This was almost snarled. 'You never told me you had a parachute. What were you doing in one?'

'The plane caught fire and the parachute landed me safely in a tree near Doris's house. That is how we met.'

Chantal's hackles began to lie flat. The other's admission that she too had been a barmaid meant that she would not be patronizing. It was annoying, but inevitable, that this woman knew more about Johnny's past than she did herself, but it would be foolish to allow it to influence her. By the time they were ready to go to table, she found herself liking Doris. Nevertheless, it would be as well to reserve judgment until the reason behind her coming had emerged.

'What a positively delicious meal!' said Doris when the coffee was served. 'Most of the food I've tasted in the West Indies has been quite revolting. I must compliment the chef.'

'My mother is the cook here....'

'Then you are a very lucky girl. I wouldn't cook for my daughters....'

'How are they?' Jonathan interposed. 'Well, I hope.'

Chantal was all ears. Now for it.

'To tell you the truth, Johnny, I don't know as much about them as a mother should know ... and that mostly from infrequent letters. Jean and her Rumanian broke up years ago. Now she seems to flit from man to man ... like a butterfly. As you may know, Gloria has re-married, but it doesn't seem to be working out very well. She married a supposedly rich man, who turned out to be not so rich, and they spend their time trying to get money out of me. . . .'

'I'm sorry . . . and the children?'

This to Chantal was what all the flimflam had been leading up to: the children. Except to say that he had two children and had only ever seen one of them, Johnny had said almost nothing about them. She had often asked herself whether this was his way of being tactful and sparing her feelings, or whether they meant nothing to him and he had forgotten their existence. Now she would know the answer.

'The children are all with me . . . at the Villa Leonora.'

All? Surely that meant there were more than two? Otherwise she would have said *both*.

'I'm afraid,' said Doris, bringing Chantal into the discussion, 'that both my daughters are very selfish young women, who care more for gadding about and amusing themselves than they do for their children.'

'Poor little children!' said Chantal, her eyes widened and brimming with sympathy.

'Edouard . . . we call him Ted . . . is a somewhat difficult child. Having been brought up . . . dragged up might be a better word . . . by servants, he resents anything which savours of discipline. Little Esther, despite the same sort of upbringing, is a sweet child. It is hard to believe that they are brother and sister. Stephen' – Doris turned to Chantal – 'Stephen, my other daughter's son, is like Edouard, only worse if anything.

'I'm afraid I haven't painted a very attractive picture for you, Johnny, but there it is. Children, especially boys, need a father's firm hand. . . .'

'They would have had mine if Gloria had not insisted on holding them. It would have been difficult here, but I would have managed somehow. It seemed then that they would have been better off with Gloria. It sounds as if I was wrong.'

'Yes, I'm afraid you *were* wrong.'

'Our son, Nico, gives us very little trouble, isn't that so?' said Jonathan, turning to Chantal for confirmation.

'He has a happy home,' said Doris. 'Perhaps that's why.'

Although greatly mollified and her earlier hostility evaporated, Chantal was still acutely aware that the true reason for Doris's unannounced visit had not emerged. Like a cat at a mousehole, she remained watchful.

'As Johnny says, Nico is a good boy. I will bring him to meet you in the morning....'

Then talk turned to other matters. How was the swimming? Was it safe? Was it always as hot as this? You're very lucky not to have television here ... so bad for the children. Is the drinking water safe? It was Doris who kept the ball of conversation rolling and did it well. Doris had come a long way, Jonathan decided. She now had the *savoir faire* which she had once lacked.

'By the way,' said Jonathan, 'what became of Fatso?'

Chantal's ears pricked.

'Johnny was very naughty,' explained Doris. 'There was an Italian prince ... well, a sort of a prince. He was a little plump, but quite sweet. Johnny one evening called him Fatso ... to his face! Long after Johnny had gone, the name stuck....'

These two had so many shared memories. Chantal's nails were digging into her palms.

'You know,' said Doris a little later, 'you two might do far worse than come over to France for a trip. I'm not often at the Villa Leonora, but even if I am, it's big enough. Make a holiday of it. It's high time Johnny saw his children. Think about it.'

'If Chantal would like to make the trip, I'm willing,' said Jonathan.

'Thank you, but no. It is kind of you to ask us, but I would not like to leave my Nico....'

'Of course not. You must bring him too. You will enjoy it and, I am sure you will agree, it's time Johnny here took a look at his children. What do you say, Johnny?'

'I agree that I should see them, of course, but it is something I shall have to discuss with Chantal. It's for her to decide.'

Whether intentionally or not, Chantal felt that she was being manoeuvred. It was and had been all along incredible to her that, having two children in Europe, he could so calmly accept being cut off from them. It had occurred to her more than once to wonder whether, if cut off from Nico, he would be so calm about it. There was a difference: the first had been idle wonderment without personal significance, but when brought down to the particular in Nico's case, the mere contemplation of such a possibility pulled her up short in horror.

'Of course you realize,' said Doris, being careful to address them both, 'that if you come over – and I hope you will – there will be no question of meeting ... either of my daughters. No good could come of it, I feel, and it might be embarrassing all round. I am sure you agree.'

Chantal hoped that her relief at hearing this did not show. Jonathan had no photo of this Gloria, but she felt instinctively that she was very beautiful ... beautiful and sophisticated. Lacking sophistication herself, Chantal felt that this was more to be feared than beauty. So far as beauty was concerned, she believed she could hold her own with any woman. 'It might be a very good idea,' she replied slowly, 'but I would like to think about it.'

'Of course, of course! Even in these days of fast jet planes it is still a long journey and not to be undertaken lightly.'

Not by me, nor Johnny either, not if I can prevent it.

'You are very kind to offer us your house. Johnny tells me that it is very beautiful. It makes me feel quite ... excited.'

Doris, with the keen perceptions of a woman into another woman's feelings and motives, was well aware that nothing would persuade Chantal to undertake the journey, which was fraught with too many hazards which had nothing to do with travel. Only Jonathan was unaware that these two had meta-phorically crossed swords.

Chantal, who wanted to know how long Doris would be staying, asked: 'If your room is not quite as comfortable and as you like it, I hope you will let me know. It can easily be changed tomorrow. But yours was the only one ready....'

'For such a short stay, thank you, it isn't worth the bother of changing. It is a beautiful room, facing the sea. What more could I ask for?'

For such a short stay ... how short I wonder?

And yet, as Chantal admitted to herself later when sleep eluded her, she liked Doris, even if she had been Johnny's *belle-mère*. The next morning, watching Nico happily show-ing her all his treasures and her convincing show of interest, some of the fears receded. Nevertheless, ways must be found of preventing her from seeing much of Johnny alone. Perhaps there would be no harm in it, but they must have many memories in common, and with instinct rather than reason to guide her, the fact that he and Doris had known one another before she had entered his life made her someone to be wary of.

Chantal had come a long way since first meeting Jonathan. Her English, if not accentless, was fluent. But her general knowledge of the world outside the islands, in fact outside the perimeter of Dabney's Reef, was pitifully small. There were so few subjects about which she could converse with someone like Doris, whose interests were much wider. Chantal's little world was bounded by her home, Johnny, Nico, her beloved bar which she had been forced to relinquish, these not necessarily in the right order of importance. She could read, of course, in French as well as English, but the whole concept of reading for pleasure, or in order to keep abreast of the world's happenings, was foreign to her. Doris's reading did not touch more than the fringe of things, confined as it was to light novels, fashion and social columns, Stock Exchange quotations and racing results. So these two soon ran out of topics of conversation and their talk inevitably returned to domestic matters, Nico, Johnny and the problems of being a mother ... and grandmother.

'I'm getting to be an old woman, you know, too old to be worried by three unruly children ... no, two unruly boys, for Esther is a darling.'

'Won't their mothers really look after them?'

'From time to time they come and see them, yes. But while I keep up that big villa and there are servants available, the girls live their own lives. Neither of their husbands, you must understand, wants another man's child around.

'Tell me, my dear, have you and Johnny decided anything ... about coming over I mean?'

'I am afraid it won't be possible this year,' replied Chantal, 'and possibly not next year either. Dabney's Reef is such a lovely place to live in that we have somehow forgotten that it gives us our living and ... well, between ourselves we are not making anything like as much money as we ought to ...'

'I understand, of course. First things first ... you need to be on the spot. But it is a pity. Whether you know it, or not, I'm very fond of Johnny, and for his sake I don't want a day to come when he will have regrets that his children are strangers to him.'

That same thought had crossed Chantal's mind many times. She believed that if Johnny ever did have regrets on the subject, she herself might regret it. She did not want a situation ever to arise in which she would be blamed for keeping them apart.

'You know, Doris, an idea has just come to me. I shall need to talk to Johnny about it, of course, but there's no good reason why the children could not pay a visit here. I would love to have them and it would be good for Nico to meet them. Let us talk of it again when we have thought about it.'

Jonathan, when brought into the discussion, also thought it a good idea and delighted Chantal by saying, 'It would have to be clearly understood that all arrangements would be made with you, Doris, not with their mothers. I think any direct contact would be a mistake.'

'So do I. That goes without saying.'

In the early hours of the next morning Jonathan was awakened by a violent jab in the ribs. 'What's the matter?' he growled.

'Johnny, I have an idea. Perhaps you were right and I was wrong ... so let us be married.'

'It's O.K. by me. Anything else?'

'No, that is all.'

A few seconds later he was snoring. In the morning he might wonder about this sudden change of heart. Meanwhile, there was the rest of the night to think up an explanation. Almost any reason but the real one would serve. Was it that for the first time she felt insecure?

On the evening before Doris was due to leave Dabney's Reef, Jonathan and Chantal were genuinely sorry to see her about to go. She had always been kind, but now to this was

104

added tact, without which kindness so often misfires. Taking Jonathan aside one day, she told him quietly that if he needed capital for development purposes, he could always call on her.

'Thank you, but no,' he said, 'you've been too generous already. You just about saved my bacon when Bookbinder's went on paying my so-called salary until the end of that year. I didn't expect it. Now, it seems, you have been a mother to my children, and I am very grateful to you.'

That evening, when it came to discussing dates for the arrival of the children, it emerged that they were at the Villa Leonora under the care of a governess who would be leaving when Doris returned.

'Shouldn't they be at school?' asked Chantal.

'Esther is at school ... in Cannes....'

'And Edouard?'

'Ted ... Edouard as you call him is kicking his heels at the villa. I sent him to a prep school in England, but it didn't work. He wasn't exactly expelled, but the headmaster wrote to say that he did not want him back for the new term.'

'Why? What happened?' asked Jonathan.

'I don't really know, Johnny, and I'm not altogether sure that I want to. The most I could get out of the headmaster over the telephone was that Ted was "not a good influence over the other boys". So you see' – she turned to Chantal – 'Ted isn't an easy boy to control. If you want to change your minds, now is the time.'

'What is the alternative?'

'Esther, as I've told you, is no problem. But if Ted doesn't come here, he'll have to be sent to another school, and if that doesn't work, Gloria will have to take charge of him and Gloria, as you realize, isn't exactly the best of mothers ...'

'Poor little boy!' said Chantal. 'It is right that he should come to his father. We will look after him.'

'Well, as the posters used to say about something, you have been warned.'

13

'We want your advice, Robbie,' said Jonathan, seating himself beside McAlister on a beach chair.

'Then you must be in a bad way. What makes you suppose that a man who can't run his own life properly can help you to run yours? Buy me a drink and you shall have the best advice I've got. What is it?'

'Chantal and I have decided to get married. That's easy. But we don't know what we should do about announcing it.'

'Then my advice is don't. Marry if you want to, but do it discreetly. My dear Johnny, nobody cares a curse about your having as the saying is "lived in sin" for eight years. Most people probably think you are married. Certainly, nobody has ever queried it in my hearing. As I say, nobody really cares one way or the other ... but now, at this late date, to draw unnecessary attention to yourselves by announcing it, would be regarded as wanton flaunting of the conventions. Don't. If for some reason you feel the urge to marry, go off to one of the other islands and do it quietly. Now buy me a drink.'

'Thanks, Robbie, I believe you're right.'

'Now, laddie, let's talk about the real reason for my visit. This time I want some advice from you. As you know, the paper and the job-printing provide me with a bare living. Margaret and I seem to get along better than most brothers and sisters do, so we've decided to end our days together here. Now Margaret has a wee income of her own, but little enough, so we've been casting around for ways of making a little more, and we've come up with the idea of starting a school....'

'How will you select your pupils?'

'The parents of the pupils will select us. I know there are a lot of people on the island who are unhappy about the low standards of the Government schools — but what can you expect when the majority of the pupils there come from such feckless homes? If people can afford the fees, know how to read and write themselves and wear boots, they are eligible parents.'

'That lets us out for a start.'

'Why?'

'Because Chantal won't wear boots.'

'All right, supposing we make an exception in your case, would you be interested in sending young Nico?'

'Yes, very much so, and I may have two more pupils for you soon, the children of my first marriage which went on the rocks. Now, Robbie, what about the advice you wanted?'

'That was only flattery, Johnny. People are always flattered when their advice is sought. What I really came for is to know whether we could use a part of La Bastide for a school house?'

'You're welcome to it ... anyway on a term-to-term basis until I've decided what to do with the old place, which is a bit of a white elephant. I'll even lend you Skefco to help clear out the rats.'

'Who's Skefco?'

'The tomcat who came ashore from a Swedish yacht and adopted us. We tried, but couldn't think of a more appropriate name ...'

Chantal, consulted on the subject of Nico's education, was enthusiastic about Robbie's idea. The McAlister Academy was a timely venture. It was a boon to the white families whose incomes were shrinking as prices rose. Most were too old to have school age children, but others, unable these days to send theirs to England, or even to pay the fees at schools in Trinidad and Barbados, welcomed the new venture. The McAlisters were, despite Robbie's addiction to the bottle, well-liked and respected.

In the slack season, when Dabney's Reef was shut down, Jonathan and Chantal slipped off quietly to Trinidad and were married. Graziella, who regarded the whole thing as foolishness, stayed at home to look after Nico.

An announcement appeared in the Trinidad newspaper, picked up from the registrar's office, but it attracted no attention. Dabneys had overflowed to Trinidad and other islands, so the name meant little. Robbie's advice had been sound.

'Do you feel any better for it?' asked Jonathan after the brief ceremony.

'Yes, Johnny, much better. Now, if that other woman, that Gloria, comes to find you, I shall spit in her eye. . . .'

'She won't come looking for me, or her children. . . .'

'Was she a bad woman?'

'No, not bad, not very good. Just selfish and with too much money. Doris, you know, is very rich.'

'That means that you still have a little *tendresse* for her. Now, wherever she is, I spit in her eye. . . .'

*　　*　　*

A voice on the public address system at Piarco airport, Trinidad, was calling for Mr Dabney. Would he please go to the nearest telephone? Jonathan complied at once.

If he would go to the office, he was told, a pass would be given to him to board the plane just in from London. The hostess who had been looking after them was anxious to be rid of her responsibilities as soon as possible. It had been a long and tiring flight.

'Something wrong?' asked Jonathan.

'I think you should hear that from the hostess herself. I'll wait for you here.'

Armed with a pass, Jonathan went out to the waiting plane. A pleasant-faced hostess was standing at the foot of the stairs holding the hand of a little girl whose face was streaked with tears.

'This is your Daddy, dear,' said the hostess when Jonathan announced himself.

Seeing this strange man standing with arms outstretched, Esther approached him reluctantly, allowing herself to be kissed on the cheeks, but without enthusiasm.

'Where is the boy?'

'I'll fetch him in a moment . . . one of the crew is sitting on him and will be glad to be relieved. We shall all be glad to be rid of him. I gather that although you're his father, you're strangers. . . .'

'I haven't seen him since he was a baby. . . .'

'Well, you have a treat in store for you. . . .'

'Has he been giving trouble?'

'You could call it that. Five minutes after he was handed over to me he called me something I won't repeat. Then he stuck his foot into the aisle and tripped my colleague, who was carrying two laden trays at the time. Food and coffee went over an old lady. But the high spot of the trip came when he got hold of some matches and set fire to a newspaper which a gentleman was reading. My hair was singed putting out the flames. That was when on the Captain's orders we had to tie him to his seat . . . and keep him tied until we landed. . . .'

'I'm very distressed to hear this . . . is there any way I can make it up to you?'

'Yes, sir, by taking him off to his cage as soon as you can. We're all nervous wrecks. But the little girl is sweet and we all loved her. . . .'

A few minutes later there was a scuffle at the top of the gangway. A uniformed steward appeared, holding an enraged boy by the scruff of the neck. One sleeve of the latter's jacket was torn and his hair was falling across his forehead, giving him an ugly low-browed appearance.

'This is my son!' Jonathan muttered under his breath.

Force had to be used to make the boy descend on to the tarmac. He fought, snarling, every step of the way.

'This is your father, Teddy,' said the hostess, doing her job to the bitter end and hating every moment of it.

'So what!'

'He's come a long way to meet you. . . .'

'Big deal!'

'Aren't you going to say something to him?'

'Yeah, *merde*, or if you like it better, *shit*!'

'A sweet child, isn't he? I wish you joy of him, Mr Dabney.'

During the short flight back to Newcastle the two children fell asleep. Esther was emotionally exhausted and the boy exhausted physically by his struggles with the plane's staff. They did not come to life until they landed. Chantal was waiting for them. Gathering Esther into her arms, she held out a hand to Ted, as they would call him. He ignored it. 'I'm hungry. I want sumpun t'eat'. Then, 'Who are you?' he asked at length, surveying Chantal from head to foot insultingly.

Arrived at Dabney's Reef, the children were given time to wash and change before going from the house to the restaurant, where savoury smells came from the kitchen. Eight or ten people were already at table. Both children agreed that they liked fried fish and chips.

As food did not arrive on the table as quickly as he thought it should, Ted prowled into the kitchen. On a side table was a platter of red peppers – the hell-fire kind for West Indian palates – stuffed with mince-meat. He grabbed one, bit it in halves and began to chew. Graziella did not approve of small boys in her kitchen, but knowing that the red pepper would shortly set his mouth on fire, she stood, arms akimbo, laughing at him. Ted's instant reaction was to stick his tongue out at her. Then, just as the hell-fire pepper was getting to work, a hot wooden spoon clipped him on the cheek smartly, causing him to bite his tongue. Roaring with rage and uttering fearful imprecations, he returned to the dining-room. There, to extinguish the fire in his mouth, he foolishly drank some cold water – it made it much worse.

'What's the matter?' asked Jonathan.

'That damned old nigger woman hit me!' he roared indignantly.

Jonathan was about to do something drastic, but Chantal shook her head and said: 'Leave this to me!'

The next thing Ted knew was that he had been seized roughly by his hair, which was too long, dragged off his chair and into the kitchen.

'You were speaking about my mother,' said Chantal in a low voice charged with menace. 'You will now say that you are very sorry for being so rude.'

'Supposing I'm not sorry?'

'Say it just the same.'

'Shan't!'

A lightning-swift slap on both cheeks followed. They hurt.

Ted's experience of women hitherto had been of the gentler sort, easily reduced to helplessness by foul language and violence. His reply to this was to aim a kick at Chantal's shins. That had always been the clincher. But this tall woman with blazing angry eyes was something new. The kick did not reach its target which, unaccountably, was not there. The grip on his hair became firmer. Chantal, for all her slender grace, was very strong. She shook Ted's head until his senses reeled. 'Will you say you are sorry now, or do you want some more?'

Ted, to whom such summary justice was entirely new, was now sobbing with fear and rage. Recognizing implacable ferocity when meeting it for the first time, he made a perfunctory apology which, as intended, was no apology at all.

Chantal, still gripping a bunch of his hair and determined to win, said: 'Now in French. My mother speaks no English ... a proper apology, do you understand? Make it sound as though you are very sorry....'

'What for?'

'For saying something very rude about my mother.'

'Well, isn't she?'

'Isn't she what?' Chantal snarled.

'A damned old nigger woman!' he shouted defiantly.

The grip on his hair really hurt as his head was again shaken violently. This delicate-seeming woman, who was anything but delicate, administered such swift retaliation that he needed to adjust his mind to the new régime.

Chantal was wearing a necklace of coral beads. Making a snatch at them, Ted broke the string, scattering the beads across the floor. She should be so busy picking them up for the next many minutes that she would forget about this apology nonsense.

But she did nothing of the sort. 'My mother is waiting for the apology ...' This with a further agonizing twist of the bunched hair.

'I'm hungry!' This came out weakly as a prelude to surrender.

Another good twist that lifted his scalp.

'*Je m'excuse, madame. Pardonnez moi,*' he said, managing to inject irony into it somehow.

Chantal let this pass, releasing the grip on his hair.

'Can I eat now?'

'When you have picked up every bead, yes. Your fish is on the table getting cold. . . .'

'I'll pick up the beads after I've eaten it. . . .'

'You won't you know,' said Chantal pleasantly. 'You will pick them up now . . . every one. There are sixty-two of them. I know because I strung them myself. If you are hungry, get busy.'

This was terrible . . . humiliating. It shattered the boy's image of himself, crawling about the floor picking up beads when ordered to do so by a woman.

When he had gathered some forty-odd, he said: 'I can't find any more . . . there aren't any more.'

'Sixty-two!' said the voice of doom.

When sixty had been counted, he kept the two others palmed.

'I'll bet you you can't find two more . . . bet you anything.'

'Then you lose,' said Chantal, forcing his hand open to reveal the missing beads.

Seizing him by the ear, she led him into the dining-room, where the other diners had been listening with interest as the struggle progressed. There had been bets on its outcome. The diners applauded as the protagonists entered the room and took their seats at the table.

'It's cold,' said Ted, pushing his plate away from him in one last flicker of revolt. Then, realizing that he was beaten, he began to devour the food with the grace and delicacy of a bull-terrier.

'You were wonderful, darling,' said Jonathan when the two children had gone to bed, tired and bewildered by their new surroundings. 'I was scared that if I interfered, I would hurt him. Now that he has learned that he can't play monkey tricks with you, perhaps we shall have no more trouble.'

'There will be more monkey tricks, Johnny, but I also have a few. Better leave him to me, as you say. When he

learns that he cannot win and that I will not give a centi-
metre, maybe he will improve.'

'It doesn't seem that he can get much worse.'

'I wish I were sure of that, Johnny. But it is not the poor
boy's fault.'

*Fault! Then whose? Gloria's? Mine? A dirty trick of
heredity? Better call it circumstances and leave it at that.*

*　　　*　　　*

Quite aside from solving the financial problems of the
McAlisters, the McAlister Academy was a success from its
inception. La Bastide was big enough to enable the very
young to be separated from the next age group. Margaret
took charge of the former, while Robbie taught the nine-to
fourteen-year-old children until it became apparent that
he could not cope with girls and boys. A retired Canadian
school teacher, a Miss Williams, then took over the older
girls, glad to earn a little money to supplement her pension.

Robbie, despite having no teaching experience of any kind,
turned out to be a born teacher, with the priceless knack of
being able to arouse and hold the boys' interest. Parents
with misgivings were delighted to observe that he had stopped
drinking to excess. The truth was that he was too busy to
drink. He was discovering the truth of the motto which,
well before his time, used to adorn the entrance of the
Hambone Club in London: Work is the Ruin of the Drinking Classes.

There was improvement, too, in the quality of the
Novocastrian, whose advertisement and circulation revenue
was creeping up, due to the influx of literate people from the
north.

When Ted, roaring protest at having to do so, came under
Robbie's wing, he was the eleventh Dabney to be enrolled
in the McAlister Academy. At the end of a month, asked how
the boy was making out, Robbie reported: 'I regret to have
to tell you this, Johnny, but your son is a graceless young
lout, and if he were not your son I would have booted him
out in the first week. His language is enough to draw down

a curse on us. Where did he learn it? As you know, a good half of the children have some coloured blood, while two or three might be called "black", whose parents are people of some standing in the community. I cannot, therefore, allow your son to call them "bloody niggers" and get away with it. Happily, when this happened, one of them, a pugnacious lad of about Ted's age and weight, saved me from forcible intervention. He punched Ted on the nose. The boy, incidentally, was a Dabney, the son of your half-brother Hugh ... It seemed to me best to see and hear nothing, so I let them get on with it. Ted, I am glad to say, took a beating, or there would have been no holding him. When his nose was being rubbed a little too forcibly in the gravel of the playground, I stopped the fight. Now what I find hard to understand is that he and his opponent appear to be good friends ...'

Ted's return from school in a somewhat battered condition had escaped Jonathan's notice altogether, but not Chantal's. If, as she believed, one of Ted's victims had turned on his tormentor, it might prove to be a salutary lesson.

That Ted had been a handful before coming to Dabney's Reef, Chantal already knew, but it was confirmed in a curious way. Pinned inside the breast pocket of the jacket in which the boy had arrived was a note which she found later. In handwriting which Jonathan identified as Gloria's Chantal read: 'Now it's your turn. Have fun.'

Slowly but surely, however, she and Ted managed to work towards a mutually satisfactory basis of co-existence. Ted, by pushing insolence, disobedience and open defiance to the limits of her acceptance, now knew pretty well how far he could go. If he went too far, he knew that vengeance, swift and furious, would follow. On more than one occasion Chantal had to give him a good shellacking. It hurt, but not too much. He bore little or no real resentment, whereas if Jonathan had administered anything approaching such punishment, he would have incurred the boy's bitter hatred. Why it should be so, none of those chiefly concerned knew. But it was so.

Between Chantal and Ted there was a certain mutual respect which, had other factors not intervened, might have turned to something warmer. Chantal had a theory that all children were bad – it was a law of nature – but that none was wholly bad. Ted, she found by experience, was truthful. Not because he loved truth for truth's sweet sake, but because he scorned to lie about things. It was sheer egotism perhaps. He would hurl defiance in all directions, but he would not dissemble. So, deeply buried under his unattractive exterior, were some seeds of virtue. If she could have had him under her control for a year, Chantal believed that a different Ted would emerge. But already it was becoming apparent to her that in her efforts, for Johnny's sake, to humanize Ted, there was the danger of neglecting Nico, her own child, and Esther whom she wished were her own.

From the very beginning, it seemed, Ted and Nico avoided one another and were never more than distantly polite. If there were ever any particular incident to foment their dislike of each other, neither spoke of it. But it was significant that after Ted had been a couple of weeks at Dabney's Reef, Nico took Jonathan aside one day and said: 'There is a Mr Mortlock at school who comes to teach boxing. He was once a Sergeant-Major, or something, Mr McAlister says. Please, Papa, I would like to learn. May I?'

This coming from Nico, who was not a combative child, was strange.

'Yes, of course you may learn, Nico, but what put the idea into your head?'

'I'm not sure, Papa, but a boy who can't box can't do much when anyone is rude to him, and I think that maybe people aren't rude to anyone they know can box.'

'Yes, that can be true sometimes. But remember that it can be better to laugh at some people than to fight them. Anyway, I'm glad you want to learn because to know that you can defend yourself if you have to makes you confident. But don't ever let it turn you into a bully.'

With a cryptic little smile, Nico shook his head.

14

ABBOTT-HUTCHINGS-McGRAW, Inc.
The Chrysler Building
New York 17, N.Y.

November 3, 1961

Dear Johnny,

Last winter, you may remember, a Mr and Mrs Hambleton stayed with you, and are booked to come again before Chistmas this year. They are a quiet couple, fifty plus. I don't know them personally, although they came to you indirectly on my recommendation. They wanted a quiet place.

I have mislaid their initials somewhere, but he turns out to be *the* Hambleton of Hambleton Hotels. (Santa Barbara, Calif.; Vancouver, B.C.; Nassau, Bahamas; one building in the Virgin Islands, and so on.)

My good friend George Napier (Napier, McCormack Travel) through whom the Hambletons booked to stay with you, quotes Mr Hambleton as saying quote Dabney's Reef is the best undeveloped site in the Caribbean unquote. Maybe you think it *is* developed, but you know nuthin from nuthin.

If you haven't yet got it, you will shortly receive a cancellation from Hambleton. He can't get away this winter. Too many commitments. These tycoons!

What's all this leading to, you are asking. Just this, that Hambleton wants to talk to you, in New York, all expenses paid. If you decide to come, my advice for what it is worth, is that you pay your own expenses. Letting him pay them weakens your position. He wants to make you some proposition. It can't hurt to listen and who knows what it might lead to?

Chantal and you might enjoy the trip. Tell her that shoes are usually worn here in Winter! Think it over. Love to Chantal and Elias.

Love to you, too.

ALICE

The Hambleton cancellation reached Jonathan two days later. He remembered the couple vaguely. They had kept very much to themselves, but all he could recollect was favourable. Passing the letter across the luncheon table to Chantal, he asked her how a trip to New York appealed to her.

'No, Johnny,' she said firmly, 'not if I have to wear shoes. But why don't you go without me? You are always saying that a long stretch here isn't good for you and that you want to feel the frost again. Ugh! People like me who have never known frost find it hard to imagine.... Besides, I couldn't leave Ted and Esther – and Ted particularly – to anyone else before they have settled down here properly.'

Over the past there had been several offers for Dabney's Reef from developers and speculators, but he had rejected them all. Perhaps Hambleton would come up with a proposition that would prove acceptable in the light of Jonathan's needs. He was reputedly scrupulous to preserve the regional characteristics of his hotels. He did not build vast rectangular rabbit-hutches, virtually indistinguishable from others of the chain. But Jonathan was determined that he would only enter into an arrangement for the further development of the Reef if he himself were included as an equal partner in its management. His thinking was inclined to be vague, but he wanted the future of Dabney's Reef to be a credit to the name of Dabney. It was not a great name, perhaps, but it was the only one he had, and he wanted it to be favourably known where it was known at all. The cold-blooded entrepreneurs with whom he had earlier discussed the question tentatively had seen it in terms of money exclusively, regarding any other considerations as flimflam.

Jonathan made preparations for his departure hopefully, consoling himself with the thought that if it came to nothing, a week or so of cold weather would tone him up. Seldom out of his thoughts was the fear of slowing down, mentally and physically, as his forebears had done to their cost.

In a letter from Doris he heard that she was spending a few weeks in New York. It would be good to see her, and to report on her two transplanted grandchildren.

Then in their weird and incalculable fashion the interlocked wheels of Fate began to turn and to weave their unpredictable patterns.

*　　*　　*

When Gloria Fooks was a little girl a more than ordinarily perceptive contemporary remarked of her: 'I like Gloria, but I would like her much more but for one thing. She only wants things when someone else wants them.'

While Gloria's mother was sitting in her suite at a small, exclusive uptown hotel, waiting for Jonathan to join her for cocktails, she little knew that her daughter was sitting in another hotel suite in New York – this in a large and garish establishment on Park Avenue – also waiting for a caller. If the electric wall clock could be believed, he was inexcusably late.

They had met not long previously on the plane from London. Sitting across the aisle from her was a good-looking, almost too good-looking, upper-class young Englishman, fault-lessly attired, an air of effeteness palliated by charming manners. 'He's a lord!' whispered the hostess, having noted the flicker of interest in Gloria's lovely blue eyes.

The young man, who had an engaging candour, was the youngest son of a slightly shop-soiled, penniless duke, whom it would do no good to name. He admitted having come to New York some months previously shopping for an American heiress, but had found presentable ones rather shy. The supply of poverty-stricken European bachelors of noble lineage tended to keep ahead of the demand, so he had been compelled to settle for the daughter of a mysterious gentleman whose name closely resembled that of an Italian soup and who was believed to be immensely rich, having close connections with the Mafia.

'He's a bit sinister looking, but seems to be a nice enough chap,' the prospective bridegroom told Gloria, 'and there's scads of money. Damned great mansion up in Westchester County ... high electric fences round the property, tough yobbos on the gate armed to the teeth, won't let you in without the password and a herd of terrifying Dobermans patrolling the grounds at night ... just like something out of a James Bond tale....

'I gather Dad has been respectable for quite a few years ... arranges all the massacres by proxy these days.'

'Is the bride-to-be pretty?' asked Gloria.

'So-so! Inclined to be a bit dumpy ... you should see her punishing the *pasta* ... but she's cross-eyed, which can be rather distressing. I never know whether Teresina's looking soulfully at me, looking out of the window to see if it's raining, or at the clock to see if it's *pasta*-time ... know what I mean?'

'She sounds sweet. When's the wedding?'

'Next week. The old man's coming over for it as soon as he's got the heirlooms out of hock. There's a diamond necklace. Mother used to wear it ... big stones the colour of amber traffic lights. Where are you staying in New York?'

Gloria told him.

So frequent had his visits been that it occurred to Gloria to wonder whether Teresina was not feeling somewhat neglected. She did not have to wonder for long.

Just when she was about to write off the evening as a dead loss, there came a gentle tap at the door of the suite. As she opened it two slender men pushed past her and closed it. They were dressed identically in dark suits with black high-necked pullovers instead of shirts. They had broadly similar faces, which seemed to Gloria quite expressionless. 'What do you want?' she said.

'Don't make a noise, lady, and you won't get hurt. Just wait for the 'phone to ring and answer it. That's all. Some-one wants to talk to you.'

The 'phone rang. Gloria lifted the receiver. 'If you know what's good for you,' said a woman's voice whose malice was projected over the line, 'you'll be out of New York by noon tomorrow.'

'And if I'm not?'

'You'll never want to look at yourself again in a mirror. Ever heard of acid burns?'

There was a soft click and the line went dead.

'Okay, got the message?' said one of the men.

'Yes, I got the message. Now get out!'

'You wouldn't do anything foolish like 'phoning the desk, would you, lady? Good-night!'

They vanished, leaving Gloria trembling with sheer terror. Things like that just didn't happen except in thrillers. That the voice had been that of the cross-eyed Teresina she did not doubt. As she had told the men: she had got the message.

Doris did not know that Gloria was in town, but Gloria knew that her mother might be and, if so, where to find her. On the off chance of finding her in, she put a call through.

'How long are you going to be in town, dear?' asked Doris, recognizing Gloria's voice.

'For as long as it takes me to get on a plane.' Her voice trembled.

'Where to?'

'I don't know ... anywhere.'

Knowing something of Gloria's exaggerated way of talking, and despite catching the note of frenzy in her voice, Doris was not at all alarmed. 'I have had a visitor this evening ... he's just left. Guess who.'

'I'm too upset for guessing games. Who?'

'Of all unlikely people, Johnny.'

'What's he doing in New York?'

'Business I gather.'

'Where's he staying?'

'I'm not sure that I remember, dear, and even if I did I wouldn't tell you. He's very happy, so leave him alone.'

'What news of the kids?'

'They're fine. Esther, as you can imagine, is enchanted with Dabney's Reef. Ted, to begin with, I gather, was a little difficult. ...'

'I'll bet he was!'

'But he's settling down, apparently, and enjoying himself.'

'Oh!'

'What did that mean?'

'Just surprise, that's all. How long is Johnny here for?'

'A week or a fortnight, no more. Why?'

'I just wondered.'

'When shall I see you dear?'

'Soon, at Antibes I hope ...'

Her misgivings might have been groundless, but Doris was glad that she had not given Gloria the name of Jonathan's hotel. Back almost as far as cradle days she had been aware of the strange quirk in Gloria's character; she had known that if Jonathan had not been engaged to Jean Gloria would not have been interested in him. Gloria was very devious. Would the fact that Jonathan and Chantal were happy together reawaken her interest in him?

That evening Gloria's mind was running in a different way: so frantically keen was she to shake off the dust of New York that when the girl at the air ticket desk told her that all the seats in southbound planes that night were booked, she said: 'Then I shall have to go north, won't I?'

Instead of dining cosily in her suite with the lordling, Gloria dined off a sandwich and two large whiskies on a plane bound for Montreal, where the best she could find for the night was a shabby little room in a third-rate hotel, and even when she was in bed with the door locked and bolted, a knock on her own or the next door – she was not sure which – left her awake and sweating with fear until a sleeping pill took over.

There was a vacant seat on a southbound plane in the morning and at around eight o'clock that evening Bill Dabney's taxi dropped her at Dabney's Reef. When the lovely girl in the office – she had to be Chantal – swivelled the register to her, she signed it with a false name. In a moment of detached admiration she was forced to admit that the touch of the tarbrush had enhanced rather than detracted from the girl's beauty. Jonathan sure knew how to pick 'em! For confirmation she surveyed herself in the mirror with satisfaction. Different types, of course, but each in its way tops!

Gloria did not want to be recognized. With Jonathan busy in New York, she was not likely to be unless she ran into either of her children, or Lawrence Dabney, the handsome young medico who had been a witness at the Caxton Hall wedding.

Feeling safe from recognition when Ted and Esther had trotted off with satchels in the morning, evidently to school, she emerged from her room and, keeping a sharp lookout for sea urchins, she went for a swim.

The frantic hurry to leave New York had sent her off without a destination. Now curiosity had brought her to Dabney's Reef, which held no pleasant memories. She was curious to see how Ted and Esther were settling into their new temporary home, which in her heart of hearts she hoped would be a permanent one.

There was no ulterior motive in coming. Gloria had no wish to break up the happy home. Rather the contrary. The longer it held together, the less the likelihood of ever having Ted on her hands again, the little monster. Esther she would have been quite happy to have again, although she might well become an encumbrance in a few years. Girls needed so much watching and then, as she herself had proved in the past, the greatest vigilance was sometimes fallible.

Seen through binoculars when he and his sister returned for lunch, Ted appeared quite docile. How had it been accomplished? He still ate like a hog, but no tantrums were apparent. Well satisfied with what she had seen, Gloria 'phoned the airport and, avoiding New York with a shudder, booked for the dogleg to Europe via Bermuda, leaving the following morning. A pox on Dabney's Reef!

*   *   *

It was late afternoon. School was over for the day. Robbie McAlister, sitting at his desk in the small upper room he used as an office, his gaze divided between the drab sweep of sugarcane which stretched for miles around La Bastide and an unopened bottle of James Talisker's Highland Dew, guaranteed ten years old, which stood in front of him. He wanted to broach the bottle and was savouring the moment in anticipation, but more than all he was indulging a rare and foolish mood of nostalgia. It was a bottle of this identical brand which, twenty years previously, had put paid to what might have been and was well on the way to being a brilliant journalistic career. When he should have been covering the biggest 'story' of the year, he was lying on the floor of a backroom off Fleet Street, dead drunk, with a bottle of whisky beside him.

My name is Might-have-been;
I am also called No-more, Too-late, Farewell.

he quoted with a groan.

The bottle, the gift of a visiting Scot, chief engineer of a banana boat, had been in Robbie's possession for some six months, its capsule still intact. It was a part of the campaign to create what the P.R. sharks called a 'new image'. Now he was wondering whether the agonies of abstention were worth while. It was necessity, not a sense of dedication, which had turned him into a teacher or, as he called it, an usher. Most small boys in his experience were dirty, dishonest, snotty-nosed little savages, on whom the flowers of knowledge were wasted. Why, therefore, bother to keep sober for them?

With one hand on the bottle and the other clutching a glass, Robbie took a final look out of the window just as the sun was touching the western horizon. He waited. As an ex-drunk he was aware that only a drunk touched whisky before sundown. Three, or, at the most, five minutes to go before virtuous resolution would permit him to open the bottle.

Then his attention was drawn to something untoward. While he himself should have been the only human being on the premises, he saw a furtive figure slip out of one door and into another where tools and paint were stored.

A friendly spaniel, a frequent visitor from below, stood wagging his tail and watching the human visitor, who emerged from the doorway bearing a can of some liquid, which he proceeded to pour over the unsuspecting dog. If Robbie's mind had not been as much on the bottle of James

Talisker – still unopened – as upon the events below, he might have been in time to grasp what was afoot and to avert a tragedy.

The figure below, dwarfed by perspective, struck a match. The dog burst into flames. In their light Robbie believed he recognized the fiend. He was not quite sure, but it would help the police to know that he would probably be suffering from burns in the face and scorched clothing. The dog, shrieking piteously in its agony, streaked across the garden and into the sugarcane. After several weeks of drought, it was dry as tinder. The trail left by the dog was soon engulfed in a sea of flame which, fanned by the rising trade wind, roared down the hill and towards the new dwellings constructed on the outskirts of the town.

The police! There was no telephone at La Bastide. Mounting his bicycle, Robbie free-wheeled down the narrow path on the side furthest from the flames.

Arrived at the bottom, he paused to think. The left turn on the cross-island road led towards the nearest police post and telephone; the right turn towards the airfield and Dabney's Reef. This was one of the moments which occur to perplex men: given the choice between his duty as a citizen and his duty towards a friend, Robbie chose the latter and swung his bicycle to the right, pedalling as fast as the rickety old machine would go. There was no need to issue a fire warning, even if he had the means to do so. The flames and smoke would have alerted the whole island and the hand-pumped fire engine would already have been trundled out of its shed to be sent on its futile errand. The fire would extinguish itself when there was nothing more to burn in its path.

15

Gloria, sitting on her balcony at the peaceful hour of sunset, was thinking that if stick-in-the-mud Jonathan would only liven up Dabney's Reef it would not be such a bad spot for a holiday. All it wanted was a big swimming pool, free of spiky and stinging sea creatures, a dance floor, a decent band and, of course, a few younger people to relieve the gloom shed by the ancient ruins who brought their ailments down from the northern winter. Yes, it could be very tolerable, if ...

Her attention diverted from these fleeting thoughts, Gloria noted with idle interest a vast billow of smoke inland. It seemed to recede and flames became visible, reminding her briefly of the exciting times when, viewed from the distance, London burned under a hail of incendiary bombs. Then afterwards, going into London and finding things much as when seen last, it had always seemed that fires looked worse than they really were.

A little later two men came down the pathway to the beach carrying an improvised stretcher slung on bamboo poles. People were always getting hurt.

Later still, after darkness had fallen, a car arrived in front of the buildings which adjoined the dining-room and bar. From it stepped the handsome Dr Lawrence Dabney – one of the sunburned Dabneys, he had called himself in front of Caxton Hall. Gloria wanted a drink but decided it would have to wait until he had gone and until she had seen the two children go to their house after supper.

Then by a path which led from behind the Dabney living quarters Ted came sauntering down to the beach, whistling tunelessly as he went. Gloria knew that whistle of old. It was, as she had learned by experience, a kind of safety-valve easing the pressure of a guilty conscience. The young hellion had been up to something, that was sure. Let someone else pick up the pieces.

Chantal and Dr Dabney emerged from one of the rooms. Then a tall gangling man on a rattletrap bicycle came down the narrow path which was not designed for wheeled traffic.

The three people remained in a huddle for a minute or two before Chantal, seeing Ted occupying himself on the beach in an unusually innocent fashion, went to fetch him, overcoming his reluctance with a good twist of his ear. Chantal, Gloria mused, knew how to handle the boy.

Dragged into the bright light under a hanging cluster, Ted fell back on the truculence he always wore as a defence when guilty of something more than ordinarily evil. It would be interesting to see how they dealt with him ... and what he had been up to.

When it emerged from the conversation that the person carried in the stretcher had been none other than Esther, Gloria's usually dormant maternal feelings were aroused. The child, it seemed, was suffering more from fright than anything else. She had swallowed a lot of smoke on the way home from a party when the wind had backed briefly. It was nothing serious, Dr Dabney assured Chantal.

Attention was then focused on Ted, who alternated between defiance and the hangdog look with which Gloria was only too familiar.

'The boy is reeking of paraffin,' said Robbie McAlister angrily. 'Ask him why ... how he got hold of it.'

'I don't know,' the boy roared under Chantal's questioning.

'What were you doing after school? What were you doing until now?'

'I don't remember ...'

'If the police question him, as they surely will, they'll refresh his memory,' said Robbie.

At the word 'police' Ted's eyes rounded in fear. Even at twenty or thirty feet distance Gloria could see the whites.

'Tell us the truth ... the truth!' screamed Chantal, grabbing him by a handful of hair and shaking him.

Further questioning was useless because Ted was convulsed

with tears interspersed with roars of fear and rage.

'Look at his singed eyebrows and hair! He's guilty as hell!'

Esther was getting over her fright. Hearing her brother's uproar, she came out of the room to investigate, and she too began to weep.

Damn her eyes! They are my children. This is where I have something to say.

Throwing all discretion to the winds, Gloria joined the little group in the pool of light shed by the cluster.

'Mama!' yelled Ted, recognizing her first, putting himself under her protecting wing. 'Stop them ... stop them!'

'Who are you?' asked Chantal icily.

'I'm his mother. Stop torturing him. What is all this about?'

'That's right, she is,' said Dr Dabney.

The two women, Chantal and Gloria, listened in a numbed silence while Robbie in his coldly factual way told them exactly what he had seen and what he suspected was the truth.

'What is to be done?' asked Gloria in shrill anxiety, now aware of the enormity of the boy's crime.

'You have two choices, madam,' said Robbie in the Caledonian accents of his youth which always emerged in moments of emotion. 'If you believe your son is innocent of this hideous cruelty, then you must stay here, wait for the police, face them and establish his innocence. On the other hand, if you believe he is guilty, there is only one thing to do. Gather his and your own passports and make for the airport ... now. In less than an hour there is a plane leaving for Trinidad. Take it and take him with you....'

'But it will take me half an hour to pack....'

'Try to put your trivial needs where they belong, woman. I don't know what they would do to your son, but it wouldn't be pleasant. At his age it would be a problem, but they would solve it ... you may count on that, and they would find a way of putting him somewhere where he could do no harm.'

Lawrence Dabney, realizing the urgency of the matter, offered to drive Gloria and Ted to the airport. 'Your belongings can be sent on to you afterwards,' he added.

Gloria went off to her room, returning with her handbag,

some papers and a few necessities thrust hastily into a dressing-case. Lawrence Dabney was about to hustle her and Ted into the car when from Esther, still dazed and muzzy from the effects of the smoke, came a cry of anguish, caused less by her ordeal than by the fact that in Ted's hour of drama she had been overlooked, thrust into the background by other urgencies which she did not understand.

'Mummy!' she screamed. 'Don't leave me here all alone!'

It did not make sense because she had more affection for Jonathan and Chantal than Gloria, while for Ted her feelings were not far short of loathing. But it was not the time to argue.

While they were being bundled into the car, Chantal had the wit to 'phone the reservation desk at the airport to make sure of seats.

In the rush there was no time for proper goodbyes. Chantal watched until the car's lights disappeared from view around the bend before returning to the bar. There, with untouched drinks before them, she and Robbie sat almost in silence until they heard overhead the roar of the outgoing plane and watched as its red and green lights swept out to sea.

Robbie lifted his glass. Chantal did likewise. 'A good riddance!' he said as he drained it. 'And now if you can let me have a bed when I fall flat on my face, I am going to give myself over to the long-deferred pleasure of drinking myself silly.'

'Robbie, my friend,' said Chantal, 'before you do that, please help me with some advice ... as a friend of Johnny's.'

'I'd do a lot for Johnny. What is it?'

'If you at this minute were sure in your mind that Johnny was *not* Ted's father, what would you do?'

'In all probability, my dear, nothing. But if you will send for a bottle of whisky, I will give the matter the attention it deserves.'

When an unopened bottle of whisky had been put in front of him, Robbie asked, 'Have you any reason to suppose that your predecessor in Johnny's affections did in fact do him dirt?'

'Predecessor? What is that? Do you mean do I think that

Johnny was *cocu*? Yes, I do. Can I prove it? No, I cannot. But I am sure just the same. . . .'

'Let us suppose that you are right, my dear, and I am inclined to believe you are, what would be the point of telling him? Ask yourself that. Would it make Johnny any happier to know?'

'Happier?' Chantal replied thoughtfully. 'Perhaps not. But surely, if it is so, Johnny should know. . . .'

'Why?' Robbie opened the bottle in front of him.

'So that he should know what a bad woman she is . . . and be happy that she is out of his life and will never be tempted to let her come back into it.'

'Ho ho! So that's the way the cat jumps, is it! You see Gloria as a possible rival and so you want Johnny to be fore-warned. Now I'm beginning to understand. . . .'

'It is not for me that I am talking to you like this, Robbie. . . .'

'Then for whom?'

'For Nico, of course. Before long, you will see, Johnny is going to be a very rich man, and I do not want Nico to be cheated. . . .'

Robbie was about to say something when Chantal cried, 'Nico! My God, where is Nico? He has not come home . . . what has happened to him. The fire! Oh God! The fire. . . .'

'Calm yourself, my dear, here comes Nico now. . . .'

Swinging his satchel nonchalantly, the boy came down towards them as the tail-lights of the bus which had brought him disappeared round a curve.

'Where have you been, Nico? I have been so worried . . .'

'You little liar,' said Robbie *sotto voce*, 'you have only just remembered his existence.'

'Don't you remember, Mama? Tonight is my boxing night.'

'Boxing! What good can boxing do . . . except turn you into a brute like—'

'Like who, Mama?'

'Er – like those rough men down at the port . . . always fighting and quarrelling. . . .'

'Mr Mortlock . . . The Sergeant-Major said this evening that a man who knows how to use his dooks doesn't need to be quarrelsome. He says that I will be able to walk in pride and fear nobody. . . .'

'Whom do you fear now?'

'Nobody, Mama, at least I don't think so.'

'Now hurry up and take your bath, and then you can eat.'

Nico brightened. 'I won't be long . . . boxing makes me very hungry.'

'Boxing!' said Chantal to the boy's retreating back. 'He is far too young. I wonder why he is so enthusiastic . . .'

'Tomorrow,' said Robbie, bringing the level of the whisky to the top of the label, 'maybe he will be less enthusiastic. Things have changed around here today . . . he'll learn it in the morning and it may change his ideas.'

They both knew what he meant.

'Advice, Chantal, perhaps I can give you some. It is this . . . always hold your ammunition against the day when you may need it. Don't blaze it off at nothing. The day will come. . . .'

'Yes, Robbie, I am sure you are right. I have seen Johnny looking at Ted through half-closed eyes . . . and wondering . . . wondering.'

* * *

On the last lap of the journey home the air hostess produced the current issue of the *Novocastrian*. Fond as Jonathan was of its founder, editor, chief and only reporter, he did not grasp it with any enthusiasm. It was never an inspiring little sheet and now, after handling metropolitan newspapers, its inadequacies were sadly apparent. There was only one real item of news under a glaring headline:

CANE FIRE DESTROYS 600 ACRES
ARSON SUSPECTED

The article went on to state what was common knowledge in the sugar islands of the West Indies: that there had been too many cane fires, due it was believed to labour unrest. Early arrests were, of course, expected. The first had started where the Montague Estate adjoined the grounds of the old Dabney property, La Bastide.

'I'd shoot the bastards!' said the man in the next seat. 'It's the only way of dealing with the problem, don't you agree?'

'No, I don't,' replied Jonathan. 'I'd be more inclined to get at the root cause of the trouble. My belief is that until wages rise as fast as prices, or a little faster, there will always be unrest. . . .'

'Go a step further. If we can get more for our sugar, we can take all these problems in our stride. You're Dabney, aren't you? With a potential goldmine working for you at the Reef, what do you care about sugar problems?'

'I don't know about the goldmine, actual or potential, but what you say is true. Things like this fire don't disturb us unless they touch us personally.'

Having, it seemed, said everything there was to say on the subject, they relapsed into silence.

The blue Caribbean, streaked with white wavelets and foam, reminded Jonathan of a lapis lazuli box which his mother had owned and which he had not seen for years. He mused about her – and his father – and the whole Dabney story.

The man next to him had no doubts about how to deal with industrial unrest. It was easy: shoot the bastards. When it came to the point he probably wouldn't do anything so drastic, but the mere expression of such a violent opinion served to remind him which side he was on, which side his bread was buttered. All he saw was the utter rightness of his attitude. The man was what the islanders called a newcomer, being only a second-generation sugar grower. Perhaps that was too short a time for a family to become as soft as the Dabneys had done. The last three generations of Dabneys, maybe more, had had none of the cold ruthlessness which must have been needed to exploit a small army of slaves and maintain their dominant position on the island through successive political and economic changes.

For the thousandth time he found himself deploring his ability to see both sides of almost any question. His father had been like that, lacking a certain single-minded ruthlessness which, in society as constituted, was the key to survival . . . material survival.

While in New York, talking to Hambleton and two of his co-directors, Jonathan realized that he had touched the fringe of Big Business. His was a skimpy knowledge of the subject, but he had sensed something of the efficiency, cold calculation and unflinching purpose which gave some of the great American enterprises their impetus. Hambleton, as Alice McGraw had said, was an uncommonly nice man, doubly so in a way because, as a self-made millionaire, there could not have been much time for niceties on the way up. He had been courteous, friendly, hospitable and, so far as it was possible to judge, completely frank. Here's our proposition, was the attitude, so take it or leave it. Put your pen to the dotted line and you walk out of this boardroom a rich man with no worries. Leave the worrying to us. It had been a fair proposition too, but what had most impressed him was the single-mindedness and lack of pretence. This was business, with no sentimentality allowed to intrude. He envied it and in a curious way admired it, if only because of his own half-toned inability to align himself squarely on the side of the angels or the devils. It would make life so much easier.

The Hambleton proposition had been starkly simple. They would acquire Dabney's Reef lock, stock and barrel. On the end of the promontory, at the point furthest from the existing buildings, they would erect a 224-room hotel of sixteen storeys, the size to be doubled later if results warranted. The lagoon would be converted into a yacht marina capable of taking up to 150 small craft. On the at present unused land between the existing buildings and the new hotel it was proposed to construct an undisclosed number of luxurious cottages. Jonathan would come out of it with $250,000 in cash and a like sum in Hambleton shares, plus the lifetime use of one of the four penthouse apartments which, being built on a flat roof, would not be penthouses.

When Jonathan hesitated, Hambleton said: 'That's our best offer. You won't get a better one from anyone.'

'But it would destroy the beauty of the place . . .'

'I'll leave you to discuss it with my colleagues,' said Hambleton, going out of the room.

Addressing nobody in particular after Hambleton had gone,

Jonathan said to the well-shaven and talcumed faces round the table: 'What you people don't seem to understand is that it's a beautiful spot ... truly beautiful, and you expect me to sit back and watch you spoil it. Besides, it's my home and you want to turn it into a kind of Coney Island in the tropics. There are plenty of them already from all accounts, but there aren't many unspoiled places like Dabney's Reef. Surely, gentlemen, there's another approach to it. It isn't a question of money ...' They exchanged shocked looks. '... I don't mind taking less money, but I won't be a party to spoiling that lovely place....'

One of Hambleton's men broke in: 'The kind of people flocking to the Caribbean these days, Mr Dabney, don't want beauty. If it hit them in the eye, they wouldn't recognize it. They want rum swizzles served by flash niggers wearing big grins and pants that are too tight and help to show off a cinder-sifting walk. In theory they like "empty stretches of coral sand", but what they really like is to lie on mattresses set as close as possible together so that they can compare varicose veins. They don't care what they eat so long as it's steak....'

'But the sewage from a place that size would soon foul the lagoon....'

'We've gone into that. The tide sweeps through the lagoon four times every twenty-four hours ... that's what tides are for.'

'What about staff? They'd have to be trained....'

'That's all taken care of. Training is of secondary importance. We insist on employing niggers who look happy ... doesn't matter whether they are so long as they look happy. People on vacation hate the sight of unhappy niggers. It makes them think. Who wants to think on vacation?'

'We have unemployment on the island, which is why some of our ... people don't look as happy as they might....'

'Excuse me, Mr Dabney ... I see you don't much care for them being called niggers. Anyway, nobody wants to press you. Think it over and let us know, but not for long, please, because we have other irons in the fire....'

It reminded Jonathan of what he had read of police methods

in extracting a confession from a suspect ... the brutal police-man who did the softening-up and the sympathetic one who caught the wretched felon on the rebound from brutality. Hambleton had reversed the process, but the technique was essentially the same. He had first exhibited the velvet glove. His colleagues wielded the mailed fist ... Hambleton's mailed fist.

As the plane began its downward glide to landing, the joy of homecoming was marred by the consciousness of his own inadequacy.

Chantal and Robbie were on the airfield to greet him. Robbie stood back while Chantal enfolded Jonathan in a fierce embrace.

In the car returning to Dabney's Reef, Chantal said: 'Well, we're waiting to hear what happened in New York.'

'A lot happened, but it came to nothing. . . .' He launched into a blow-by-blow account of the interviews.

'I just don't understand people like that.'

'What do you think they thought of you?' asked Robbie. 'Maybe you were even harder to understand. They're in business to make money and they paid you the compliment of believing that you were, too.'

'Compliment? They're bandits ... soulless bandits and yet, when I first talked to Hambleton I thought he was a very nice chap.'

'Don't rule out the possibility that he is one at heart, Johnny,' said Robbie. 'The Henry Hambleton you met was his public image. The world is allowed to see what is good for it to see. The personalities of these tycoons are shaped by the public relations sharks. In every room of every hotel in the Hambleton chain is at least one original oil painting. It's featured in every brochure. Down in New Mexico some-where ... near Santa Fé, I think it is ... they run a factory where a team of deadbeat European artists turns out "original art" by the yard. So Henry Hambleton is billed as a great "patron of the arts". The bog seats in every bathroom are "sanitized", which means that a paper cover is put on it, often without the formality of a good wipe after the last user. H.H. gets a medal for that from some crank society that pioneers

134

hygiene. But it's all a fake, Johnny, just a front like the Pony Express office in a Western movie. Strip that front off and there's a bandit underneath, not necessarily because he's a bandit at heart, but because he has to be one to survive. Underneath that – and I am only theorizing – he may be a very nice chap. If Alice McGraw says so, he probably is ... but what can a man like that think of a softie like you?'

'Go now, Johnny,' said Chantal. 'Take a bath, change and we'll have a drink waiting for you.'

'You two look conspiratorial ... something's happened here. What is it?'

'It'll keep, Johnny. ...'

The other two had waited for Jonathan and they drank their drinks in silence. 'Now, before we eat,' he said, 'let's have the bad news.'

'Why do you think it is bad news?' asked Chantal.

'Because, stupid as I may seem, I know that if it had been good news you couldn't have kept it to yourselves. Also, if you hadn't bamboozled Robbie into helping you break it gently, he would have been propping up Tucker's bar now instead of playing gooseberry here. So, one of you or both of you, let's have it.'

With an expressionless face he listened in a kind of frozen silence to the horrifying story.

Robbie left them alone. 'What are you thinking, Johnny?' asked Chantal when the silence had become oppressive.

'I wasn't so much thinking as wondering ... wondering how much of it all was my fault.'

'Maybe much, Johnny, maybe none at all. But don't wonder any more because you will never know the answer.'

Uncounted hours later, as a breeze stirred and crept through the louvred shutters of their room, Chantal murmured: 'Try to sleep Johnny. It is better.'

'I'm not worrying about ... that. I was just wondering whether I have the right to be so happy.'

'Everyone has the right, Johnny, but everyone does not have the chance. Now go to sleep.'

16

Time, as always, brought changes to Dabney's Reef, but time of itself had little significance. There was a clock of sorts in the dining-room, visible from the kitchen, but the moist salt air did something peculiar to the works, causing it to gain or lose as much as ten minutes daily. Jonathan possessed a watch, a good one, guaranteed waterproof, which stopped dead when, forgetting that he was wearing it, he swam the length of the lagoon. He would have to do something about it. The only really reliable timekeeper was the sun, which rose around 6 a.m. and set around 6 p.m. with insignificant seasonal variations.

A change which left a void was the decision on the part of Dr Elias to end his days in Trinidad with a married daughter. Before leaving he sold his little motor cruiser *Jane* to Jonathan for a trifle. 'Her bottom is fouled with barnacles and weed,' he said ruefully, 'and her timbers are worm-ridden. But patch her up and she will serve you well.'

Graziella's decision to return to Martinique came about less peacefully than Elias's departure. Arthur Dabney, working a couple of miles offshore from the reef and using beam nets which flapped like a bird's wings, made a big catch of flying fish, almost beyond dispute the most delicious and delicate fish to come out of the Caribbean. For a cook they involve a lot of work in preparation, which Graziella did not care to leave to her ham-handed kitchen help. Cleaned, split open with their backbones removed, she salted and peppered them lightly, squeezed fresh lime juice over them and did not begin cooking until people were at table. In flavour flying fish is not unlike the fresh sardine, but far less greasy. They vary in size, but the largest are as big as small herrings.

Graziella was a kitchen artist whose chief reward was to see people rolling their eyes and showing the other signs of appreciation as they ate.

The first to be served were two couples from Detroit who shared a table. Smoking hot, two to a plate, the flying fish were put before them. Graziella, beaming in anticipation of her vicarious satisfaction in watching their enjoyment, stood framed in her hatch surveying the dining-room.

One of the woman reached for a bottle of tomato ketchup, which she proceeded to slop over her own and her husband's fish. Worse was to come. For sweet that day there was to be a kind of pancake, so on each table there was a small jug of honey. Graziella stood transfixed with horror as they desecrated the fish by pouring a puddle on to their plates.

This was too much to be borne in silence. Graziella's horror turned to rage. Removing her apron, she screwed it into a bundle and hurled it at the feet of the offenders. Then, discretion thrown to the winds, she let off steam in Martinique French, which mercifully nobody but Chantal fully understood. When, invective at an end, she fell silent, she overturned the table on which the flying fish, all ready for the pan, were waiting. Then, with a snarled *'Canaille!'* she stormed out of the kitchen never to return. Michael Angelo asked to paint a barn door could not have felt more insulted.

When Chantal pleaded with her mother to stay a short while longer in order to teach a successor, she was met with a blunt refusal.

The underlying reasons why no cuisine worthy of the name has evolved in West Indian islands under British domination is less important than the fact. Part of the reason undoubtedly had to do with the absence of good raw materials in the early days. Slave food, in the form of salt beef and pork brought down from the north in barrels, became the staple of the master race. The brine was so strong and the flavour so revolting that the only way to make it edible seemed to be to disguise it with hell-fire chillies, stew it for days and call it a pepper pot. This was not a propitious environment for the development of culinary skills. As a result cooks, if they ever existed, fled the islands, leaving the preparation of food to clods.

So it was that efforts to fill from local sources the void left by Graziella's defection seemed hopeless. The new Tucker hotel, where the food was only just edible, had a kitchen staff turnover of above twenty per cent per month.

Chantal and Jonathan had to lose Graziella in order to learn what a priceless boon she had been.

The accommodation at Dabney's Reef had never been more than mediocre. People had come for the charm of their surroundings and for the food, so far beyond anything to be found in the neighbouring islands as to defy comparison.

'Don't waste time or money advertising,' said Robbie McAlister. 'Anyone on the island who knows how to boil a kettle without burning it has been tried out by Tucker and sacked.'

Chantal could not cook. None of her mother's skill had rubbed off on her, or she might have tried to take over. Nor did she feel herself capable of watching over the kitchen except to stop excessive thieving.

While trying to decide what was best to be done, events took charge. There was an outbreak of what in Mexico is variously called the *turista*, the Curse of Cortez, or the Toltec Trots. Those untouched by the scourge fled, hoping that they would not be seized during the flight home. The rest sweated it out on a diet of boiled rice, praying for release.

A sad-eyed sanitary inspector sent from Port Lewis to investigate the cause of the outbreak gave it as his opinion that the kitchens were no worse than others he had inspected. His only recommendation was that cloths used to wipe the floors should not do double duty wiping kitchen utensils. He added as a rider that as the cook's assistant appeared to be suffering from what looked like contagious itch, it might be as well to employ him elsewhere until he had ceased to scatter scabs when he scratched himself.

From several of the departing guests there were threats of lawsuits, but Zachary said these could be disregarded owing to the impossibility of proof. 'Any one or all of them might have brought it with them.'

All future bookings were cancelled and agents advised that 'due to unforeseen circumstances' Dabney's Reef had closed and would remain closed until further notice.

'Now what are we going to do?' asked Chantal who, badly rattled by her mother's defection, could not take its aftermath calmly.

'For the moment, nothing, darling,' said Jonathan. 'If you understood simple accounting you would realize that far from being the calamity you think it is, it could turn out to be a blessing in disguise . . .

'The amount of profit we've been making,' he went on to explain, 'isn't worth a fuss.'

'Where did we go wrong?' asked Chantal.

'I don't know, but I intend to find out. We may have had too many people on the payroll. They may all have been stealing us blind. Maybe we weren't charging the guests enough . . . any one of those reasons or all three. But don't worry, darling. We aren't rich, but we have more than enough for our needs, and if we sell the place we could be very rich . . . *If* we sell Dabney's Reef, that is. . . .'

'No, not that Johnny! We will, we must find some other way. . . .'

'I hoped you would say that, and meanwhile let's enjoy life. We have each other. We have Nico. We live in what many people have called paradise, so what have we to be unhappy about? Before we even think of re-opening to visitors we must wait until all the scandal dies down.'

After a couple of weeks, during which Chantal took charge of the kitchen, Jonathan was heard to say: 'I made a great mistake.'

'What mistake?'

'I should have married your mother.'

Despite the atrocious food, there began for these three an idyll lasting several months. They rose with the sun, swam across the lagoon and back, and with their early tea ate fresh pineapple, cold from the dew, big ripe mangoes when in season, papaya sprinkled with lime juice. Sometimes it was varied with scooped-out passion fruit.

Chantal and Jonathan had the gift of silence. They lived

their happiness, feeling no need to chatter about it. Whether Nico followed their example or inherited it, he was a quiet, silent boy who spoke only when he had something to say.

Neither Jonathan nor Nico cared much for fishing as pleasure, but when Elias's *Jane* had been repaired at Port Lewis they made many expeditions together, building up a good relationship at the same time. They fished strictly for the pot, keeping fish which they knew to be good eating and throwing back the rest, often without even knowing their names. Cavalli, mullet and crayfish were the favourites, the latter especially provided they were not too large and coarse. When the turtle were running they were a welcome change, a turtle steak being vastly better as meat than any local beef, which had the consistency of leather.

Nico, if he was not learning much at school – for it became apparent early that he was not the studious type – was learning self-reliance. He was virtually amphibious, healthy and even-tempered. At the age of ten he understood the principles of an internal combustion engine and was happy tinkering for hours at a stretch with *Jane*'s old engine. Clever fingers plus a boundless curiosity about how and why were a clue to his future.

The day came when the McAlisters said that they had done all they ever would be able to do for Nico. Next to be decided was where he would go for the rest of his education.

The views of Jonathan and Chantal on this question seemed quite irreconcilable. 'Education!' said Chantal contemptuously. 'What is that? You are educated, Johnny, but what good has it done for you?'

'I am not educated,' he protested. 'I wish I were. When I left school, instead of going on to a university, as planned, I went into the R.A.F.'

'Yes, I know, and you went looking for that woman ... that Gloria, in your parachute. Maybe it *would* have been better to be educated, then you would not always be reading those stupid books.'

Chantal knew a little simple arithmetic, fairly fluent spoken French and English, something of French history in so far as it touched France's West Indian possessions, and very little else. Nor, fortunately for her happiness, was she conscious of the need for more.

How to get across to her without storms of protest that in the larger world beyond Dabney's Reef and beyond the Caribbean the key to material success was highly specialized education?

The McAlisters joined forces with Jonathan in trying to batter down the walls of spurious logic Chantal had built around her son. They cited a Mr Ayling who had visited Dabney's Reef several times. He was an eminent consultant chemist reputed to be making a huge income. 'Where would he have got without education, do you suppose?' asked Robbie.

'Do you see Sam over there?' she countered. Sam was the dim-witted son of one of the ancient servitors at La Bastide, employed to pick up litter if there was any, otherwise to sit in the shade. 'Poor Sam had no education' – she pronounced the word viciously – 'but look at him. He did not need education to know that it is wrong to wear one black shoe and one brown at the same time. That is what Mr Ayling did. When Sam eats he does not spill his food all down his front ... like your educated Mr Ayling....

'You, Robbie, are educated, yes? But you do not make much money.'

'But I drink, Chantal. I still have occasional lapses. In one life there is not often room for money-making and drink. Besides, education helps with many things as well as making money....'

'Tell me one ... just one.'

'Education is the only sure way to success, but even then it is not sure. What *is* sure is that without education, without knowledge, Nico will never amount to anything.'

'Knowledge!'

'You are right, my dear, to be so contemptuous of knowledge, for without understanding it can be very bad. But tell me, what is in your mind about Nico's future? What do you want him to become?'

'It is not what I want ... it is what he wants, and he will become an engineer. Already he understands motors. Ask

Johnny what he did with the motor of *Jane*. Also, he is clever with his fingers.'

'Yes, it sounds right that he should become an engineer, or something of the kind. But where will he learn that? Not here, you may be sure. There is no school of engineering here ...'

'School! You are always talking about schools. Mr Simpson down at the electric power station is an engineer. He could teach Nico.'

'You don't really believe that, Chantal. You are just putting up these arguments because you ... you, as his mother, don't want Nico to go abroad to learn.'

'Where would he go?'

'To England, Canada or the United States ... France or Germany if you like. Anywhere where there is good teaching.'

'Always you want to send him to cold countries where I could not go with him.'

'There is nothing to stop you going with him to any of these countries.'

'Johnny says that if I go to a cold place I must wear shoes.'

'Then wear shoes, my dear. It is a small price to pay for your son's career and future happiness.'

'A small price! That is what you think. I know better.'

Chantal would not listen to reason because her whole attitude was emotional rather than reasonable.

'What does Johnny think of this?' asked Margaret McAlister.

'Johnny thinks much as Robbie does,' said Jonathan, weary of the storms which raged around the question, 'and he hopes that when the time comes Chantal will see things the same way.' He looked across at Chantal, whose face resembled a house with drawn blinds.

Despite everything, Jonathan had his reservations, which he kept to himself, not because of a desire to be secretive, but because he despaired of Chantal ever looking dispassionately at both sides of any question. To her it came naturally to be sweetly reasonable about things which did not touch her deeply, violently passionate when they did, without it ever occurring to her that there was a middle road.

When thinking of Nico, he recalled vividly some of the events of his own schooldays in England. He had been one of a group of what he now thought of as rootless boys, whose parents were in India, the Sudan, on the China Coast, in East and West Africa, hot and unhealthy places then regarded, and probably rightly, as prejudicial to the health of growing children.

These boys, or those of them who had no close relations in England who would give them a home during the holidays, were put in charge of a housemaster who stayed at the school the year round. He and his wife were kind, warm-hearted people who did their best for these orphans of circumstances. Jonathan could still feel the pain shared by this little group when at the term-end the rest of the boys, full of the delights of the holiday ahead, went off home happily without a backward glance.

It had been among those who were left behind that Jonathan had made his friends. Several of them had not survived the war, but the rest had kept in touch as far as possible, and from what Jonathan knew of their careers, the survivors had turned out to be a more than ordinarily successful group, although no longer a group. He himself was not a good advertisement for the system, but this he attributed to other causes. As his father had said once: 'We've too many generations behind us of people who haven't had frost in their beards, or known what it was to beat their arms to get circulation going.'

Nico had perhaps inherited all the Dabney decadence, while from his mother was the added handicap of mixed blood. What was best to do for the boy's own sake ... not for his father's pride or to satisfy his mother's possessive love. If only there were someone to turn to for advice!

The McAlisters were right in saying that there was nothing more they could do for Nico. They had both retreated too far from the turmoils and problems of latter-day living to be of much practical help. When the moment came to decide matters, Jonathan knew that the decision would have to be his and his alone, and he shrank from it, fearing what it might do to disrupt an otherwise ideally happy marriage.

Were parents competent to make the decisions regarding a child's future, Jonathan asked himself, or should they be left to the state, or some other impersonal body? He faced the possibility that some parents were competent, but in his own case he had grave doubts. What was there about his own relative failure which entitled him to supppose that he could draw a blueprint of Nico's future? Then there arose the question of Chantal's competence to make the decisions which, he believed, would most likely turn out more disastrously than his own. Chantal's inexperience and small horizon would of themselves impose fearful limits on the boy's future.

If Nico remained in the setting in which he had been born he might, with the aid of some inherited money, become a large frog in a small pond. But to amount to anything by his own efforts elsewhere, he would need specialized training.

17

Of all the changes which had come about at Dabney's Reef, the one which had touched Chantal most had been the loss of her beloved bar. Behind the bar, dispensing drinks, exchanging persiflage with the customers, dominating the scene, she had been someone. She could control rowdy behaviour and foul language with a frown. When a customer in her opinion had had enough to drink, she had the knack of being able to lengthen the intervals between drinks, or give short measure, or both, without the customer being aware of it. It was the one thing she did supremely well and she knew it.

Paradoxically, it would have been hard to find anyone less interested in money for itself; she loved punching the cash register. In a drawer, hidden even from Jonathan, she preserved a bundle of the long slips taken from the cash register at the end of every day, showing the items and the grand total of takings. She disliked ambiguity and there was something so utterly satisfying about a cash register's unambiguity. One couldn't argue with it. There it was.

The events which led to the bar's reopening were simple. Dabney's Reef offered far and away the best swimming on the island. Elsewhere the few beaches were overcrowded, garish with umbrellas, mattresses, and littered with cigarette packages, ice-cream cartons and the like which, since nobody was responsible, nobody troubled to clear.

Fastidious people and those less fastidious who knew of the existence of Dabney's Reef came over to swim. Jonathan had no objection to their coming so long as a precedent was not established prejudicial to the rights of ownership. Zachary gave it as his opinion that people could not be prevented from swimming there, but they could be prevented from crossing privately owned land to get there. On Zachary's advice, therefore, the land was fenced against access from the road and at the gate was posted a notice to the effect that the land was private property, but that the gate would be opened for pedestrians only during daylight hours if visitors would ring the bell.

The small tips which most people offered became the perquisites of Sam, who prospered as never before.

Most of the people who availed themselves of this were well behaved. Someone asked Jonathan why he did not open a bar there? Why not somewhere where food could be obtained? If not a restaurant, then a sandwich bar?

After some thought it seemed a good idea. Chantal, consulted in the matter, was delighted. Carefully concealing her delight, she agreed that it might be a good idea. It was left to her to make all the arrangements.

It took a few days to enter into an arrangement with a coloured couple named Wilcox. He had worked in the kitchens of a mail ship running from Southampton to South America, but had left the sea when a leg was amputated as the result of an accident. His wife Araminta was a pleasing, smiling young woman in her early twenties. She had had no experience of bar-keeping, but Chantal undertook to teach her all that was necessary.

The arrangement was that the Wilcoxes would provide all food and fuel at their cost and keep all the profits, if any, from the sale of snacks. Araminta would keep a proportion of the bar profits.

While it lasted it turned out to be a very good arrangement for everyone concerned.

Thus Dabney's Reef came to life again and thus also, by a circuitous and quite unpredictable chain of events, the problem of Nico's education was solved.

Among those who from the first availed themselves of the swimming privileges was a young, good-looking Englishman who came alone. After a few days he came with a group of young men and women. Jonathan and Chantal exchanged greetings with them, but it did not go beyond that. Then one day a handsome, hard-faced woman in her fifties came with the same people. Chantal, who missed very little, noticed that the latter's presence had the effect of putting a damper on the party. She observed no particular incident, but that was the impression she gained. On two successive afternoons, just before sundown, the older woman – who turned out to be his mother – and the first young man left together before the others.

At the bar, before the rest went, the talk was that the young man was painfully tied to his mother's apron strings. The young man's name was Hendrikson. His mother was a twice widowed woman, now known as Mrs Scully. She owned a house on the land which Jonathan had sold near the light-house and was reputed to be wealthy.

Then came a day when Mrs Scully did not put in an appearance. The word was that she had flown off to New York to consult someone about financial matters. Someone else said that she had gone to see a nerve specialist. Another theory was that she had a boy friend and was teetering on the edge of a third marriage. Very likely all three theories were wrong. But the salient fact remained that she no longer came to the beach.

Two of the group were exceptionally lovely girls, but Hendrikson seemed less interested in them than a man some ten years his senior.

Chantal misheard and misunderstood much of the chatter, because it was in Mayfair argot, which she had never heard. There were times when she wondered if it were really English she was hearing. The day came when, the holiday presumably over, the group disappeared and was seen no more. Hendrikson and the other man continued to come.

One morning when Jonathan was passing the gate a col-oured family arrived. The man, whom he knew by sight, was a schoolmaster, conspicuous because of his great size and the fact that he was really a black man, as opposed to the great mass of the population who, known loosely as Negroes, were of all shades of brown.

Sam, the guardian of the gate, was in the act of refusing the family admission when Jonathan came on the scene.

'I'm very sorry about this,' he said. 'Poor Sam's instructions are to keep out rowdies and unaccompanied children. The gate is there to preserve my rights as owner of the land.'

'Then there is no exclusion of coloured people?'

'How could there be when my name is Dabney? But there is exclusion' – he glanced at the portable radio the other was carrying – 'of that. We live here.'

'For that I am grateful,' said the schoolmaster. 'I only submit to the noise for the sake of the children.'

The family spent a happy day on the beach, cleared up all litter, smiling their thanks as they left for home in the afternoon.

A few coloured people, mostly of the prosperous class, on realizing that there was no change of policy at Dabney's Reef, availed themselves of the opportunity to swim and picnic there. They were well behaved. They did not mix with each other unless they were friends, which was true of the white people who came. The ban against portable radios was enforced for all races. One group of white people made a fuss. The man, by way of being a sea-lawyer, talked about 'high-handed interference with individual freedom'.

'You are free to make all the noise you wish on the other side of the gate,' Jonathan reminded him. 'Here I make the rules.'

Best of all, there was no apparent friction between the races. White and coloured children tended with a few exceptions to mix happily. Nico mixed with both quite naturally. He seemed oblivious to colour, which delighted his parents.

One hot afternoon Jonathan, who was writing letters, heard Nico come up from the almost deserted beach spluttering with laughter. 'What do you think I have just seen?' he asked Chantal who, to fall in with his mood, made several perfunctory guesses.

'I saw those two men' – he pointed along the beach – 'and they were kissing each other. It looked so funny.'

'I expect you made a mistake, darling. Now go and have your afternoon sleep. It's much too hot out there.'

'If he speaks of it again,' said Jonathan, 'don't behave as though you are shocked, or surprised, or anything. Let's hope he will forget what he saw. Meanwhile, I'll deal with it ...'

'Deal with what, Johnny?' she asked with a bewildered air to his retreating back as he went out into the afternoon blaze.

Going along the beach, his footsteps muffled by the soft sand, Jonathan came abreast of the two men unheard by either. Suffice it to say that their behaviour left more or less nothing to the imagination. They were Hendrikson and the older man.

'If you two dirty animals are not off this beach and outside the gate by the time I reach a telephone,' Jonathan told them, 'I am sending for the police.'

'Who the hell are you to take that tone?' blustered the older of the pair.

'Get going ... now!'

They went.

'Why did you send those men away?' asked Chantal a minute or so later. 'I don't understand why you are so angry.'

'Because I don't want Nico corrupted by such sights, that's why.'

It soon became apparent that Chantal had not grasped the significance of the episode. So with a great distaste for his task, he explained matters in as general terms as possible consistent with making his meaning clear. It was an aspect of life of which she had been spared any knowledge.

'What are they called, these men?'

'By a dozen or more names, which you don't need to know.'

'But I want to know, Johnny, so please tell me.'

'They are called queers, pansies, poofs, queens, fags and many more.'

'What do you call them?'

'I call them buggers.'

There was a long silence while Chantal was digesting things. 'Why do men become like that?' she asked at length.

'I'm not sure that I know the answer to that,' he replied. 'When doctors and others try to explain it they use a lot of long words that I don't understand. I wonder sometimes whether they do. Some think they are born that way. I don't know and I don't want to know. Nobody has ever explained why people become murderers, traitors, thieves....'

'People steal because they are poor and hungry....'

'Yes, but not all. The rich and well-connected thieves are called kleptomaniacs.'

'That isn't fair, Johnny.'

'No, darling, it isn't fair, but although I'm not a very wise or experienced man, I find that the more closely one examines things, the less fair they are. It has been said that all men are born free and equal, but that some are more equal than others. Don't let's bother our heads about these things. Let someone else reform the world.'

They dropped the subject, but it was much on Chantal's mind, which did not permit her to view such things in the light of general human problems. Chantal's was a much circumscribed world, largely bounded by Nico, Jonathan and perhaps her mother. Flames which did not scorch them were hardly flames. She was warm and friendly to many other people, but only to the degree that they were warm, friendly, and contributed to the welfare or happiness of those nearest and dearest to her.

A few days after this unpleasant episode, the McAlisters, taking advantage of a school holiday, came out to Dabney's Reef to spend the day. On the bus which brought them out was a white woman unknown to them, who turned out to be Mrs Scully, the mother of Hendrikson. Sam, knowing no reason to the contrary, admitted her. She chose a shady spot and, fumbling in her bag for a paperback, went through the motions of reading, from time to time glancing to where Jonathan, Chantal and the McAlisters were sitting on the cool verandah. Nico, wearing diving goggles, was happy out in the lagoon watching underwater life. Except for Mrs Scully, the beach was deserted.

'In a few moments,' said Margaret McAlister, 'that woman is going to come across to us. I wonder what she wants.'

There was not long to wait. Mrs Scully appeared to come to a decision of some sort, rose quickly to her feet and, opening her sunshade, approached the little party.

It was plain from a distance of twenty feet that her mission was not a friendly one, for her face was contorted with anger.

'Is there something I can do for you, madam?' said Jonathan politely.

'Yes, take me to some place where I can talk to you alone.'

'I have nothing private to discuss with you, so please say whatever you have to say here.'

'Very well,' she said after some hesitation. 'I have been away for a week or two. On my return yesterday I learned from my son that he and his friend were grossly insulted here. I want an explanation.'

'Madam,' said Jonathan icily, 'if your son were even half a man he would not send his mother on such an errand. . . .'

'Errand! How dare you!'

'. . . And I assure you that your son was not insulted.' He paused for the final thrust. 'After what I witnessed, it would be an impossibility. I have known better behaved animals in a farmyard. And now, unless you have anything else to say, may I remind you that this is a private party on private property.'

The blood left her face and she rocked back on her heels as though from a blow.

'There,' said Robbie when she was out of earshot, 'goes the perfect example of the domineering female who emasculates her sons by mothering them to death.'

'I wish you would not use such long words, Robbie. Please explain what they mean,' said Chantal wearing a little frown of bewilderment.

'What I mean, my dear, is that women like that keep their sons tied to their apron strings and prevent them from ever developing normally. When they do finally enjoy a little freedom from mama they are at best only half men. Ask Johnny to explain the rest to you if you must know. . . .'

'I have done that already,' said Jonathan, 'and now I'm inclined to wish I hadn't.'

'I'm glad that I know,' said Chantal intensely. 'If I do not know about ugly things, how can I guard against them . . . for my Nico?'

'You don't need to worry about what Nico saw the other day. He just thought it was funny. He's not referred to it again, has he?'

Chantal shook her head. 'But if what Robbie says is right,' she went on, 'I shall be a bad mother if I keep my Nico tied to me for too long. I will not be a bad mother, because I want him to be a real man.'

'Don't distress yourself, darling.'

'How can I be not distressed?' Chantal raged. 'I love him so much I want him always to be with me, Johnny! Now maybe I think you were right. Even if it breaks my heart, we will send Nico away to school.'

All eyes turned towards Nico who, dragging his feet in the sand, was coming towards them carrying a crayfish he had speared near the reef.

'Nico,' said Chantal, gathering the boy to her, 'if you were to go away to school, which country would you like to go to?'

'I don't care, Mama, so long as I can play football.'

Thus simply was the course of Nico's future mapped out for him.

'That,' remarked Robbie when the boy had gone off to bath, 'is what is known as the inscrutable ways of Providence. The dear lad will never know that what he saw on the beach led to the first great turning-point of his life. May he never live to regret it.'

18

Jonathan believed in all sincerity that sending Nico to school in England had been in the boy's best interests. The kind of education he might have picked up in the West Indies, academically speaking, probably differed little from that available in Britain at secondary schools where middle-class people sent their sons. But a school's curriculum was far from being the whole answer. The few good West Indian schools might be well enough for boys who, from choice or circumstances, would spend their lives in the West Indies. But for a career in the greater world outside the Caribbean such schools were, Jonathan believed, too cramping. In Britain Nico would meet a different kind of boy: not necessarily better, but with broader outlook, background and interests. There were, too, climatic advantages. Nico, except for the mere dash of coloured blood inherited from his mother, was a Nordic and as such needed the climate which nurtured Nordics.

That all this was true, Jonathan had no least doubt, although ruefully he was bound to admit that in his own case the results might have been better.

It was, however, the means by which this desirable end had been brought about which troubled Jonathan and lay heavily on his conscience. He and Robbie between them had 'conned' Chantal and exploited her fears by allowing her to believe that domination by a mother, as in the case of young Hendrikson, was the sole cause of turning a healthy young man into a pansy. It seemed likely, as both of them knew, that this was one of the causes, but there were many others, known and unknown.

There were plenty of bad habits and contacts to be encountered at an English boarding school. With memories of his own youth to guide him, Jonathan had chosen a school whose known policy – which did not appear in the prospectus for obvious reasons – was not to employ bachelors or celibate curates as assistant masters. Whichever way one turned there were risks, of which the greatest were probably in the boy's own character. All kinds of theories were aired freely, but none of them held water and none gave the complete answer.

Despairing of ever making Chantal see this in well-rounded perspective, Jonathan wished that her swift agreement to Nico going abroad to school had been brought about more honestly.

Martinique, where Chantal had been brought up, lived by lower middle-class French standards and customs. A few, but very few, families sent their sons back to France to be educated, these from a stratum of society far removed from Chantal's. Jonathan was at pains to tell her how, at his own school, there had been boys from every corner of the world, cut off from their parents for years at a time. It had seemed quite normal then, but to Chantal it was horrifying.

At Nico's school there was a hard-and-fast rule that on Sundays boys should write to their parents. This delighted Chantal, who welcomed any link, however tenuous, with her beloved Nico. In her turn she devoted one day weekly to replying. Letter-writing did not come easily to her, even in French, while in English her epistles were painfully inadequate. Another school rule, which imposed a censorship on all in-coming and out-going mail, caused Nico acute embarrassment at times, in fact almost as much as if his mother had turned up barefooted on Speech Day.

It seems to be inherent in small boys to be ashamed of any parental deviation from the accepted norm. What they themselves think of such deviations does not matter: it is what the other boys think which counts. As between his mother and father, Nico had a far greater affection for the former, but despite this he wished that his father would do the letter-writing for both of them. On the few occasions when Jonathan *had* written, the letters had not bubbled over with affection, but their form and content had not been such as to cause Nico any embarrassment, knowing that other eyes than his saw them.

Being a passionately demonstrative woman, it amazed and appalled Chantal that Jonathan did not wear his heart on his sleeve. When Jonathan had flown to New York, Chantal had stood back in shocked amazement when he had parted from Nico with nothing more than a handshake and 'So long, old chap. Look after your mother.'

Jonathan, although 'country-bottled', had all the ordinary Englishman's dislike for emotional scenes in public. Affection, or the lack of it, did not come into the matter, but Chantal interpreted it as irrefutable evidence of a soul-chilling indifference.

If Chantal's letters to Nico were difficult ... sometimes impossible to understand, the same could be said of those in the opposite direction. Nico's letters seldom referred to anything which had happened, or might happen, at Dabney's Reef. It was as though he had never lived there: his interests, if his letters were a true guide, were narrowed down, in order of priority, to football, food, school personalities, occasional lukewarm mention of cricket, all liberally besprinkled with school slang. It infuriated Chantal when, anticipating that she might have trouble understanding some of the references, Nico suggested that Jonathan might be able to interpret them for her. The clear implication was that his father understood him and his problems better than his mother did, a suggestion which she refuted hotly.

One letter, which had evidently been posted on the q.t. to avoid censorship, referred to the school food as 'swill' and to the headmaster, whose name was Timothy Charteris, as 'Timothy Tightarse'. For some unstated misdemeanour the latter had given Nico 'six of the best'.

For Chantal's benefit all this required laborious explanation, and when told what 'six of the best' meant, she had the pretext she needed for an emotional storm.

'What kind of a father are you that you sit there smiling and allow a strange man to beat your son?'

'He is not beating my son. He beat him last month and I haven't any doubt that Nico deserved it. In any case, you can be sure that Nico has forgotten all about it by now, so don't get worked up over a trifle.'

'Trifle! Maybe a trifle to you, but not to Nico. Poor boy! Maybe that brute beat him so hard that he is in hospital. You are a brute, too, a heartless brute. . . .

'What about Ted and Esther? They are your children, hein? What do you care! Have you ever written to them? No, you have not. What country are they in? You do not know. Why do you not know? I will tell you why, Johnny. It is because you are a brute without a heart. . . .'

And so on and on and on. Even if he had wished to reply, or to interject a few words, he would not have been allowed to do so. The storm must be allowed to blow itself out.

Jonathan picked up a copy of the paper just arrived from Trinidad and began to read. This, as he knew it would, enraged Chantal, who began to bombard him with ripe mangoes from a basket which had been left on the verandah. Without saying a word, Jonathan went to the refrigerator, taking from it a jug of iced lime squash, which he proceeded to pour down the front of her dress. 'If that doesn't cool you off,' he said quietly, 'there are two more where that came from.'

The calm, deliberate way in which this was done aroused Chantal's ire more surely than if Jonathan had flown into a rage and done something violent. This, by her curious standards, was clear evidence that Johnny had no heart, on a par with his quiet acceptance of Nico being beaten by a faceless monster on the other side of the ocean.

Realizing that she could not provoke Jonathan to violence, Chantal gave herself over to tears. Her sobs were audible far into the night. No further word on the subject was exchanged until after lunch on the following day.

'This morning early, while we were drinking our tea at dawn,' Chantal began, breaking a long silence, 'you looked across the lagoon. Fishes were jumping. The palms were waving gently in the little breeze. It was very beautiful and you, Johnny, you said: "It is so beautiful, almost too beautiful. It makes me very happy, and I hope it makes you happy, too, darling." Do you remember?'

'Yes, I remember. Go on.'

'Then I will tell you something, Johnny,' she said, leaping to her feet and spitting out the words ferociously. 'I am *not* happy. I have lost only one son, my Nico, and I will not be happy until he comes back to me. But you, Johnny, have lost two sons and one daughter and' – her eyes blazed – 'you are happy. How is it that you are happy? I will tell you, Johnny, it is because you have no heart. It has taken me a long time to find out, but now I know that my Johnny has no heart.'

Thus Dabney's Reef entered upon what Jonathan would always think of as its Dark Age. If he were to go to England, take Nico away from school and bring him back to his mother, thunderclouds would give way to smiles. But as he saw things this would have been to sacrifice the boy's best interests to satisfy his mother's ill-considered whim. If she were determined to be unhappy, see no other viewpoint but her own, nobody could stop her and reason could not enter into the private enclave of the heart, where misery ranked as a luxury and intrusion was forbidden. So he did not intrude.

Once each year for two months beginning in late July the clouds of gloom were lifted. A little patch of blue sky would appear in early July when arrangements for Nico's return were completed. The dull resentment in Chantal's eyes would recede. A little of their former sparkle would appear and, when she believed herself to be alone, she occasionally sang.

If only Jonathan would show signs of missing Nico as much as she did, Chantal might have relented. But she was incapable of believing that those who did not wear their hearts on their sleeves had any hearts.

People whose children are always with them are like gardeners who can watch the slow natural growth of plants. But the Nico who would leave Dabney's Reef in late September bore little resemblance to the Nico who returned the next July. The latter was taller, his features less rounded and more mature, his mode of speech was changed and the interests which had absorbed him the previous year forgotten.

These processes, perfectly natural in the circumstances, outraged Chantal, who would have regarded an eclipse of the sun as a personal affront. An appallingly emotional scene was enacted at the airport when Nico arrived one day, his voice broken. With the passage of two years he had become a man without his mother's knowledge or permission. That he seemed scarcely aware of the phenomenon himself made it even worse in her eyes.

Nico was at the awkward age when, after an absence of ten months, he viewed his parents critically. What right had they to change as they had? Why were they so silent? Why were they so stupid as not to know who Jenkins Major was, when everyone should know that he was Captain of Football. He was now able to view his parents through cool, detached, critical eyes. They wore such peculiar clothes, he thought, comparing them unfavourably with those worn by other parents visiting the school.

What his parents did not know and would have been horrified to learn was that he could survey Dabney's Reef in the same detached way, and that the thought of one day living there never crossed his mind. Larger horizons were beginning to open.

While Nico was and would remain the bone of contention between his parents, the emotional climate varied from day to day and there were times when only the most discerning outsiders could have detected anything wrong in their relationship.

During one of the bad patches, as Jonathan chose to think of it, Chantal voiced a vague intention of returning to Martinique to spend some time with her mother. Jonathan thought it an excellent idea, which was interpreted by Chantal as a desire on his part to get rid of her and caused her to abandon the project.

Relative idleness did not suit Chantal, giving her too much time to nurse her grievances. She felt thwarted by Jonathan's reluctance to see her presiding at a busy bar; it was the only occupation which – aside, of course, from hourly contact with Nico – because she knew she did it well, satisfied her and gave her great happiness.

158

Going back to first causes, the inability of these two to see problems in anything like the same light, stemmed from their ethnic differences. Jonathan, because he came of Nordic stock, tended always to take the long view of anything, while Chantal's few drops of African blood blinded her to any but a short view. There was nothing of the squirrel in her nature: what she wanted she wanted *now*. She was quite unable to look ahead into an uncharted future for the rocks and shoals which might strew the path of her son decades thence. The significance of education escaped her. She saw it as a pretext to separate her from Nico.

*   *   *

At the far end of the beach where, if Jonathan had agreed, Hambleton would have erected an hotel, was a big outcropping of coral, thrown up by some submarine upheaval centuries – perhaps millennia – earlier. When and if Dabney's Reef were to be exploited, Jonathan was determined that coral should be the building material used.

Weighed down as he was by the sense of failure – his own as much as that of the Dabneys – he felt the need to do something useful or creative. He had wanted to do so much, but had done so little. A life of *dolce far niente*, with the thunder of the surf against the reef in his ears, the rattle of the palm fronds in the breeze, the hot scented nights and Chantal's sweet presence, which was once so desirable, had palled. The fact that Chantal's presence was no longer so sweet accounted, at least in part, for the change.

He became impelled not only to do something useful, but something arduous and even dangerous, which would, he believed, help to stifle his sense of guilt.

*   *   *

The theory and practice of quarrying, Jonathan soon discovered, were as far apart as the poles. After causing miniature earthquakes with dynamite, the fragmented rock turned out to be useless for his purpose. It was either too small or in pieces so large as to be unmanageable. On the far side of the island, where a similar reef of coral was being worked, he heard of a Barbadian named Holt, reputedly a wizard as quarryman and stone mason, who was just ending his engagement. Naming a wage that was high, but not excessive, Holt brought his skill to Dabney's Reef.

Sections of rock too large for the small power-driven circular saw, bought from the importer in Bridgetown, had to be sawn by hand into building blocks, using the sizes of blocks in the original Dabney weekend house as guide. Holt, a giant of a man, with muscles rippling under his shining black skin, made light of his end of the cross-cut saw. But an hour at first was more than enough for Jonathan. Finally, four hours daily of the gruelling work was the most he could do. Under this punishment every scrap of superfluous fat vanished. He became tough and lean once more – and too fine-drawn.

'Why you do this, Mister Dabney?' asked Holt one day, observing Jonathan in a state not far short of collapse at the end of a day. 'You don' have to. Me, I have to, so I do it. You b'long to the master race, that's it, en't it? You the first white gennelman I ever see take off his coat excep' to play games. . . .'

'Why do I do it? I wonder, but I'm not sure that I know why. It goes something like this, Holt. All this rock we're cutting comes from Dabney's Reef. Some day someone is going to use it to build fine houses here. People won't see it, but my name will be on those blocks. Some of them will have been wet with my sweat . . . the first Dabney sweat that came from doing something useful in a long time. Does that make sense to you, Holt?'

'Yes, I guess it does. You know, Mister Dabney, slave days were bad for the black man an' maybe they was worse for the white man . . . on'y he didn' know it,' Holt ended on a note of good-natured laughter.

This exchange was, as Jonathan reflected later, a good summation of the relationship between the two races. But the barrier of misunderstanding remained. Holt was bewildered, long experience having taught him that although some white men appeared to have changed their attitudes, they were still at heart oppressors of the black man. What, he wanted to know, was Jonathan trying to prove?

When Jonathan reached home the light was just fading. On the verandah sat Chantal and Robbie McAlister, the latter with a bottle of whisky in front of him. 'Man, you're all in,' said Robbie. 'When's all this foolishness going to stop?'

'When I've got it all out of my system, I suppose, or when I can't take any more punishment ... which, maybe, isn't far off. I'll drink some of that whisky, Robbie. I hope it will taste better than it did the last time. I'm not much of a man for whisky ... but wait! There's still some of that old rum left. You drink your whisky and I'll drink rum....'

'Like hell you will alone, laddie. I promised your father I'd help you drink it and, by God! Robbie McAlister isn't the man to break his word to an old friend.'

It had not escaped Robbie's notice that Chantal and Jonathan had exchanged no greeting. He had seen for a long time that all was not well between them. While the latter was off filling a decanter with rum, Robbie asked: 'What gives between you two? What's wrong?'

'Everything, Robbie, everything!' Sobbing, she went into the house.

Although Robbie was his only confidant, Jonathan found it hard to broach the subject uppermost in his mind.

'Well, laddie, oot wi' it! What's your theme-song for this lovely evening?'

'In one word, Robbie, it's failure....'

'That has a familiar ring ... it's where Robbie McAlister lives. Failure, eh? Tell me more.'

'It's a long story, the Dabney story. In his last years you knew more of my father than I did. Well, I'm just the next instalment of the same story.'

'Aye, I mind it, the old riches to rags tale he was so fond of telling when he was full of rum. He wore out the record, Johnny, for at the end he was a sad, sad man. A failure, yes he was that, but there came a time when he was proud of it, which is fatal. Now I'm a failure, laddie, but I've the grace to be ashamed of it. May I ask what particular brand of failure you have on your mind, aside from that of your ancestors whom you didn't choose.'

'I'm an all round failure, Robbie.'

'Aye, that's bad. Now my failure wasn't an all-round failure. Mine was painfully specific, easy to identify. I just surrendered to the whisky bottle and allowed it to take charge. So don't you talk to me in generalities, Johnny. Be a little more specific.'

'You don't need me to tell you I've made a mess of my marriage. You've seen that this evening. I'm a failure as a father. Chantal will tell you that ... a man with three children and where are they? Ted, likely as not, behind bars. Esther, half way to becoming a nun and mumbling about eternal damnation when she ought to be laughing with a boyfriend. Then there's Nico ... Nico the sweet, gentle, obedient lad you remember. How do you think his headmaster describes him in his last report? ... Just one word. Nico, he says, is "belligerent". Belligerent! Did you ever hear such nonsense?'

'All right, laddie, we'll take it as read that you're a bad husband and a bad father. What about yourself other than as husband and father? What makes you tear the guts out of yourself pulling on one end of a crosscut against a buck big enough to eat you for breakfast? What are you trying to achieve?'

'Justification, I suppose, justification for my existence. I set out to do something and ... well, I've done it, something more than sitting comfortably in the shade, smoking Cuban cigars and drinking rum swizzles surrounded by poor blacks toiling under a pitiless sun. I've done it, Robbie, don't you see? One small achievement that nobody can take away from the name of Dabney....'

'What does Chantal have to say about it?'

'Nothing. She probably thinks I'm crazy.'

'A young woman of discernment evidently. More to the point, Johnny, what are you going to do about it?'

'What can I do?'

'Is that a question, Johnny, or a meaningless remark indicative of despair?'

'Either or both.'

'Then I'll take it as a question, Johnny, and tell you what's to do, knowing as I say it that I'm wasting my breath. Have you got a pair of medium weight rubber-soled shoes?'

'Yes, but—'

'Then take one, either one, go into the house, grab Chantal by the hair, put her over your knee and go on walloping her until she says she's sorry.'

'Sorry for what? She's done nothing, poor girl.'

'Precisely! Won't you understand, laddie, that your cold, passionless, gentle remonstrances are utterly foreign to her nature. In other circumstances she would have married a man who beat her from time to time on general principles and if he forgot to do it she'd have felt neglected. Justice? Justice doesn't enter into the matter. Nobody with a drop of African blood in his veins knows the meaning of the word. The strong oppress the weak, the rich oppress the poor. A ten-word history of Africa. You may not think it justice ... and you're probably right. But Chantal would take it in her stride and become her sweet self again. They don't say it with flowers where she came from ... they say it with bruises, which explain themselves without a lot of damn silly talk. ...

'But tell me, laddie, what has Chantal to say about Nico's alleged belligerence?'

'Nothing! In the first place, she doesn't know the meaning of the word and won't let me explain it to her. In any case, she knows that he's perfect ... she's utterly unreasonable.'

'Knowing that, Johnny, why waste time appealing to non-existent reason? It is that very absence of reason which is a great part of her charm, and now, if it's all the same to you, I'm tired of the subject and I'd like to concentrate my attentions on this wonderful rum ... but don't waste time talking to me about failure. No man is a failure until he's tried something and failed. What in hell have you tried? No, don't answer me. I'd rather not hear ... you have an unfortunate tendency to blather ... some other time.'

19

It enraged Chantal that she had to rely on matter-of-fact, terse school reports to learn about Nico's progress. The reports left so much unsaid, omitting the one thing she passionately desired to know: Was he happy? If he really managed to achieve happiness without her, she would see it as an affront to herself. It would be so unjust because her happiness away from him was inconceivable. Did that mean, she asked herself, that she wished him to be unhappy? No, of course it did not, but it was all too involved and none of these soul-searchings would have been necessary if she and Nico were living closely as mother and son were supposed to live.

Nico, as she could see for herself, had filled out. He no longer looked a delicate boy. From all accounts he excelled at sports, particularly athletics.

The boxing instructor at school – another ex-sergeant-major like Mortlock – gave it as his opinion that when the time came Nico would walk away with the public schools championship. This made Chantal shudder: they were trying to turn him into a brute. Boxing!

Then the news came that Nico had passed the Common Entrance examination. Chantal was impressed. Her Nico, it seemed, was an intellectual giant. Having no least idea of what this signified, she flew into a rage when it was explained to her that the Common Entrance (to her the end of education) was merely the preliminary to acceptance at a public school, part of the cruel conspiracy to keep them apart. Although she allowed Jonathan and Robbie to batter down her resistance to the idea of a public school, she remained unconvinced that this surfeit of education was in the boy's best interests. In due course, however, Nico went on to

Bracknell, one of the lesser public schools.

Being themselves largely unconcerned with matters revolving around colour, Jonathan and Chantal had by tacit agreement brought up Nico to ignore racial differences. Thus it was that the boy reached adolescence without an awareness of the great importance assumed by colour in some parts of the world. He would learn about such things later. Why cross the bridge before it became necessary? So he was quite unprepared for what he might and probably would have to face later.

*   *   *

On the top of the main classroom block at Bracknell was a flagpole from which the Union Jack was flown on certain high days and holidays. The hauling up and down of the flag was done by one Tompsett, groundsman and general handyman. Tompsett fell ill two days before the school Speech Day, when the governors and other notabilities were due to arrive. When an assistant master undertook to haul the flag to the masthead, he bungled the job, and the flag became tangled in the halyards and stuck at halfmast.

There was a long consultation about what to do next. Like all committees it did nothing but talk. Just when someone proposed calling in a fireman, a figure was seen walking across the roof ridge. It was soon identified as Dabney who, ignoring loud protests from the ground, shinned up the flagpole, disengaged the tangle and slid down.

The assistant master who had originally bungled the affair, relieved to see Dabney safely on the ground again and wishing to show appreciation, made a somewhat foolish remark to the effect that perhaps Dabney's ancestors had come down from the trees later than most. There was no *arrière pensée*. To those in earshot it was most humorous. A few days afterwards an educational colour film was shown depicting primates in the African rain forests. One episode showed a very black African engaged in placing a still camera and flash apparatus on a high bough. Some wag called: 'Well done, Dabney!'

Thereafter, as boys will, they chewed it to death. One boy, bigger than Nico and two years older, just about to leave for the university, carried the joke too far. It happened in the changing rooms. Nobody afterwards was quite sure what was said, but everyone heard Nico's retort: 'Say you're sorry, or take the worst beating of your life.'

The offender was a prefect. To apologize was unthinkable. He took the beating then and there. He needed medical attention when it was over. It came to the ears of authority, but no official notice was taken of it.

While the school was asking why Dabney was so sensitive, Dabney was remembering things which made him wonder whether there *was* anything unusual in his pedigree. As such things will, it became an obsession. Putting two and two together quietly, he realized with a great shock that among all the Dabneys he had ever met only one appeared wholly white and that was his father. From books he gathered a lot of misinformation about throwbacks, and from then on he began to imagine jibes.

There was a school rule against bare-fist fighting. Differences had to be settled with boxing gloves in the gymnasium if the protagonists were reasonably well matched.

Nico participated in several gymnasium fights, but authority could never get at the underlying cause of them, so that the not unreasonable assumption was that Dabney was a naturally quarrelsome fellow.

A summer holiday at Dabney's Reef intervened, during which Nico's doubts were dispelled. The Dabneys were half-breeds, a word he had learned from stories set in the Canadian backwoods. The fact did not distress him in the smallest degree, but he determined that anyone who threw the jibe in his face would pay for it. So, as his headmaster observed, he went back to school in a belligerent mood.

The famous and final incident occurred during an inter-house football match. There were charges and counter charges of foul play in which Nico was involved. A boy on the other team called him 'Nigger'. When a master and several team-mates finally overpowered Nico and dragged him off the offender, the latter had to be taken to hospital.

166

The headmaster, admitting that Nico had acted under extreme provocation, put in a transatlantic call to Jonathan and requested him to remove his son from the school. There was no enquiry into the rights and wrongs of the matter and Nico would in all probability not have been expelled had a group of parents not seen the incident. The altogether fallacious theory was that schoolboy differences were trifling, easily resolved and not to be taken seriously. Sometimes, although not often, they engender bitter lifelong hatreds.

The sweet-natured tractable boy who had first left Dabney's Reef for school in England returned as a surly adolescent burning with resentment and with a chip on his shoulder he was destined to carry for a long time.

'Where is the fine gentleman you promised me when you stole my Nico from me?' said Chantal through a storm of tears after the short ride home from the airport, during which he hardly spoke.

When asked what had happened at school, Nico took refuge in silence. His parents interpreted this as remorse for having done something shameful and did not press him further.

Dr Lawrence Dabney, having come out to Dabney's Reef to treat Jonathan for a poisoned foot, was troubled to see Nico loafing about the place with a hangdog air, obviously at outs with the world. 'What's eating you?' he asked. 'If there's anything I can do to help, come out to the house one evening. The boys will be glad to see you. Then after dinner, if you feel like it, we can have a chat.'

The doctor, a wise and kindly man, believed he had an inkling of what lay behind Nico's behaviour. He had known what it was to be a brown-skinned man, one of a tiny minority in a mainly white community. It had been a searing experience. Reason had come to the rescue. He went through a phase of earnest enquiry to satisfy himself on one important point: Was there any aspect of life in which by virtue of his pigmentation and blood line he was the proven inferior of his contemporaries? Academically, he soon learned that he was the equal of the best. In games, which never enthused him greatly, he was as good as he wanted to be and could always hold his own. By a process of elimination he came to the conclusion that his Achilles Heel was in the matter of temperament. He found that he brought to human relationships a slight, but to others perceptible, humility, conveying in some subtle way that he felt apologetic about his origins. When good sense told him that he had nothing to be apologetic about, the cloud lifted. Other men of colour, he knew, went through the same soul-searching. Some went to the other extreme and became arrogant as though to prove that a black skin was vastly preferable to a white one. When satisfied intellectually that there was no element of superiority or inferiority inherent in pigmentation, he no longer dwelled upon it and as it passed from his mind, it passed from the minds of others. From that point onwards he became a sanely balanced and well co-ordinated man, determined as far as it lay in his power to lead a happy and useful life.

After the family evening meal the doctor took Nico into his consulting room, ostensibly for some unstated treatment. 'Remember, Nico,' he said, 'I don't want to press you into telling me anything. But I see that something is troubling you and I'd like to help.'

Nico for the first time found he could talk. 'I'd like you to answer a few questions, Uncle Lawrence ... the truth straight from the shoulder.'

'You'll get the truth, or nothing....'

'Then tell me, have my father and I any coloured blood?'

'Your father to the best of my knowledge and belief has none. You have a little ... just exactly how much I don't know....'

'Then I must get it from Mother....'

'Of course. Didn't you know?'

'Then why, Uncle Lawrence, wasn't I told about these things? Why did I have to go to England to find out?'

'I'm afraid I can't answer you there, Nico. But my guess would be that your father, like me, assumed that you knew. Why not ask him?'

'Maybe I will one day. I can't now.'

'Well, don't go carrying a grudge about it. A grudge can weigh a ton and can crush you.'

'I've no grudge but they should have told me....'

*　　*　　*

Then out of the blue there came a letter from Doris to Jonathan. She was spending the winter in Barbados. Would she be welcome if she came over for a few days?

Jonathan referred it to Chantal, whose first reaction was negative. She liked Doris, but it was hard to forget that she was also the mother of that woman ... that Gloria.

'All right, let her come,' Chantal said grudgingly.

'Only if *you* want her to come. If for any reason I wanted to see her, there's nothing to stop me flying over to Barbados.'

No, that wouldn't do at all. If contact with Doris were to be renewed, let it be there at Dabney's Reef where she – Chantal – could keep them under her eye and break it up if Doris and Jonathan were getting too chummy.

'Yes, Johnny, I would like her to come. I was only thinking that we couldn't make her very comfortable.'

Even as she spoke she was thinking what a great pity it was that in life so many small lies served better than the truth. Chantal was by nature truthful and outspoken, but she had learned that although lip-service to truth was the rule, people seldom liked it when it conflicted with artificiality.

Problems, problems and more problems! Doris, unless handled with care, could prove to be one more.

20

Port Lewis was metaphorically rocked to its never very substantial foundations one morning by the sight of five white men of uncertain age, clad in dirty rags, their features obscured by mats of hair giving them a simian appearance, who stepped ashore from an inter-island schooner. They were carrying their possessions in untidy bundles. They slouched into the shed marked 'Immigration – Passports' where they produced their papers. These apparently in order, they were admitted. The five then climbed over the railings of the Victoria Garden and, in the shadow cast by the statue of Queen Victoria herself, promptly went to sleep.

Nobody in living memory had ever been to sleep there before, but as there was no law to prevent it, they were left undisturbed. In mid-afternoon they roused themselves, scratched suggestively under their filthy garments and, separating by arrangement, went on a systematic begging tour of the town. White people had been known to do some very odd things in Port Lewis, but begging was not one of them. At European homes and establishments doors were slammed in their faces and they got nothing. From the more prosperous coloured people, likewise. In a quarter where the poorest of the Negroes lived in rusted corrugated-iron and tarpaper shanties and where hunger was no stranger, they were given some stale bread, bananas and from one house a bottle of beer.

At the new hotel Tucker sent for the police when they presented themselves, but as there was no bad language or threatening behaviour, the police could do little but warn them to keep out. The five posed an entirely new problem and policemen everywhere prefer to be guided by precedent, so they fell back on the move-along-there technique. When the five found a pile of fishing nets down by the harbour, using it as a mattress, it was no-sleeping-allowed-here. After a three-night crossing as deck passengers they were in a state not far from exhaustion.

Two of the five knew, or knew of, Dabney's Reef, claiming to have been there crewing for a yachtsman. A kindly coloured policeman told them that it was on the other side of the island some nine miles distant. If they had the price, there was a bus. If not they would have to walk. They walked some five miles of it until they came to the long grass at one end of the airfield runway. There, hidden from view, they spent the night and, soon after dawn, roused by the sun's dazzle and heat, they trudged the rest of the way to Dabney's Reef.

Old Crazy Sam, as some people called him, let them through the gate without question and they made straight for the beach where, finding a shady spot, they resumed their interrupted sleep.

By late afternoon they were ravenously hungry. The coloured couple running the snack bar – there had been a succession of them – drove them away with curses when it became apparent that they had no money. Chantal, who was just opening the bar, refused to serve them on any terms.

Hearing the uproar – Chantal's voice – Jonathan came out to see what was happening. 'What do you chaps want?' he asked with less hostility than was expected.

'Something to eat,' said their spokesman. 'Our bellies think our throats are cut, and when we've eaten ... anything will do ... we want some sleep. ...'

Jonathan did not like the look of the five, but it was contrary to his every instinct to refuse food to hungry men. Rummaging in the storeroom, he found some rice, sweet potatoes, a freshly caught schnapper and a piece of tough, stringy local beef fit only for stewing. The fresh water tap used by bathers was drinkable. Seeing that they carried their own cooking utensils, he gave them the food and told them to get on with it and to clean up any mess afterwards.

As he was returning to the house, Jonathan heard the

'phone ringing. The police post near the airport was on the line to say that five bums were believed to be heading for Dabney's Reef. 'If they make the smallest trouble, give us a ring,' said the officer in charge. 'We'll be glad of the excuse to put them back on the schooner which brought them.'

This offended Jonathan's sense of justice. Time enough to raise the issue when the men had made trouble. Chantal, when he told her of the call, agreed that it was not fair. But being eminently practical, she asked: 'If they have no money and no food, what are we to do with them?'

'Let's give them some bread, tea, a tin of condensed milk in the morning and warn them that it's all they can expect.'

'It might be better to give them some work to do and offer to pay them for it. Let them pull on that saw for a few hours every day. We shall need the building stone sooner or later. No work, no pay.'

Jonathan was delighted with this unexpected co-operation and interest. For a long time it had been 'I', never 'we', but she had said 'we shall need the stone'. Was it a slip of the tongue or, as the commentators on international affairs were fond of saying, indicative of a thaw?

Soon after dawn the makings of breakfast were given to the men. 'From now on,' Jonathan told them, 'any food you get here will have to be earned.'

'How?' came an uneasy chorus.

'Enjoy your breakfast and I'll show you afterwards.'

Shown the block and pulley for lifting the large pieces of coral, the crosscut saw and other tools and on being told what was wanted, there was a shocked silence. The whole idea of doing something useful was repugnant to them. It was to escape such barbarous ideas that they had come to the languorous tropics where, if one waited long enough in the shade, ripe fruit would drop from the trees.

'But that's work for niggers!'

'If you stick at it you'll be able to do it nearly as well. . . .'

'What about something easier?' asked one who had detected no irony.

'That's the only work available here,' said Jonathan firmly but pleasantly. 'Take it or leave it. Nobody is pressing you.'

'Not for me!' said one. 'Nor me!' said two others in chorus.

'Well, you know where the gate is,' said Jonathan. 'But if you'll take my advice you won't walk back to Port Lewis in the heat of the day.'

'We'd rather stay here.'

'Stay and work, or go.'

'Why should we work for you?'

'I thought you wanted to eat. Otherwise, there's no reason at all, so make up your mind.'

Three of the five walked disconsolately towards the gate. This was worse than the town where at least nobody had suggested anything so degrading as work.

The two remaining men conferred briefly and the spokesman said: 'We'll have a stab at it, but you may as well know now, we're not very handy and we're a bit soft, too.'

'Never mind that. Nobody expects miracles,' said Jonathan cheerfully. 'I was on one end of the saw that cut the pile you see here now. I admit it's tough, so don't try to overdo it at first. You'll find me reasonable if you do your share.'

The two men did not get much done that day, but they tried. At noon they took a three-hour break, cooked the food given to them, swam while it was cooking, and went to sleep afterwards. Plainly, they were flabby, strangers to any work harder than rolling their own cigarettes.

At the end of three days, when it became apparent that they were making a serious effort to master the gruelling work, Jonathan arranged a scale of piecework agreeable to both sides. The two drew rations in the manner of a detached army post and were debited with them at cost price. A beach shed was cleared of assorted lumber and turned over to them, together with two old mattresses.

'I may as well have your names,' Jonathan said one day. 'Not that I'm curious, you understand, but I have to call you something.'

'I'm Bill,' said the hairier one of the two, 'and he's Joe. Okay?'

They were not communicative about themselves, and their rather furtive behaviour and disinclination to talk to or be seen by strangers led to the assumption that they were on the run from something. At the end of ten days or so, there was a change. The rhythm of the crosscut saw became steadier and at the same time more relaxed. Instead of pulling against each other, they began to lean into the saw on the return stroke with an appearance of ease. The breaks for rest and a smoke came at longer intervals and were of shorter duration.

'If you'd like to eat a turtle steak,' Jonathan told them, 'come across at noon when I whistle. There will be a bottle of beer apiece at the bar.'

They grunted acknowledgment and went on with their work. No effusive thanks. Nor did they seem to expect favours.

'What are you planning to build out there?' asked Hairy Bill when they came to collect the turtle steak and beer. 'Buckingham Palace?'

'A block of flats ... some time.'

'Nice place for those who can afford it,' said Joe rather sourly. 'Some people get all the luck.'

'*Bon appétit!*' called Chantal gaily as they went back to their shed.

In the late afternoon when the men had resumed their work, Jonathan heard Nico speak of them disparagingly.

'At least they are earning their keep,' Jonathan retorted angrily. He would have said more but for being uncomfortably aware that his own sweat glands had not been working overtime lately. With indecision heavy upon him, he was not cutting a very impressive figure, and he knew it. Also, he did not want to start an altercation with Chantal, who resented the smallest criticism of her beloved Nico. It was a surprise therefore when a little while afterwards she, having observed Nico lolling in the vicinity of the two men sawing, said angrily: 'People do not like to be watched while they are working. It is not kind or polite.'

'Who cares what they like, or don't like?' Nico retorted indifferently.

'I do,' said Chantal hotly, 'and you should. They are working like ...'

'Like what?' snapped Nico before she could finish. But it went over her head. Going into the house, she wept softly for her loving, gentle boy now a sulky lout. They had once been very close to each other, sometimes it seemed to the exclusion of Jonathan. Now, however, there had been a subtle change, subtle in the sense that although Nico was surly and morose with both his parents, he seemed less so with his father. Was it just a boy's natural leaning towards his father in time of stress, or was there some deeper reason? What did the occasional blaze of resentment in his eyes mean? It seemed almost accusing to Chantal. The old warmth and affection were gone. It was like getting to know a hostile stranger. If this was what education did to a boy, she wanted none of it.

The arrival of Doris helped to break the monotony of life at Dabney's Reef.

'It's good to see you both,' she said that first evening. 'You may believe me when I say that to me you are more family than my own daughters. When I see them, or hear from them, it is because they want something. Jean is still in South America with a third husband. I haven't seen her for five years. . . .'

Doris was about to talk of Gloria, but thought it more tactful not to do so.

'And your other daughter?' asked Chantal, making it easy for her.

'Gloria is married to a crazy Scot, who married her for her money. He owns a ruined castle in the Highlands – about all he does own – and when they give a party the poor guests have to endure the screech of bagpipes during dinner. It covers up his lack of conversation. But they spend most of the year at Cap d'Antibes and, I need hardly say, do most of their entertaining there ... at my expense ...

'Then there's the boy, Ted. There's nothing but bad news there, too. I may as well get it over with and tell the whole story ... then we can talk of something else. . . .'

Jonathan braced himself for what was coming.

'Yes, as I was saying, Ted ... he's turned out even worse than I expected. He'll never be able to go back to France again. He and a young friend burgled the Villa Delphos a little further down the Cap. The family was out, but the old housekeeper interrupted them. Although they wore some sort of masks, she recognized them. The young fools didn't hurt her, thank goodness, but they locked her in a room, where she wasn't found until morning. The boys bolted across the frontier into Italy, taking the money they found in a drawer and leaving some jewellery behind. They were tried *in absentia*, as the French call it, and given, I think, six months each. If they ever set foot in France again, they go straight to prison....

'Not a nice story, I'm afraid. There have been ... other episodes, but we don't have to go into them.'

'And what about Esther?' asked Jonathan, conscious that of all those concerned in the broken marriage she had fared worst.

'Esther, poor child, is also a problem, but of a different kind,' replied Doris. 'She was sent to a convent school where she became so devout that ... well, I for one find it hard to swallow. If it had made her happy I would have nothing to say. But it hasn't. Instead it has turned her into an introspective bore with a muddy complexion....

'And Nico, what of him?' Doris went on.

'Aside from the fact that he's disgruntled, sulky, ill-mannered and carries a chip on his shoulder, he's a delight to have loafing around. He wasn't exactly expelled from school, but I was invited to remove him ... a distinction without a difference. I've never been able to get to the bottom of it, but from being a gentle boy he became something very different. There was a quarrel during a football game ... the other boy finished in hospital.'

'Don't you, either of you, let it depress you too much,' said Doris in an effort to be cheerful. 'From all my friends with children, or grandchildren, I hear the same story. The young seem to be in open revolt everywhere....'

'Some of it *must* be our fault,' said Chantal, 'but where we went wrong we do not know. I am very unhappy,' she added tearfully.

'I understand that, my dear, but don't take it out on each other. It's none of my affair, except that I'm fond of you both ... I hate to see you straining to be polite. You still have each other, so be thankful for it.'

Between Doris and Jonathan, almost from their first meeting, there had flowed a warmth and understanding. Some of it had overflowed to include Chantal, who thought of Doris as a friend instead of being merely the mother of 'that Gloria'. The latter, who might have been expected to be a link between Jonathan and Doris, had been a wedge rather than a link. Doris had seen clearly before either of those chiefly concerned that the marriage of Jonathan and Gloria would not work out well and, if in decency she could have done so, she would have prevented it.

Inevitably one evening, the talk came around again to Ted. The three of them were alone, Nico having gone off on some mysterious errand.

'I keep asking myself what I ought and can do for the boy,' said Jonathan. 'While I admit that he lost my affection by the way he behaved here, the fact remains that Ted is my son and I have a duty to him. . . .'

'I wouldn't let that worry you too much, Johnny. It might turn out like putting salt on a bird's tail . . . you'd have to catch him first. Last year he was involved with drugs. I don't know the exact details. If she knew them herself, Gloria didn't tell me. All I know is that he was sent to Borstal, or some sort of reformatory.'

'If you can let me know where he is, I feel I must try to do something for him. . . .'

'Yes,' said Chantal surprisingly, 'Johnny is right. If Nico did something very bad, I would expect Johnny to stand by him.'

Chantal was amazed at hearing herself say this, more amazed when she re-examined it to know that it was a reflection of her true feelings. As she had once said to Robbie McAlister, she believed that Jonathan was not Ted's father. But she was nothing like as sure as she implied. What really mattered in her eyes was not so much whether it was, or was not so, but what Johnny believed. If, believing that Ted was his son, Jonathan were prepared to write him off, then in similar circumstances, it followed, he would be prepared to write off Nico. Thus, using the logic of the heart, she found herself in the position of championing Ted whom she detested for what he had done and resented for what he was. It all sounds very complicated, but to Chantal it had an elementary simplicity.

'My solicitors handled the matter for Gloria,' said Doris. 'I'll write to them and let you know what they say. But so far as money is concerned, Johnny, you don't have to worry. I've made provision for him in my will. There's a trust and trustees. If Master Ted wants to benefit, he'll have to toe the line.'

On hearing this, Chantal had to restrain herself from kissing or making some other demonstration of affection for Doris. Ted was no longer an obstacle in the path of Nico.

In all this Chantal saw 'that Gloria' as the arch villain. That she could be as indifferent to the welfare of her son as she apparently was, made her a bad woman, so that it was almost possible to think of Ted again as the 'poor little boy'.

21

The telephone rang very early one morning; too early unless it were an emergency. Chantal answered it. 'No,' Jonathan heard her say, 'there's nobody of that name here. Sorry.' She rang off.

'Somebody wanting someone called Sanderson,' she said, resuming the interrupted breakfast.

The telephone rang again shortly afterwards. Jonathan answered it this time. 'I'd like to talk to Sanderson,' said a rough-edged voice.

'You must have the wrong number. As you've been told already, there's nobody of that name here.'

'He's working for you, so you ought to know his name....'

'Tell me your name and where you can be reached by 'phone,' said Jonathan, 'and I'll try to find out.'

'My name don't matter and I can't be reached by 'phone.'

Jonathan hung up. Later in the morning, when the sun was too hot for sawing, he found Joe and Bill stretched out in the shade dozing. 'Either of you chaps named Sanderson?'

'Who wants to know?' asked Joe, the less hairy, suddenly alert.

'Someone who wouldn't give his name rang twice and asked for Sanderson.'

'What'd you tell him?' asked Joe, with the edge of anxiety in his voice.

'That there wasn't anyone of that name here.'

'That's right. There isn't, is there?' said Joe, the relief in his tone almost palpable.

Late that same afternoon, a motor cruiser registered in Savannah was seen to cast off its moorings and make for the open sea. Coiling a wet rope on the foredeck was Joe and that was the last Dabney's Reef ever saw of him. Something had evidently caught up with Joe. It was a great pity because the two men had been working together well. There was even a little money due to Joe, whose reasons for the hurried departure must have been good.

The man who arrived by bus later in the day and began to nose around, got little change.

'If you're the man who telephoned here this morning,' said Jonathan, 'you've already been told there's nobody called Sanderson here....'

'He could just as easily be using some other name. I was told he was working here and I want to see him.'

'There was a man working here until today, but he's gone.'

'Where's he gone to?'

'I don't know, and even if I did I wouldn't tell you without knowing much more about you. Let me tell you also that unless you want to walk back to Port Lewis tonight, the last bus is about to go.'

'Is his mate still here?'

'I'm answering no questions until you've answered a few.'

'If you knew,' the visitor persisted, 'what those two had been up to....'

'I'm only concerned with what a man does here, not what he's supposed to have done before he came here, or what he's going to do when he leaves. The man who said his name wasn't Sanderson worked hard while he was here and earned every penny he received. I dare say the police would be interested to talk to you....'

Taking the hint, the man turned just in time to catch the bus.

From the other side of the hibiscus hedge where this conversation had taken place stepped Hairy Bill. 'Thanks!' was all he said.

*　　　*　　　*

Jonathan wondered what Hairy Bill would do now that his friend had left so precipitately. Would he slope off again? Without a partner, he could hardly go on sawing blocks: it takes two men to pull on a crosscut.

180

He did not think it fair to penalise him because Joe had bolted, so, for the time being, he continued to provide him with food. This, obviously, could not go on indefinitely, and after several days, in which Bill made no move, Jonathan made it the subject of open discussion. 'If all we want is someone on the other end of the saw,' said Bill, 'what's wrong with him?' He nodded towards Nico, who was loafing within earshot. 'He looks healthy enough.'

'Well, what about it, Nico?' said Jonathan. 'Want to give it a try?'

Nico hesitated, showing no enthusiasm.

'Maybe his lordship is too delicate,' jeered Bill. 'Something easier, like making daisy chains, is more his style.'

Jonathan stood back, saying nothing. This was better settled between the two youngsters. Privately, he hoped Nico would rise to the taunt and for a change do something useful. A father should be able to take some pride in his son and it was sad to feel he could not. As Chantal had said, something bad had happened to the boy back there in England. But what?

Nico's face gave no indication of what was passing in his mind. In fact it was as though he had not heard. Then, pulling himself upright, chin tilted aggressively, he walked across to Hairy Bill, looked him squarely in the eyes and said: 'It may take me a day or so to get the hang of it, but don't fool yourself that there's anything – anything at all – you can do that I can't do as well, or better, and that includes knocking your block off if I have any more of your lip.'

For a moment it looked as though there was going to be a fight. There would have been if Bill had not had the sense to realize that Jonathan would have been compelled to stop it.

Much the same thought was going through Jonathan's mind. Of the two Bill was the stronger. He was inclined to be squat, built like a bruiser, with the air of a youngster who had survived many fights. Nico was lighter on his feet, with a longer reach. The muscle was there but it lacked the other's coarse lumpiness. If it came to a fight the result, Jonathan believed, would hang on guts rather than physical qualities.

'Well,' said Bill cheerfully, 'what's keeping us? We can

put in an hour before the sun gets too hot.'

When Jonathan left them, a minute or so later, they were pulling on either end of the saw. 'Take it easy and let the saw do the work,' Bill was saying.

During the weeks of idling Nico had become soft. When he came to eat at noon, his face was showing signs of strain. It was gruelling work. Nico ate quickly and, finding a spot in the shade, fell asleep almost instantly. At four o'clock, when the sun had lost some of its ferocity, he went down to the promontory to resume work.

Finding Chantal watching the two youngsters from a distance, Jonathan expected indignant protests. Instead she said: 'It is good. It will not hurt him unless he does too much.'

'He'll soon get tired of it.'

'Yes, he will soon get tired of it, but he will not stop. To stop would hurt his pride.'

'I am glad to hear you say that,' said Jonathan, 'because we could not let him go on as he was.'

'He must learn what it is to be a man,' she said soberly.

Beginning with two hours daily on the end of the saw, Nico was soon able to manage four hours. Remembering the strain it had been on himself, Jonathan made this the limit.

There was an almost frightening intenseness about the way these two worked. From the very beginning each realized that the other's mode of expression was inflammatory so, wisely, they hardly exchanged a word, working with set faces, and when the work was done, turning their backs on each other and going their separate ways until the next session. They sawed for about fifteen minutes at a time and when by a kind of telepathy they agreed to stop, they threw themselves down in the shade, their rib cages working like bellows. To maintain the balance of salt in their bodies – a trick Bill had learned elsewhere – they quenched their thirsts with a mixture of sea and fresh water.

Jonathan when watching them through binoculars sometimes had the feeling that their grim silence was bound to lead to an explosion, and there were moments, of which he soon had the grace to be ashamed, when he hoped that it would. Anything was better than to see them glaring at each other like caged beasts, pulling on the saw, neither giving an inch.

'You lads don't seem to like each other much,' said Jonathan, taking them a cold drink one day. 'Anything wrong between you?'

'What d'you want me to do,' asked Bill, 'kiss him?'

Chantal spent a lot of time, too, watching them uneasily through binoculars, with the growing certainty as the days passed that there would be a flare-up. Her feelings on the subject were curiously mixed, torn between a mother's fear that her only son would suffer a brutal beating and her hope that when and if the crisis came, he would be equal to it. Her feelings were even more complicated by the fact that she had a sneaking sympathy for Hairy Bill who, although quite plainly on the run lest his misdeeds catch up with him, was trying to redeem himself by hard work. Perhaps it would be best if they never came to blows and neither of them was hurt.

Matters came to a head, but in an unexpected way.

'What does your old man pay you for this?' asked Bill during one of their rest periods, opening his mouth for the first time except as the needs of work demanded.

'Pay me? Nothing.'

'That's not right.'

Nico replied with a shrug.

'A man does a nigger's work, he's entitled to a nigger's pay, that's what I said and ...'

Before he could finish the sentence, Nico was on his feet. 'Say that again and I'll beat the shit out of you!'

'You and who else? You don't have to get all steamed up. Even if you are a nigger, you can't help it.'

There was nothing more to say. The time for words was over. Bill belonged to the hit first and hit hard school. Few of his fights had lasted more than a minute. He had the makings of a good bar-room bruiser. Crouching low, he leapt into the fray, using his tried and true technique, but without touching Nico. The latter, using a straight left and his longer reach to advantage, drew blood in the first minute with what looked like a mere tap to the bulb of the other's nose. It hurt, stinging Bill to fury. Neither displayed good footwork in the soft sand, which slowed them down.

Bill's wild haymakers hit thin air. Relatively speaking, Nico's blows were light, but they were blows and having delivered them he was quickly out of reach and untouchable.

'What is this ... a dancing class?' Bill jeered. 'If you're going to fight, then fight.'

'Try that for size,' retorted Nico with a left to the jaw and a right to the belly-button which knocked the wind out of Bill who, try as he would, could not get to close quarters.

Bill was getting the worst of it. He was up against a boxer and knew it. They fought on doggedly until sheer exhaustion overcame them, too out of breath even to exchange insults. They lay two or three yards apart face downwards in the sand.

'Say, what were we fighting about?' asked Bill, the first to speak.

'What the hell does it matter? Want any more?'

'No, I've had plenty.'

'So've I, so let's call it a day.'

They grinned, both embarrassed by this display of weakness.

Chantal, who had been watching the encounter with the binoculars, saw the grins and was unaccountably happy. Jonathan was in Port Lewis and, unless the boys were badly marked, need not know about their fight. She would not tell him.

Nico's place at table that evening was empty. He arrived in the house after the evening meal had been cleared away. 'Bill and I ate on the beach,' he explained. 'We ate a fish wrapped in banana leaves under the ashes of a driftwood fire.'

'Was it good?' asked Chantal.

'Wonderful!'

'I had the impression that you and Bill didn't much care for each other,' said Jonathan.

'Bill isn't such a bad chap when you get to know him.'

22

It was the dawn hour. The sometimes wearisome breeze had died away. Outlines were softly limned by an opalescent haze. Jonathan sat back drinking in the beauty of it all, thankful that he was not one of the tens of thousands battling in and out of the London Underground amid the smells of fog, damp raincoats and cold remedies. To be living at Dabney's Reef, limited as the life was, made him feel highly privileged. He had just eaten his half of a large papaya, chilled by the dew, its flavour relieved by a sprinkle of inimitable fresh lime juice.

Tea arrived on the table in a big brown teapot salvaged from La Bastide. Before pouring himself a cup he was waiting for Chantal to arrive. She always managed to look her best in the early morning at the expenditure of fifteen minutes of time. There was not long to wait.

Relations between Chantal and Jonathan were, inexplicably, happier. Although Jonathan had never been told of the fight between Nico and Hairy Bill, it all dated from then. All he knew was that the two youngsters who had seemingly detested each other had become inseparable. Anything which made for harmony was to be welcomed: the whys and wherefores did not matter. All that had suffered was the output of sawn coral blocks now that the hostility at the opposing ends of the saw had vanished.

When Chantal had news the decibel output in conveying it to others varied with its importance. In another age she might have made a good town crier.

'Johnny!' Something important was coming. 'I just went into Nico's room to wake him. He has not slept in his bed....'

'Perhaps he slept on the beach.'

'The *Jane* has gone from the mooring.' This much louder.

'Perhaps the boys have gone fishing. I hope they catch something good. I'm tired of cavalli.'

'Johnny!' she yelled, determined to shake him out of his apparent indifference. 'Someone broke into the storeroom during the night. Many things are missing. A bag of rice has gone, almost all the canned things, tea, sugar, coffee, matches ... two bottles of Robbie's special whisky.'

'Sit down and drink your tea while it's hot ...'

'Tea! Who wants tea?'

'I do for one. Calm yourself.'

'Listen! There is no noise of sawing this morning. The boys are gone. Where do you think they went?'

'My guess would be that at this minute they are in Port Lewis filling the tank with fuel and charging it to my account. After that it's anyone's guess.'

'Aren't you going to *do* something?'

'No.'

'Aren't you worried?'

'No, not in the least. In fact I'm delighted. Like all boys ... girls, too, I expect ... Nico has passed through several phases. There was a time when we both thought he was inclined to be rather namby-pamby. That passed and he became a sulky, ill-mannered young lout, a misery to himself and everyone else. Now, I hope and believe, that has passed, or is passing, and he is in process of turning into a normal, healthy adolescent. When I was his age we didn't have a motor-cruiser, but I like to think that if we had I would have borrowed it, filled it with stolen stores and gone off adventuring somewhere. Good for Nico! Has it escaped your notice that so far as we know he has never had a friend? He has never even mentioned any friend he might have made at school. Well, now he has a friend. Even that hairy young ruffian Bill is better than no friend.'

'You think so?'

'I am sure so.'

'But we know nothing about Bill except, as you say, he is running away from something.'

'Stop for a moment, darling, and ask yourself how much

we know ... really *know* about Nico. Like all parents, if the truth be told, we just hope for the best.'

'But he may be shipwrecked....'

'If he went to Martinique, he might be bitten by a *fer-de-lance*. Here he might be bitten by a tourist. Whatever one does, there is risk ... the biggest risk of all is life itself.'

'I hope he does not buy a parachute.'

'Why? Because one saved my bacon?'

'No, because it took you to that woman ... that Gloria.'

'I suppose you would rather I had left it behind ...?'

'Yes.'

'Now drink your tea and stop fussing.'

'I shall drink coffee this morning.'

When Chantal returned to the table with a pot of coffee, she had calmed down. 'Perhaps, Johnny, you are right. It is time my Nico became a man and in his own way. I must try to remember that he is no longer a little boy.'

*   *   *

Dr Elias's little cruiser *Jane* was as seaworthy as she had ever been, which was not high praise. In reasonably sheltered waters or in river estuaries, she was adequate, but she was never intended for deep sea work. Neither lad knew even the rudiments of navigation. There was a chart in the cabin. It told them that in all directions but north there was open water. Northwards, the Grenadines, a long chain of rocky islets, stretched up to St Vincent. They were waterless and by repute uninhabited.

'How much money have you got?' asked Hairy Bill when, having taken on a full load of fuel in Port Lewis (and as predicted, charged it to Jonathan's account), they headed out to sea.

'None, not a cent.'

'I haven't got much more. Your old man's looking after mine. Going to be a bit awkward, isn't it?'

'We haven't any papers, so we can't go into any place where money's any use....'

'What happens when we've eaten all the stores?'

'We shall have to catch fish,' replied Nico, quite untroubled by the prospect.

'How long do you figure on being away?' asked Bill who, although the older of the two, was out of his depth and looked to Nico for leadership. Nico's sure touch and air of competence with the engine gave the other some reassurance. The truth was, and Bill was becoming uncomfortably aware of it, that he knew very little of anything and was entirely in Nico's hands.

During the afternoon of the first day the wind freshened. Not alarmingly, but enough to make the prospect of a night at sea undesirable. There was no sign of any habitation on the rocks and islets they passed. On one, which appeared to be over a mile in length, they ran in close enough to see some goats browsing. There was a sheltered cove on the lee side of the island. Making for this, they crept in carefully and dropped anchor close in shore.

Nico, who was an amphibian, speared a huge crayfish among some rocks. It was a disappointment, for it turned out to be too big and coarse to eat. By mutual consent an octopus speared at the same time was thrown overboard. By then it was too dark to fish, so for the evening meal they ate a can of bully beef.

'What do you figure your old man will do when he finds us and the boat gone?' asked Bill.

'There isn't much he can do. My guess is that he'll do nothing at all for a few days. Then he'll pass the word among the schooner captains to keep a lookout for us.'

After breakfast the next morning another thought occurred to Nico. 'Have you got a passport?' he asked Bill.

'I had one, but I burned it.'

'Why did you do that? It might have come in handy.'

'Well, the chap I ... borrowed it off had been in bad trouble. There was enough on my plate without being picked up for what he'd been doing. Besides, don't you see, I wasn't much like him to look at. That's why I hid behind this hedge,' he added with a laugh, indicating his hairy face.

Nico's first reaction to this was to be shocked. Having

been sheltered from the need for illegality of any kind, it was hard to adjust his mind to the kind of thing implicit in the other's frank admissions.

'You see,' continued Bill as though reading Nico's mind, 'you put one foot wrong and if you don't want to get caught, you've got to do something else, and before you know it, you're in it up to the neck.'

'Did you do anything very bad?'

'Depends how you look at it. Anyway, the cops thought it was bad, and I wouldn't like to go back ... not until it's blown over.'

Next morning the wind was blowing too hard to venture out into open water, so they fished inside the cove.

'How's about catching one of those young goats,' Bill suggested. 'I dare say they're pretty good eating.'

Nico was willing, but by the time they had found out that wild goats are not easy to catch, the shadows were falling and they were too tired to do anything but cook some fish and go to bed.

Three more days of rough weather took some of the gilt off the gingerbread. On the last day a shark was seen prowling round the cove, effectively frightening the fish out into deeper water.

Still heading north at the maximum speed of six knots, they came abreast of an island which looked greener and lusher than the rest. Another and smaller island not more than two to three hundred yards from it made a good natural harbour. Alongside a ramshackle wooden pier a typical inter-island schooner was moored. Clearly visible through glasses, she was being unloaded by six men. There was no sign of habitation on shore.

Creeping between the islands, Nico brought the *Jane* close to the schooner and dropped anchor. Building material was being unloaded. The work was being rushed as the schooner captain wanted to get away before nightfall. Soon after she had sailed, there came a hail from shore. A coloured boy standing on the pier asked if he might come aboard. Told that he might, he ferried himself out on an improvised raft. He appeared to be around the ages of Bill and Nico.

'Ah doan' want nuthing,' he explained, ' 'cept I'se lone-some. Skeered too. If you folks doan' mind, I kin sleep on deck.'

'There's only the two bunks,' Nico told him, 'but you can have a mattress on the cabin floor. What's your name?'

'Ma name's Henery ... Henery Holt. I'se Bajun.* Mostly dey calls me Sambo.'

'I know a Bajun named Holt. He worked for my Dad. Big, big man.'

'He comin' here nex' week ... biggest black nigger you ever see. He ma Dad.'

According to Sambo the island had been bought, or leased, by a wealthy American, who intended to build a house there for part year occupation. First there was going to be built a big water reservoir with a concrete catchment on the slope of the hill. On the point exposed to every wind there was going to be a steel tower windmill to generate electric current. He evidently intended to make himself comfortable. Sambo didn't know his name, but the talk was that he was very rich.

'You know,' said Bill, when he and Nico were alone, 'you knowing Sambo's old man and he having worked for yours, there might be something in it for us.'

'Such as?'

'I'm thinking of that big pile of coral blocks back at Dabney's Reef. Some day your dad's going to need builders, so what's wrong with us? Why don't we learn something about building right here ... maybe pick up some money while we're learning? You see,' Bill went on earnestly, 'I've gotta have money. If things catch up with me, I shall have to scram, and a man can't scram without a passport. Maybe I could knock one off from a tourist ... but even then I'd need money. Whichever way you turn it comes back to money.

'Here, don't you see, I'm safe. Nobody asking questions or wanting passports. We get back to Dabney's Reef and it's the same thing there. So I've got to stay here, or there, until things blow over. Then I can cook up some tale about losing

* Colloquialism for Barbadian.

190

my passport and apply for another. You can go back home if you want to and leave me here....'

Having made a friend, his only friend, Nico refused to contemplate losing him. Bill's problems were his problems. They were in this together and would see it through together.

'What do they want you for?' asked Nico, the ubiquitous *they* becoming the common enemy.

'I ran away from school.'

'That's not too bad. They can't do much to you for running away, can they?'

'That depends what kind of a school you run from,' replied Bill coyly.

'I see,' Nico said, but he didn't really and on due reflection decided that on the whole he preferred not to know. The past belonged to Bill. It was enough that they intended to share the future.

The building contractor, who arrived by schooner a week later, was short-handed. Men showed no enthusiasm for being isolated for weeks in the Grenadines. He was a coloured Barbadian, related to Holt and, therefore, to Sambo. He agreed to employ Nico and Bill as unskilled labourers. 'Nigger wages, of course,' he said, with no desire to be offensive, although coming from Barbados where colour lines were drawn strictly, there was a certain small satisfaction about exploiting the needs of two white boys as his own people had always been exploited.

At the end of three months, still a long way from being skilled builders, Nico and Bill had absorbed the rudiments of the craft, and when the time came to return to Dabney's Reef, they did so with some regret. There was also the uncertainty about the kind of welcome to expect when they got there.

On the eve of departure Nico was compelled to admit that unless someone showed him the way, he was quite incapable of navigating the return journey. Happily, the schooner was calling at Port Lewis, so *Jane* was able to follow tamely in her wake.

*　　*　　*

'Stop worrying, darling,' urged Jonathan, seeing Chantal's drawn face at the breakfast table. 'If you can only make yourself believe it, there was far more cause for worry when Nico was here. His behaviour was unnatural. Now that he has behaved naturally, you should be rejoicing not looking at things through red-rimmed eyes.'

'What is so natural about a boy who runs away from home without a word to his parents? Doesn't he love us?'

'It depends how you interpret love. Yours is a smothering kind of love. A boy's isn't. Nico is being natural because he *has* broken away from us for a while. A boy of his age, almost a man, isn't complete unless he kicks over the traces – that's what we say of a horse which does not submit kindly to harness.'

'My Nico is not a horse!'

'Looking back, darling,' Jonathan went on, 'I know, now that it is too late, why I am such a dull fellow. I didn't kick over the traces. At school there wasn't much opportunity, while in the R.A.F. I was too busy trying to stay alive.'

The breakfast table was Chantal's favourite forum for displaying her miseries. There was a bleakness about a day which began without the prospect of seeing Nico and knowing all was well with him.

A few breakfasts later a schooner was seen to lie hove to off the reef. A dinghy was rowed ashore. It brought a well-written letter from Holt, giving news of the boys' whereabouts and what they were doing.

Chantal that day was heard to sing one of the gay and somewhat lewd *chansons* she favoured when in a happy mood. Nevertheless, she would have been even happier if Nico could have been *there*, where she could see and touch him. A son's place was near his mother: otherwise, what good was it to be a mother? She could not subscribe to the idea that any outside influences took the place of the mother's love. Cats sometimes eat their kittens sooner than allow them to be touched. Chantal understood it.

23

Each generation seems to have its own measure of time. To a schoolboy the three months of a school term seem like an eternity, whereas to older people they pass all too swiftly. Nico and Bill, without putting it into words, were comforted by the feeling that after the lapse of four months their peccadilloes at the time of their departure from Dabney's Reef would have fallen into a convenient oblivion. The truth, of course, was that it all was as fresh in the minds of those left behind as though it had occurred a few hours previously.

Chantal, watching from the verandah as the rim of the sun touched the horizon, saw the *Jane* come furtively into the lagoon. At least, to her somewhat jaundiced eyes its arrival seemed furtive. To any other observer it would have appeared quite normal. During Nico's absence Chantal had blown hot and cold, at one moment consumed with fear that he was in danger and at the next consumed with rage at his callous neglect and failure to communicate. In short, she was consumed.

Nico, Hairy Bill and Sambo, Nico in the lead, came up from the beach jauntily. Chantal, who saw them coming, gave way to floods of tears and retired to her bedroom. Jonathan was at his desk writing letters. The first he knew of the prodigal son's return was hearing him shout: 'Hey, there! Anyone at home?'

Now that Nico had returned, Jonathan was still undecided as to what attitude to adopt: the stern father calling an errant son to account, or the loving father, so pleased to see his son back safe and sound that he was prepared to overlook anything. Coming out on to the verandah in response to the hail,

Jonathan realized with some dismay that the decision had been taken out of his hands. When he saw Nico striding up the beach followed by Hairy Bill and the very black Sambo, he saw at a glance that this was no frightened boy trembling in anticipation of his father's wrath.

Actuated by some sort of delicacy, Bill and Sambo stayed on the beach out of earshot, allowing Nico to go forward alone.

'Well,' said Jonathan, 'aren't you going to say something?'

'Hello, Father, I'm home.'

'Is that all?'

'What would you like me to say?'

'It might be in order to say that you're sorry for causing your parents so much anxiety.'

'That would be a lie, because I'm not.'

'I see,' said Jonathan for the sake of saying something. 'You're looking well.'

'Thank you, I feel well. Hard work seems to have agreed with me.'

'Quite a change, eh? By the way, who is your sunburned companion?'

'That's my friend Sambo. You know Holt, his father. Thanks to Sambo and his old man, Bill and I got jobs. We've come back rolling in money. There wasn't any way of spending it where we've been.'

'Would it be indiscreet to ask where you have been and what you have been doing?'

'No, not a bit. We've been doing nothing we're ashamed of.'

'I'm glad to hear that.'

'We've been helping to build a house in the Grenadines. If the place had a name we weren't told it. It was built for a man with more money than sense, I think. But that doesn't matter. It's his affair. What does matter is that we learned a lot. We aren't highly skilled builders, of course, but when you feel like turning that pile of coral blocks into something useful, we're ready to go to work.'

'I notice you say "we" all the time.'

'Sure. Bill and Sambo are my friends.'

'Isn't Sambo a ... well, rather an odd kind of a friend for you to have made?'

'Surely, Father, it isn't the colour of his skin that makes you say that?' said Nico with a malicious grin.

'Well, you must admit that it's somewhat ... startling.'

Chantal, listening to this exchange from inside the house, found herself trembling with fear.

'Surely, Father, you of all people don't draw the colour line? That would really be a wonderful joke.'

Jonathan flinched as though from a slap in the face. Search as he would for the right thing to say, he could find nothing, so he said lamely: 'It isn't a question of colour....'

'Then, if it isn't colour, Father, what is it?'

'Although it's not a word I care to use, Nico, it's a question of class. I dare say that he is a very fine young man. Knowing his father, I don't find it surprising. But one only has to look at him to see that he isn't ... well the kind of person one would care to sit down to a meal with.'

'Would you like him better if he wore boots?'

'Perhaps that would be an improvement.'

Jonathan was not prepared for the bellows of laughter which followed. 'That's lovely, Father,' said Nico when his mirth had subsided. 'I must remember that.'

Inside the house Chantal, who had heard every word of this exchange, looked down at her own bare feet and gave herself over to unrestrained weeping.

'Talking of class, Father,' Nico went on with an amused expression on his face, 'you may have a point there. He happened to mention one day that his grandmother's maiden name was Dabney. All the same, it isn't fair to hold that against him, is it?'

Chantal, realizing that unless she made an appearance there would soon be a violent altercation between father and son, dried her eyes and came out on to the verandah. Flinging her arms around Nico, she wept again, this time for joy. A tear-stained face looks much the same whether the tears are of grief or joy.

'I am so happy to have you back, Nico ... nothing else matters.'

'It's good to be back, Mama.'

She needed time to think, so she hugged him to her and hid her face on his shoulder. There was a struggle going on between the two people she loved best in the world. One of them was sure to be hurt ... wounded in his tenderest feelings. Which was it to be? Chantal knew that the choice lay with her.

'That's Bill down there, surely?' she said. 'Ask him and your other friend to come up and drink something. I expect you are all thirsty.'

'Talking of drink, Father,' said Nico, covering up the awkwardness while Bill and Sambo took their places at the table, 'I've brought back those two bottles of whisky I borrowed. We might have needed them, but we didn't.'

Chantal disappeared for a moment, returning with a jug of ice-cold lime juice and water, which they all drank with apparent enjoyment. One crisis was, if not averted, at least postponed.

'Now I expect all you boys are hungry,' said Chantal, retaining the initiative. 'What would you like to eat?'

'Anything in the world except fish,' said Nico. 'We're all starting to grow fins!'

'There are some Canadian cold-storage steaks in the freezer. How would they be? But I warn you, they'll take some time to thaw out.'

'I don't know about you chaps,' said Nico, 'but I'd like a swim. Up where we were,' he added, turning to his parents, 'we hardly dared swim at all. Sharks cruised into the cove all the time.'

While the boys were swimming, Jonathan avoided conversation by going into his office. Chantal went into the kitchen to consult with the cook, a pale-skinned, good-looking girl named Charlotte.

'Mr Dabney and I won't be eating steaks,' Chantal explained. 'They are too heavy for us at night. We'll just have an omelet. So three steaks will be enough ... unless you'd like one, Charlotte.'

'No thanks, ma'am. I'se eat already. But,' she added in horror-stricken tones, 'you don' need to feed steak to that black nigger Mas'er Nico brung back with him ...'

'He's Master Nico's guest and he must have the same as the others.'

'Then, ma'am,' said Charlotte, flouncing out of the kitchen, 'you mus' cook it yo' own self. I won't cook for no black nigger ...'

Crisis piled upon crisis. The snobbery of colour, Chantal knew, was one of the hard facts of life. The pecking order went by shades of pigmentation. By her own standards Charlotte was right. If Chantal did not mind demeaning herself by cooking for Sambo, she could get on with it. Chantal knew with a slight sense of shame that to some degree she shared Charlotte's feelings, but deeming them unworthy, she stifled them. Her formative years having been spent on a French island, she was far less colour conscious.

Jonathan, meanwhile, spent the time of waiting in his office, trying to work out some not too obvious way of avoiding sitting down to table with Sambo, and trying also to find out just how honest he had been in using class as a way of hiding colour prejudice, which he had always denounced so righteously. Gritting his teeth, he knew that the only way in which he could maintain the façade of tolerance was by eating with the rest. Were shades of colour so all-important? He found himself wondering.

Sambo's enjoyment of his steak when Chantal had cooked and served it was spoiled by the consciousness that he was out of place at this daintily appointed table, eating with people who were accustomed to such surroundings. Nevertheless, Sambo ate delicately by comparison with Bill. Knowing that Bill did not suffer from over-sensitivity, Nico asked him: 'Would you be happier if you took your steak on to the mat?'

Bill thought this a very good joke, continuing to talk at the same time as chewing great lumps of steak with his mouth open, the while holding his knife and fork in his fists and waving them for emphasis. 'Thank you,' he said graciously at the end of the meal, 'it's a long time since I ate so well.' There was even a note of appreciation in the resounding belch which followed.

During the next few days Chantal trod so carefully that she might have been walking on eggs. There was no actual unpleasantness between Jonathan and Nico, but the threat of it hung implicit in their cold over-politeness. As the invitation to meals was not repeated, Nico ate on the beach with Bill and Sambo and, judging from the sounds of laughter wafted up to the house, they all enjoyed themselves.

To Jonathan the difficulties of the situation seemed insoluble. Manifestly, he and Nico could not continue to behave like strangers. While it was no longer possible to talk to Nico as to the boy who had vanished so suddenly months previously, equally he could not bring himself to acknowledge him as having the stature of manhood. Chantal was no help. Her response to the situation was as always emotional: her husband and her son were at loggerheads and she was miserable.

When it became apparent that Hairy Bill and Sambo were in process of putting down roots at Dabney's Reef, and that if they were ejected Nico would follow them, Jonathan chose what he thought was a favourable moment to broach the subject. 'You realize, I hope,' he said, 'that some considerable time must elapse before we start any building here. The first thing to be decided is what kind of building we want. Next we have to find an architect ...'

'Why are you saying all this, Father?' asked Nico in an entirely non-committal tone.

'Because I don't want to mislead your two friends into supposing that there's going to be work for them for some while. It wouldn't be fair.'

'Meaning that you'd like them to clear out?'

'I didn't say that....'

'No, but you thought it....'

'Very well, if you must know, I don't want them hanging around indefinitely.'

'Okay, you're the boss. We'll go.'

'What will you do?'

'We'll get jobs somewhere on the island. I may as well tell you that Bill can't leave here until he gets a passport. He's been in trouble, and until that's all cleared up he can't apply for a new one.'

'What sort of trouble?'

'I don't know, or care. He's my friend ... thanks to you my first real friend, and I don't intend to lose him.'

Ignoring the 'thanks to you', Jonathan went on: 'While I know that you didn't have much of an education, surely you can do something better for yourself than work as a builder's labourer? I hope to sell La Bastide shortly, and with part of the money I would like to see you trained for something ... well, more important. It isn't too late, I believe ... why not try training to become an architect? Building seems to interest you.'

There was no response to this.

Chantal, hanging on every word, knew that this was all leading to a showdown, although that was not the word which occurred to her. She dreaded what was coming, without knowing what it was.

'Since we're being frank, son ...'

'Who is?'

'... Do you realize that I haven't the smallest idea how far you progressed with your studies at school?'

'Not very far. Didn't you read my reports?'

'Yes, of course, but they weren't very informative. The only thing I remember is that the headmaster complained of your belligerence. You were such a gentle boy ... what made you become belligerent?'

'I didn't like being called a nigger. The last chap who called me that wound up in hospital.'

Chantal gasped with horror. Jonathan was left speechless.

'... It was foolish of me, I know, but it didn't seem foolish then. Now, of course, I don't mind who calls me a nigger.'

'What caused you to change your mind?'

'Knowing that I am a nigger, of course....'

'Now you are being absurd, Nico. You are not what you call a nigger, a word that I detest....'

'In the Southern United States, Father, the slave states, one drop of Negro blood in your veins makes you a nigger.'

'That's perfectly ridiculous,' snapped Jonathan, 'and in any case we're not in the United States.'

'I notice that you don't deny it.'

'You are exaggerating things out of all recognition, Nico, making a mountain out of a molehill. It is true that your mother has some coloured blood and she must, therefore, have transmitted a little to you. But that's nothing to be ashamed of.'

'I'm not ashamed of it.'

'It isn't fair to blame your mother.'

'I don't blame Mother,' he shouted angrily. 'I blame *you*. You had no right to send me out into the world without telling me what I was ... letting me learn it from other boys' jibes. It was cruel and unfair ... and I doubt whether I shall ever be able to forgive you.

'If I've made a mess of things early in my life ... and I did ... it's all your fault. Now you jeer at me for being content to become, as you put it, a builder's labourer. I don't intend, feeling as I do, ever to leave this island. Nobody here is ever going to jeer at me, or call me a nigger. There are too many people in the same boat. They understand and are sympathetic and – what a laugh! – most of them seem to be Dabneys.

'But don't worry, Father. I'm not feeling sorry for myself. In fact, all things considered, I'm glad. I'm free now in a way I never was before ... free to live the kind of life I want to live, among the kind of people I like, without bothering my head about the stuffy little nothings whose only claim to importance is that their fathers and grandfathers didn't take a pretty little nigger wench to bed....'

Nico looked wonderingly at his father, who seemed to have shrunk physically, with tears streaming down his face.

'So, Father, if you want us to go, you have only to say the word. Let me know in the morning. Good-night!'

Jonathan and Chantal – she had heard everything – lay awake all that night, speaking only occasionally. At dawn's first light Chantal broke a brooding silence. 'He was wrong to speak to you like that, Johnny. It hurts me to say so, but he was wrong. What is to be done?'

'He was wrong and he was right. It was something we –

he and I – had never mentioned. There seemed no purpose to discuss ... you. I took it for granted that he knew. I was wrong and even if he ever forgives me, I shall never forgive myself. But to make threats and conditions to me, his father, is too much. If these others, Hairy Bill and Sambo, mean more to him than we do, darling, I feel we must let him go. ...'

Chantal was a long time pondering the matter: she was called upon to make the most difficult decision of her life. 'Yes, Johnny, as you say, you were wrong, but you are right. Unless he comes to us and says he is sorry for speaking like that in temper, he must go. Bill is not a bad boy ... perhaps he was bad, but he seems to have learned some sense ... and the other, that Sambo, Nico brought him as an insult to me. He too is a good boy ... but not as a friend.

'There is a great pain in my heart, Johnny, but you are right and if it is what he wants, he must go.'

In the morning, after breakfasting on the beach, the three young men gathered their small belongings and prepared to leave. With Nico in the lead they walked in grim silence across the beach and up the narrow path to where the bus stopped. Jonathan and Chantal, looking as helpless as they felt, watched them go. When, having mounted the steps of the bus, the trio was lost to sight, Jonathan turned to Chantal. 'I wish I understood where I failed,' he said in a dead voice, 'but fail I did. Just one more Dabney failure. I seem to have failed Nico, as I failed my other two children and' – seeing the tears which streamed down Chantal's cheeks – 'I seem to have failed you, too.'

'No, Johnny, not that. We are such little people and sometimes life is too big for us.'

Nico and their differences about him, which had once threatened to drive them apart, were now unwittingly healing the rift between them.

24

Weeks ran into months without any direct contact between Dabney's Reef and Nico. The news which filtered through was to the effect that he and Hairy Bill were working together at the site of a new hotel in course of construction a few miles out of Port Lewis. What shocked both Jonathan and Chantal – neither for quite the same reasons – was that they were working alongside and apparently on terms of equality with unskilled black labourers. Chantal was not ashamed of the African blood she had inherited, but was only too well aware of its disadvantages. That she herself had the relatively light pigmentation of her father rather than that of her mother, she regarded as great good fortune. It was, she believed, easier to be white than black. Nico in her view had taken a retrograde step which, if he continued as he was going, might cost him dearly, diminish his social standing in the eyes of island society, thus adding to the burden of guilt on his father's shoulders.

Jonathan, on the other hand, did not see Nico's backsliding as a result of his mother's well-diluted blood so much as being a legacy of his own tired, worn-out Dabney blood. For himself Jonathan had long lived in terror of becoming such another as his own effetely elegant and ineffectual father. The Dabneys had been fighting a losing battle for so long that now it seemed hardly worth continuing it.

The only person with whom Jonathan could discuss his fears was Robbie who, being weak himself, understood weakness. 'Johnny, my boy,' said the latter, 'you've got it all out of proportion. Instead of moping you should be rejoicing that at long last Nico, a Dabney, is doing something more useful and constructive than planting his backside in a long chair while he laps up rum punch. I've seen him at work, stripped to the waist and holding his own with the best of them. The contractor tells me that Nico and Hairy Bill between them are worth any three men on the job. They may not know much about the paperwork involved, but they'll turn out practical builders in the end. You mark my words!'

'But a common black labourer! Surely I'm entitled to want something better for my son?'

'Johnny,' said Robbie, raising his voice in high indignation, 'you're nothing but a bloody hypocrite. Aren't you the man who made the proud boast that at Dabney's Reef there was no colour bar? What was the hokum that Alice McGraw sold you? It isn't the colour of your skin that matters, but the way you wear it ... something like that.'

'He's not your son, Robbie,' – this in a voice loaded with reproach – 'or you wouldn't be talking like this.'

'That I wouldn't. I'd be too proud and happy for talking ... proud of a son with the guts to practise what his father preaches. Which reminds me that there's another father who feels strongly about colour ... Holt, the father of young Sambo.'

'That doesn't sound like Holt, who's as black as the ace of spades ... a fine chap, Holt.'

'Am I to infer from this that in your judgment a jet-black skin debars Holt from the luxury of colour prejudice?'

'No, Robbie, I don't mean any such thing and you know it.'

'Then what do you mean? Out with it, Johnny!'

'I mean that Holt, because of his blackness which, as you well know, places him low in the West Indian pecking order, is unlikely to be guilty of colour prejudice. That's all.'

'Colour prejudice, Johnny, isn't solely the prerogative of white people. Our friend Holt takes the view – and I agree with him – that Sambo's close association and apparent friendship with Nico and Hairy Bill will do him more harm than good. Society is not quite ready for such an association and Holt has the good sense to see it. He is not concerned with questions of superiority or inferiority, but he believes that until there is a change of heart in the world, black should cleave to black and white to white. It's people like your randy ancestors who caused so much harm and unhappiness. Equality is a fact, or it is nothing. Mere assertions of equality don't mean anything.'

'I don't care about Sambo. He isn't my problem,' said Johnny, 'but I am concerned about the effect of all this on my son.'

'Just as Holt is concerned about his. Won't you understand, Johnny, that in every person of mixed blood there is a constant tug of war going on between the two races? Nico, from what you've told me, is passing through a phase in which his mother's blood calls to him more loudly than yours. He is torn between sympathy with the black man and a sense of guilt because in his heart of hearts he despises those with a darker skin than his own. Like plants which climb to reach sunlight, the goal of mixed blooded people is a lighter skin. It is not a coincidence that there is a direct connection between material success and a light skin. Take your own half-brothers as an example: Lawrence and Hugh, the two successful ones, are married to women with lighter skins than their own. It's all very simple really, but instead of being able to digest it all gradually, poor Nico was almost overwhelmed when he had to learn of these things the hard, the cruel way, and if he is full of resentment, who can blame him. Meanwhile, don't waste time in self-recrimination. There's nothing to be done about it. It's like whisky.'

'What has whisky to do with the matter?' snapped Johnny, believing that Robbie was having fun at his expense.

'Everything, my lad, everything! When the Sassenach mixes water with his whisky, there's nothing that can be done about it. Once mixed, whisky and water can't be unmixed, and it's the same with blood, except that the consequences are longer lasting.

'Miscegenation, as they call it, was an inevitable process as soon as man began to travel. Now with the speeding up of all forms of travel it is assuming gigantic proportions. It happened in the Mediterranean before and during the early centuries of the Christian era when what we now call the Mediterranean type evolved. Walk the streets of Marseilles,

Naples, the Piraeus, Palermo, Alexandria, Tunis and Algiers ... anywhere in Andalusia or Portugal. The people you will see are no longer varied types, but one type, the product of Phoenician and Arab pirates, Roman soldiers, Greek traders, Jews and assorted Levantines, the blue-eyed Norman conquerors of Sicily, Nordic sailors and Negroes from south of the Sahara ... come ashore after the hardships at sea to scented evenings and the arms of willing maidens.

'If Nico were to go to any one of those cities, he would feel at home. He would pass unnoticed wherever he went ... just another Mediterranean type. The people don't talk nonsense about pure blood or long pedigrees ... they don't even think about it. We are what we are, they say, and they get on with the business of living.

'Now the voyages are longer in distance, shorter in time and greater in frequency. We count the travellers now in tens of millions. From the very beginning it was inevitable that from being a Mediterranean phenomenon ... problem ... call it what you like ... it should spread to every corner of the world. There are so far as I know no miscegenation statistics issued in New York and Detroit. They would tell a story. Do you suppose that the tens of thousands of air crews circling the world, the uncounted commercial travellers, officials, pleasure seekers and the rest lead immaculately celibate lives with evenings to kill in Cairo, Bombay, Singapore and Hawaii? I doubt it, my lad. People of mixed blood are being born by the millions every year.'

'All very interesting, Robbie, but what in hell has it got to do with me or, more to the point, Nico? How does it help him to be happy about his mixed blood in a world that despises it?'

'Chantal has mixed blood, Johnny. Does it bother her?'

'For herself, no, but in so far as it affects Nico, yes.'

'Try to understand, Johnny, that it is only for horses, cattle and dogs that pure blood is greatly prized. In humans it was never more than an empty boast ... now it is just a joke. If pure blood ever existed, it was so long ago that it is meaningless today. The future belongs to the people of mixed blood ... the half-breeds, the mongrels. In the predictable future, although I won't live to see the prediction fulfilled, it is a mathematical certainty that the overwhelming majority of the great-grandchildren of anyone living today will fall into a type which has a somewhat sallow complexion, hair with more than a suspicion of kink in it and eyes inclined to be slanted. The Caucasian, Negro and Mongol blood streams will have merged into a mighty river on whose banks, in bewildered little huddles, stand the remnants of the pure-blooded peoples, vainly conscious that the world has passed them by and that they fit into no known pattern. Nico's descendants will regard them as we regard circus freaks.'

'Even supposing you are right, Robbie, and you may well be,' said Jonathan heavily, 'I can't look as far ahead as that. Nico's descendants will adjust themselves to conditions as they find them. Let unborn generations solve their own problems, as they always have and always will. I won't look beyond Nico, who is my son and to some degree my responsibility. He has one little life and I want it to be a happy one. You talk in cosmic terms, which are of no comfort to Nico.'

There was little comfort for Chantal either who, because she had faith in Robbie's good sense, had listened to every word of this exchange. The only crumb of comfort was the realization that essentially she and Johnny were concerned only for their son. Her world was painted on a very small canvas. The big canvas on which Robbie had painted his word picture was beyond her understanding.

*   *   *

Christmas was approaching ... Christmas without Nico. Chantal was inconsolable.

Doris had written from Jamaica, where she was spending the winter, asking if she might spend a few days at Dabney's Reef. She was not happy among strangers and her two daughters were no comfort to her. All they wanted from her was money ... and more money. There was, she was forced to admit, an element of justice in this, because money was really all she had ever wanted from their father, Fook, who had so stoutly resisted the stupidity of ffoulkes. It was strange

206

that she felt closer to Jonathan and Chantal than to her own daughters, but it was so.

Doris's good business head had always told her that Dabney's Reef was, as others believed, a potential goldmine, but now that she was older and more mature, she saw things more clearly. If these two had enough money for their simple needs, why spoil the place by turning it into a vulgar tourist trap?

Christmas nostalgia brought another visitor to Dabney's Reef in the person of Graziella, who had come from Martinique to spend a little time with Chantal. It was her first visit since leaving in a rage after seeing people slop tomato ketchup over her carefully prepared flying fish. There had been a certain satisfaction in knowing that efforts to replace her in the kitchen had ended disastrously.

Observing Jonathan and Chantal in low spirits, it did not take her long to learn the cause. When she had not been too busy in the kitchen, Graziella and her grandson Nico had been close. There had been a warmth and understanding in their relationship. She knew, none better, the problems Nico would have to face because of his mixed blood. Saying nothing to anyone, she went in to Port Lewis determined to find Nico and bring him back home, if necessary by force, forgetting that he was now a young man strong enough to tuck her under one arm and walk off with her.

Graziella arrived by taxi at the building site where Nico and Hairy Bill were working, feeding a cement mixer whose hungry maw kept them fully occupied. She chose for her visit the last working day before Christmas, after which construction would halt for a week. It was some little time before she was able to distinguish Nico from the others working on the site. Long hours of exposure to hot Caribbean sun, bare from the waist up, had burned Nico's skin unrecognizably.

A few minutes after Graziella arrived, a pretty girl riding a scooter entered the site and dismounted at the door of a shed which served as the contractor's office. On the pillion seat was a canvas bag which she struggled to remove. She could have removed it unaided, but a pretty display of helplessness served her purpose better. Smiling at Nico, she made a dumb show of seeking his help. Unable to leave the cement mixer at that moment, he called out, 'With you in a jiffy!'

Hard on the heels of the girl riding the scooter a battered pick-up truck arrived with two men. Similar vehicles were coming and going frequently, so this one attracted no special attention. The two men left the pick-up, strolling nonchalantly towards where the girl stood beside the scooter at the door of the shed.

Graziella was an eye-witness to what followed, but it was some moments before she fully understood what was afoot. She had no means of knowing that this was pay day and that the girl had come from the bank in Port Lewis with the week's pay swelled by Christmas bonus payments.

When one of the men seized the canvas bag, the girl tried to prevent him. The other man thereupon struck her a brutal blow in the stomach which left her writhing on the ground.

Nico and Hairy Bill were the nearest of the men working on the site: most of the others were in the building or high up on the scaffolding.

Nico's rage was concentrated on the man who had struck the girl, whose name was Rosalie. She was his first love and they were at the stage of 'walking out' in the evenings. Interposing himself between the men and their pick-up, Nico hurled his shovel, blade first, at the offender. It struck him in the neck, causing him to collapse in a gush of blood. The other man, divining Nico's intention of serving him in much the same way, pulled a revolver from his pocket and fired one shot, which struck Nico in the upper arm. Hairy Bill, until then slow to realize what was happening, began a mad bull charge across the thirty-odd feet between him and the drama taking place. Bill's reckless charge was opportune ... for Nico. The armed man, his pistol aimed at point-blank range, would assuredly have killed Nico if he had not seen Bill just at the moment when he was about to fire. He fired at Bill instead, the bullet hitting him in the chest. As Bill did not check in his stride, it seemed to the onlookers that the shot had missed. Bill's momentum carried him across the few feet separating him from the would-be killer. With head lowered he proceeded to butt the man in the stomach, driving all the wind out of him. Whereupon Bill began to dance on the man's face. It was, all things considered, a most impressive performance. It impressed Graziella, who knew a surge of gratitude towards the young savage who had by his disregard of danger saved Nico's life.

The entire episode, from the attack on Rosalie to the last, had occupied little more than thirty seconds. It was all over before most of those working on the site knew what was happening.

There was little serious crime in Port Lewis and the rest of the island. Drunken brawls, occasional knifings, wife-beatings and petty thefts were commonplace enough, but nobody remembered such a thing as armed robbery.

Graziella's taxi took Nico and Bill to hospital. She herself was given a lift into town in the police car which soon came on the scene. Refused permission to see the two injured young men, she took herself back to Dabney's Reef, where the news had already been received by telephone. Dr Lawrence Dabney, who had been in the accident ward when the two were brought in, took charge of the cases and later he was able to assure Jonathan and Chantal that there was no great cause for worry.

The attempted hold-up had taken place on a Thursday, the day on which the *Novocastrian* went to press. When Nico and Hairy Bill had breakfast brought to them on the Friday morning it was to learn from flaring headlines that they were heroes. Robbie McAlister pulled out all the stops, but in trying to do justice to the occasion, Robbie encountered one well-nigh insuperable obstacle: nobody at Dabney's Reef, or elsewhere, seemed to know Hairy Bill's surname. The item was spotted with such phrases as 'Nicolas Dabney's gallant young friend Bill.' Who, people asked themselves, was this modest hero?

Among those who asked the question was Major Pilkington, the Commissioner of Police: and there was no answer. Was he born on the island? Apparently not. Then in that event there should be some record of his arrival.

Realizing that Hairy Bill was somewhat coy about his antecedents, Dr Lawrence Dabney kept would-be questioners at bay for as long as possible. This, naturally enough, heightened rather than diminished curiosity on the subject. In recognition of Bill's hero status – Major Pilkington was a kindly man – further enquiries were for the time being dropped.

Of the two young men Bill's wound was the more serious, for the bullet had grazed his lung. Nico would have been allowed to return home on the third day, but elected to wait until his friend was discharged from hospital.

There had in the meantime been a tearful reconciliation between Nico and his parents. Then it became necessary to receive a deputation comprising the Mayor of Port Lewis, bearing an address of thanks to the two young men and an inscribed gold watch to each of them. Next demanding admission to the sick beds was Rosalie, accompanied by her parents and a photographer who took a good photo of her kissing Nico. Implicit behind the visit was the loud and clear peal of wedding bells, and this was not the moment for Nico to say that marriage had not exactly been his intention. Rosalie was pretty and charming, but she was also embarrassingly black, embarrassingly because of his avowed preference for people of colour. Was he, he asked himself, being untrue to an ideal? Marriage, after all, was a serious step: surely he had the right to second thoughts?

Less embarrassing was a visit from the building contractor whose uninsured payroll had been rescued. But even here there was an awkward moment when, having given Nico a cheque for £50, he turned to Bill and said: 'What name shall I put on your cheque?'

'Make mine out to Nico,' said Bill, closing his eyes in feigned sleep.

Being a hero raised complications.

Friendship, as these two interpreted the word, demanded total acceptance: neither felt entitled to ask questions which the other might resent as intrusive. Nevertheless, Nico would not have been human if in the privacy of his own mind he had not wondered about the closed chapters in the other's life, the real reasons why he was so coy in the matter of his identity. There were so many unanswered questions.

'Bill,' said Nico on what was to be their last day in the hospital, 'I don't want to poke my nose into your affairs, so shut me up whenever you want to....'

'Say anything you feel like saying.'

'Well Bill,' he began haltingly, 'I've been thinking....'

'Ask nurse for an aspirin.'

'I've been thinking,' Nico went on, 'that whatever it was you did back there' – the gesture which accompanied this seemed to embrace both time and place – 'this might be a good time to clear things up ... if you know what I mean....'

'What *do* you mean?' asked Bill with the bluntness of someone who does not deal in subtleties.

'Well, what I mean is that now, when you're the blue-eyed boy ... wounded hero and all that ... would be a good time to ... well, straighten things out a bit so that you can use your real name, whatever it is. See what I mean? "Hairy Bill" suits you all right, but you must admit that it's ... it's a bit strange. Suppose, for example, you were invited to Government House, you couldn't very well be announced as Mr Hairy Bill, now could you?'

'Between the two of us, Bill, I don't care a damn what you did over there' – again the wide gesture – 'but whatever it is you're running away from, now if ever is the time to do something about it. You didn't commit a murder, did you?'

'No, not quite.'

'That's good because I'm told murder is hard to square and, whatever it was, you must have been pretty young at the time and, well, what I mean is that you're a man now and you're not likely to be pinched for what you did as a young boy. They'd put it down to high spirits, or something like that. Give it a thought,' Nico concluded, feeling that he had said all he decently could.

'I've been giving it a thought for a long time,' said Bill soberly, 'but I don't seem to get anywhere with thinking....'

'What about your father and mother ... couldn't they help in some way?'

'My father kicked me out of his home a long while ago, while as for my mother, I wouldn't ask her the time. She doesn't know or care what's happened to me. So that's out. Any more bright ideas?'

'What about my father? He'd help ... now. After all, you saved my life....'

'Balls!'

'Now don't come the modest hero with me. You've made a friend for life, so use him. That's what friends are for. My old lady, too. Why, if you'd shave off that filthy looking mat of hair, I believe she'd kiss you. But Bill,' he went on soberly, 'you've got to do something. You can't go through the rest of your life calling yourself Hairy Bill. If you ever make any money you won't be able to open a bank account. "Hairy Bill" would look good on a cheque, wouldn't it?'

There followed a long silence full of unspoken thoughts. Bill's churning indecision was almost visible. 'Haven't you ever wondered who I really am?' he asked at length.

'Yes, often....'

'But you've never asked.'

'If you'd wanted to tell me, you would have and if you didn't ... well that was all right with me. I don't care who you are, Bill. I suppose everyone has parts of his life he wants to keep private. But unless you want to call yourself Hairy Bill for the rest of your life, you may as well tell me what your name really is.'

'My name's the same as yours, Nico. I'm Dabney ... Edouard Dabney, the one you knew as Ted.'

'The Little Monster, eh?' said Nico, laughing. 'It was a long while ago, but I seem to remember you disappeared rather suddenly. One day you were at Dabney's Reef and the next you weren't. What happened?'

'Didn't they tell you why?'

'I don't think so. All I remember was a lot of whispering....'

'Perhaps it's just as well, so let's skip it....'

'Like that, eh?'

The enormity of what he had done still weighed heavily on Ted's – let us revert to calling him Ted – conscience. The screams of the poor dog as, enveloped in flames, it died in agony would, he believed, always haunt him, and it would always be a mystery to him how he had committed such a barbarous act. It was this memory, far more than what may be called his juvenile delinquencies in Europe, which had caused him to return to Dabney's Reef furtively, disguised behind a mat of hair. Behind his return had been the belief that when the time was opportune he would be able to declare himself to his father. But the time never had been opportune. More than once he had heard himself described as 'that little monster Ted', once when he was on the point of declaring his identity. If that was how they regarded him, he could not come out into the open.

The return to Europe, with his mother's recriminations ringing in his ears, had been an experience, and her subsequent neglect of him had earned for her an undying resentment not far short of hatred. His rebellious behaviour and stupidly criminal acts thereafter had been a devious way of revenging himself upon her.

Back at Dabney's Reef, no longer on the run, Ted had wasted no time making good resolutions. Without being conscious of doing so, he had purged his past in hard work. It was as though the torrents of sweat had by some mysterious alchemy leeched away what a magistrate had once called his criminal tendencies. Whether or not this were the true explanation behind his changed ways, he was discovering that one rose or fell in general esteem according to one's behaviour. He realized that after all it was worth while treading the straight and narrow path. None of it, of course, was quite so clear cut in Ted's mind.

One of the rewards had been Nico. Hitherto Ted had been friendless in the world. There had never been time to stay still and acquire friends: the wake of his passage through life had been strewn with enemies thirsting for his blood.

Now, metaphorically licking his lips as he savoured the possibilities implicit in his new status as a hero, Ted gave himself over to undiluted happiness. For the first time he could remember he was at peace with himself.

* * *

213

Hair is said to improve some faces. Beards can and occasionally do, by hiding weak chins, create an illusion of strength. Ted did not have a weak chin. Nor to a purist could his matted tangle of hair be called a beard.

Doris, who greeted her hero grandson with as much warmth as she could muster, but nevertheless with a certain reserve, suggested that before Ted take his place at the welcoming dinner, something should be done about it. Ted, practical and not over-fastidious, employed for the first stage a pair of dog clippers found by Nico. When a safety razor completed what the clippers had begun, a new and unrecognizable Ted emerged. He was, by general consent, an improvement on the other, which was not necessarily high praise. It was hard to believe that he and Nico were half-brothers, so utterly unalike were they. Indeed, if it had not been for Doris's identification, there might have been doubt on the subject.

Graziella, whose memories of the small Ted were not entirely happy, set aside her prejudices, remembering only that he was the saviour of her grandson, Nico. They were soon engaged in animated talk, she in her Creole French and he in the Riviera argot which passed for French.

Doris, who knew more than anyone at the table about Ted's exploits in Europe, knew little enough. But there was something about his gay blue eyes, the wrinkles of good humour beside them, the pugnacious jaw and his general swashbuckling, devil-may-care appearance, which made it easy to believe that what he had done had been all in a spirit of good clean fun and, true or not, that was the spirit of his welcome back into the family.

It was Jonathan who cast a small shadow on the evening by insisting that the first priority was to regularize Ted's legal status. Legally, which is to say officially, he did not exist. Hairy Bill had vanished into thin air. Who was to take his place?

It was left to Zachary to work out the details, but it was several weeks before officialdom could be persuaded to relax its stiffness. It was all very well to say that this was Edouard Dabney, but what had Edouard Dabney been up to elsewhere to make his clandestine arrival so necessary? In the end they were persuaded to conclude that whatever it might have been, word of it had not reached the island. Ted would always be the object of some speculation, but his reckless bravery would help him to live down the past.

*　　*　　*

The talk went round in circles. There was plenty of capital available for the 'development' of Dabney's Reef, but always at a price Jonathan was not prepared to pay. The speculative 'developers' would, if they had their way, destroy the peace and beauty of the place, while the conditions under which bankers would lend money were too onerous. 'Bankers,' as Doris insisted, 'are glorified pawnbrokers, who want none of the risk and all the profits. Why not let me be your banker? I have the capital available and I believe it would be a good investment. Think about it.'

The conversation took place under the arcade outside what had once been the restaurant. Present were Jonathan and Chantal, the two grandmothers, Doris and Graziella, Ted, Nico and Robbie McAlister. The gathering was to mark the imminent departure of Doris for Europe and Graziella back to her native Martinique. It turned into a round table discussion of the future of Dabney's Reef.

Ted and Nico, neither of whom had anything which could be called financial acumen, or interest in money as such, played no part, their minds elsewhere.

Before the gathering broke up Doris agreed on terms to be worked out in detail the next day to make available a large sum of money which would obviate the need to go hat in hand to a bank. Zachary, acting for both parties, would be asked to prepare a workable agreement.

'Well, that's that,' said Doris, happy at having reached what she considered a fair and sensible understanding. 'And you two boys' – she turned towards Nico and Ted – 'will in the course of time be the owners of a very valuable property. Let us hope you will still be good friends and will not quarrel over it. Long may you live to enjoy it.'

So saying, Doris raised her glass and a ragged toast ran

round the table where every face but one was smiling. Chantal sat scowling, her face black as a thundercloud, tears of what looked like rage coursing down her cheeks.

Doris was distressed, for she was fond of Chantal. 'What is the matter, child?' she asked, forgetting that she was addressing a woman approaching forty. 'Has someone said something to upset you?'

Ignoring Doris, Chantal turned towards Jonathan, her eyes blazing with indignation. 'Dabney's Reef belongs to my Nico ... you promised!' Her snarling fury knew no bounds.

'But darling, think,' said Jonathan quietly. 'Thanks to Doris half of Dabney's Reef will be worth many times more than the whole of it is now. Also, do not forget that Doris is Ted's grandmother.'

'Ted, it is always Ted! I am tired of his name.'

'Do not forget also that it was Ted who saved Nico's life, so please say nothing that you don't mean. . . .'

In a paroxysm of weeping, Chantal fled to the living quarters, leaving a stunned silence behind her.

The rest were too shocked to speak. It was so ... ungracious was the word which came to mind. Even Graziella bit her lip in vexation. Although the talk had been in English, which she did not understand, she had been able to grasp the salient fact that Chantal, despite everything, regarded Ted as an interloper, begrudging him his share of the inheritance. She understood, but did not approve.

Doris knew that Chantal had no real grasp of money matters. Allowance had to be made for that. Entries in a ledger were not money to Chantal. Money was what came out of a cash register to be counted and checked at the end of a day. All Chantal was able to grasp was that Dabney's Reef belonged to Nico by right of having been born there. Come what may, she was now determined by fair means or foul to block this conspiracy to steal half of it from him. Steal and conspiracy were strong words, but where Nico's interests were concerned, only strong words would suffice. Yesterday the whole of Dabney's Reef was his: now if they had their way, only half. What else was that but theft?

✳   ✳   ✳

Chantal required time before she would become approachable. Doris approached her after a night of weeping behind a locked door, when some of the hedgehog prickles had subsided. 'Surely dear,' she began, 'you know me well enough to know that I would not do anything to harm you ... or Nico? Won't you understand that in a curious kind of way I sometimes think of Nico as my grandson. Why? Because, my dear, I am very fond of Johnny. To me Johnny is the son I never had. Ted, as you know, *is* my grandson. He and Nico, partly because they are close friends and good for each other, have equal places in my affections ... and both of them, don't forget, are Johnny's sons.'

'Ted, as you say, is your grandson. I do not forget ... anything. But' – Chantal's face became a vicious mask – 'my Johnny is not his father. Ted is not a Dabney, so why should he have half the Reef?'

'Who told you this?' asked Doris in blank astonishment.

'Nobody *told* me. I have eyes and I did not need to be told. You have only to see Nico and Ted standing together in swim trunks to know that they are not, cannot be, brothers, even half-brothers. You do not wish to admit that your Gloria is a bad woman. I can understand that, but you know, as I know, that Johnny is not Ted's father. It is not right that because your Gloria took into her bed an ugly man like a gorilla, my son is to be cheated of what is his. . . .'

There were no tears now. Chantal maintained an icy calm.

Doris liked Chantal, with a liking not far short of love. Her fresh spontaneity, so lacking in both her own daughters, had a strong appeal for her. Where Nico and Ted were concerned, her affections were uninvolved. She was prepared to write them both off. Anything she was prepared to do for Nico was because of her real devotion to Jonathan. Nico, it seemed, was a troublesome boy who hadn't the sense to know on which side his bread was buttered; paradoxically, her impatience with him stemmed largely from the fact that he was so undiscerning as to have formed a close friendship with Ted, whom she had had cause to regard as a criminally minded young monster who – she cringed at the realization – happened to be her own grandson. For the moment Ted was basking in public acclaim as a hero, but it did not impress Doris, who had always known that he was plucky, being, as she saw him, too stupidly brutish to recognize danger when he met it. He might just as easily have been the payroll robber as the hero who foiled it.

Now what irked Doris most was that in trying to save Jonathan from the clutches of the bankers, she was in danger of causing him incalculable hurt.

'Before you do anything which you might regret, dear,' she said to Chantal, who sat like a statue staring at nothing through unblinking eyes, 'I want to be sure that you understand clearly just what the position is. I am very fond of your Johnny, but you know as well as I do that he is not clever in business matters. If he borrows money from the banks, or some speculator, he will end by losing Dabney's Reef. I want to help him, not to rob him.'

'But you want to rob my Nico, to steal half from him.'

'All right, my dear, you must think what you please. But there is another way ... a way in which the whole of Dabney's Reef will belong to Nico.'

Chantal's eyes came alive for the first time.

'I have known for a long time that Johnny was not Ted's father, but I have said nothing because his mother is my daughter and also because I did not want Johnny to be hurt.'

'How hurt?' Chantal's eyes were at once full of concern.

'Hurt in his pride, my dear, a man's tenderest spot. Now Johnny is very proud: he has two sons who are heroes. For too long he has been ashamed of the name of Dabney and now that he is proud of it I do not want to destroy his pride.'

'How?'

'By telling him that he is not the father of Ted, who has not one drop of Dabney blood in his veins. Ted then becomes my responsibility. He is my grandson. I will find money for him when the time comes. Johnny will have to borrow from the banks and your Nico will risk losing everything. If we do as everyone ... everyone but you agreed, my dear, your Nico will be a very rich man one day.'

'And Ted also?'

'Of course. Neither of the boys is more important to me than the other, although Ted *is* my grandson. But if you do not want him to share Dabney's Reef with Nico, it is very simple. Just tell Johnny the truth ... that another man is Ted's father. Everything will go to Nico and everyone will be happy ... everyone but Johnny. It is for you to decide, my dear.'

There was a long silence while Chantal's mind ticked furiously. There it was, the moment had come for a clear-cut decision: it was what the bull fighters were supposed to call the moment of truth. She must decide between the two people she loved best in the world. Either the little monster Ted must have half of what she believed rightly belonged to Nico, or she must deal the final blow to Johnny's pride by denying him the satisfaction of believing, now he had redeemed himself, that Ted was his son.

Looking at the thin-lipped determination on Doris's set face, Chantal realized that a cunningly laid trap had been set for her. With eyes wide open she walked into it, and in a curiously twisted way was happy to do so.

'Your way is best, Doris. It would be too cruel to tell him now. He is my Johnny ... *mine*,' Chantal said fiercely, 'and it is a small price for our Nico to pay.'